HEARTS OF GOLD

*A romance set against the background
of the Australian Gold Rush*

Western Australia, 1890. Sarette Maitland is
orphaned when her father dies of a snake bite
on the goldfields. Rescued by adventurer John
Kern, she takes the place of his own dead
daughter in his heart. When tragedy strikes and
Kern is killed, Sarette is introduced to Kern's
nephew, Magnus – whose honesty and heart
are tested when he discovers his uncle has left
Sarette a considerable fortune...

HEARTS OF GOLD

Janet Woods

Severn House Large Print
London & New York

This first large print edition published 2011
in Great Britain and the USA by
SEVERN HOUSE PUBLISHERS LTD of
9-15 High Street, Sutton, Surrey, SM1 1DF.
First world regular print edition published 2009 by
Severn House Publishers Ltd., London and New York.

British Library Cataloguing in Publication Data

Woods, Janet, 1939-
  Hearts of gold.
  1. Guardian and ward--Fiction. 2. Love stories. 3. Large
  type books.
  I. Title
  823.9'14-dc22

ISBN-13: 978-0-7278-7912-7

Severn House Publishers support The Forest Stewardship Council
[FSC], the leading international forest certification organisation. All
our titles that are printed on Greenpeace-approved FSC-certified paper
carry the FSC logo.

Printed and bound in Great Britain by the
MPG Books Group, Bodmin, Cornwall.

Welcome to the world
Emelia Thomas
18th April 2008
Love you lots

One

Jack Maitland lay on a stretcher under the shade
of the eucalyptus trees. The death adder's venom
had done its work efficiently. He'd been dying
for three hours now. It had started with a headache then progressed to sickness that had
drained his body of moisture. Pallor had crept
under his tan, turning it a sickly yellow. His lips
were blue and his body rigid, except for an
occasional jerk. He no longer seemed to know
Sarette, and would not sip the precious liquid
from the water bag his daughter held to his
mouth.

Tears trickled from her eyes as she gently
waved a mulga branch over her father's body to
prevent the bush flies from settling in the
corners of his eyes and mouth. *Damn the snake!*
Sarette thought. Startled by her father's foot on
its skinny lure of a tail the reptile had barely
scraped its fangs against his skin in defence of
itself before it had slithered off in fright.

'It will take more than that little scratch to kill
me,' her father had said, giving his great boom-
ing laugh as he'd spit on his kerchief and rubbed

7

it over the wound. But she'd seen the fear in his eyes as the venom had begun to take effect.

It was a hot afternoon. Above them, the canopy of a tree swayed in the breeze, and the sun dappled the ground with moving patches of light and shadow. A pair of rose-breasted cockatoos began to squabble above them. Didn't they know that her father was dying?

'Shut up!' she yelled at them, but they began to screech louder, until she threw a stone up at them. They flew to a neighbouring tree.

Was her father still breathing? She couldn't tell. Sarette leaned forward to place a hand against his heart and her ear against his mouth. There was still a faint breath.

His eyes opened. Usually they were a clear green like her own. Now they were dark with blood, as though he was bleeding inside. His voice was barely discernible. 'Why is it dark?'

Tears sprang to her eyes. 'It's not dark. Papa, please don't leave me,' she begged.

'I love you, Sarry girl, I'll never leave you,' he whispered, then the slow, erratic heartbeat against her palm stopped so abruptly that she found herself unprepared for it.

She sat back on her heels. There was a strong sense of release in her, that her father was no longer suffering. There was also a yawning sense of bewilderment. He'd been a big man; how could something as small as a snake take his life away? It had happened too quickly, before she was prepared. He looked different without his life, smaller and vulnerable, and even though she knew that nothing could harm him now, she wanted to protect him. A sorrow so deep hit her that she didn't quite know how to handle it. *He was dead! Dead!* Never again would he tell her that he loved her.

Throwing herself to the ground she beat her fists against the earth, the violent act sending up orange puffs of dust. And she shouted out her grief in her fury. 'Isn't it enough that you took my mother? Did you have to take my father too, and before his dreams were even realized?'

When her rage was spent Sarette became aware that the world would go on without her father, and so must she. Her mouth tasted of dust. It was everywhere, in the air that she breathed and in her hair, turning the dark length of it a dull copper and gritting against her scalp.

'It's Godforsaken country that doesn't give anything back easily,' her father had said of the place. 'We'll give it six months.' That six months had become three years.

Rising, she brushed the dirt from her skirt. It was one that had belonged to her mother, though it didn't fit her yet and she tied it around her waist with a rope. There was another gown. Dark blue with lace on the bodice. Sarette was small for fourteen, she knew. She was saving the dress for when she was bigger and needed something special to wear. All the same, she was strong, and could dry blow the dirt for several hours before she became tired, dropping panfuls to the earth. While the dust drifted away on the incessant wind, any heavier flecks of gold in it were left behind to be carefully collected.

The flies had begun to cluster. Shoing them

9

away she gently closed her father's eyes, covered him with a ragged sheet and waited for Flynn to come back with the horse and cart, for she'd sent word to him.

The Irishman didn't have much to say for himself, as usual, but began removing her father's clothing.

'What are you doing?'

'If I bury Jack in his clothes somebody will dig him up for them. Besides, I could do with his boots and his clothes mesself. We'll tie him in that auld sheet. Turn your back, now, girl. A neked man is not a sight for an innocent girl to look upon. We'll bury him with your mother, God rest her poor innocent soul, and we'll say a prayer over him to speed him on his way.'

She didn't want to part with him. 'Can't we bury him tomorrow?'

'No lass. It's too hot for a body to be left unburied.'

Before too long her father was tied up like a long, dirty-grey parcel. She helped Flynn lift him on to the cart, holding his legs so they didn't flop around. The horse plodded off towards the cemetery with Flynn at the reins. Sarette sat next to him.

'Men took their hats off and held them against their chests as the cart passed, calling out, 'Who is it?'

'Jack Maitland ... snake got him.'

'Poor sod!'

And more piously. 'May God gather Maitland's soul into his keeping.'

Without being asked one or two men picked up

10

their shovels and began to follow the cart, the others went back to work, their muscles bulging and their skin shiny with dust-streaked sweat.

When they got to the site the men began to dig. Eventually the one in the hole with the bandanna over the bottom half of his face gave a nod to the others and they hauled him out.

An odd smell hung about him that attracted the flies.

Sarette knew he'd dug down to where her mother rested, and she leaned forward and tried to look down into the grave. She caught a glimpse of a dirty piece of rag and a bone, before Flynn pulled her back. 'No, girl. It's not a sight you should be looking at, now. Remember her as she was.'

Her father was lowered into the grave with her mother. The dirt was thrown back into the hole and heaped over the top, a prayer said.

There was a flat piece of oddly shaped stone, with her mother's name on it. Died from typhoid. Sara Jane Maitland August 1892 and her unborn infant.

'Do you know the date of your papa's birth, Sarry?'

When she shook her head, Flynn took a small pick from the back of his trousers and scratched in her father's name, with the date underneath, and the word that from now on would make her blood run cold. Snakebite.

They stood and looked at it in awkward silence for a while, Sarette thinking that, even though she wore her mother's clothing she couldn't really remember the woman who'd given birth

11

to her all that well. Her presence had faded, and Sarette had long stopped crying over her. So the memory of her father would fade too in time, and become easier.

'What will you do, now?' Flynn said, breaking in on her thoughts.

Sarette gazed at him, not quite understanding what he meant. Everything had happened so quickly that she hadn't had time to think of her future. She didn't like Flynn Collins much but she had nobody else. 'I'll look after things and help dig for gold, like I always do.'

Flynn avoided her eyes. 'I'll take you back to the tent, then I'm going off to the grog tent to have a drink with the boys. A bit of a wake for your father.'

Sarette ate some of the stew she'd made. The small kangaroo her father had shot was tasty, and she'd thrown a handful of barley in to thicken the gravy. As the sun went down the air cooled, and the campfires began to twinkle amongst the trees. After relieving herself, she crawled into her swag, curled up and cried herself to sleep. She felt lonely without her father for company. She slept soundly, her brain ignoring the rustles and snaps in the bush, the sounds of snickering horses and the wind soughing in the canopy above her.

When she woke things felt different. Flynn hadn't come back, and they'd been robbed. Pots, pans and shovels were missing. During the night someone had cut a hole in the tent, had scooped a hole in the earth and removed the tin containing her father's small stash of gold. When the tin was full they'd been going to leave this place and buy themselves a house in the city. It was a woeful amount that had been stolen, nothing like the large strike at Fly Flat that had brought Sarette's family here to seek their own fortune.

The thief had also taken the water bag with the last of the water, and the pot with the remains of the stew, which had been hanging over the campfire. They were careful with water here in the dry landscape of the Coolgardie gold diggings, for it rained only rarely. The water was collected from a well at the base of a granite rock and was carried some thirty-five miles overland every day in a tank on top of a wagon. It cost at least a shilling for the gallon, and often more, so they had to eke the liquid out as long as possible, and make sure there was enough left over at the end of the day for the horse to have a drink. Her father's partner reckoned that the water carrier collected more gold for his labour than the miners dug out of the ground.

Sarette had never felt so alone in her life, or so scared. She had nothing of value, and would have to beg for water unless she could earn some money to buy it with.

It was cool under the trees, but by the time she reached the more sparsely vegetated area the sun was beginning to bite into her back. She slowed down, then flicked a dry tongue over her lips and trudged on. The scrubby sand was alive with lizards that had come out to soak up the sun. A spider loped off with a fast, ungainly gait, heading for the safety of a hole thatched by a patch of spinifex grass. A hawk floated in a circle over-head.

As she walked towards the town others were heading out. Some were new, people lured by the thought of riches, as her parents had been. They didn't know how hard life in the goldfields was yet. Those who did were going in the opposite direction. She felt like keeping on going herself, but a few hours on the open road without water and she'd be dead. And if she happened to reach the city, what then? She must find Flynn.

The town consisted of a straggle of shacks amongst the trees, the grog tent and some other buildings, though the land was still being cleared. She walked the length of the street then walked back again. There was a group of men sitting in the shade of a tree. She approached them. 'Have you seen Flynn Collins anywhere?'

'Who wants to know?'

'Sarette Maitland. He was my father's partner.'

'You're Jack's girl? I'm sorry to hear about your pa. He was a decent man.'

She nodded. 'Somebody stole our things from the camp, including my pa's gold. We've got no water and I can't see the horse and cart anywhere.'

The men exchanged looks, then one mumbled, 'Flynn headed out.'

'Headed out where? He can't take the horse and cart. It belonged to my pa. Do you know where's he gone?'

The man shrugged. 'He didn't say, luv.' Fishing around in his pocket he came out with a shilling. 'Here, this will buy you some water.'

'He's taken the bottle.'

The man looked at his two companions. 'Come on, you two. Last night you were giving her pa a send off. Spare a shilling or two for the kid.'

One of the men spit into the dust. 'I haven't got enough money for mesself, let alone any to spare.'

'Nor me. Perhaps Bessie will give her a job.'

'She's just a kid.'

Sarette put her hands on her hips. 'I'm fourteen, and I can work as hard as any man. Where does this Bessie live?'

He jerked a thumb towards the bush. 'Over yonder. Some men like them innocent. I reckon she'll get a nice price for you. They'll be queuing all the way to Southern Cross.'

When Sarette realized what he was talking about, she blushed and didn't know where to look.

The first man rose to his feet. 'Nay, lass. Take no notice of him. You come with me and I'll see if Benstead will let you help him in the store. At least you'll get fed.'

But Mr Benstead didn't have any paid work for her. 'Her father owed us money for provisions when he died. She can work off what he owes.'

'As long as you feed her.'

'I didn't say I'd feed her. She's not my problem.'

Mrs Benstead came through from the back room, where she'd been listening to the conversation. 'It's our problem if the debt's not paid. It's only right that she should work it off. And I reckon I can manage to feed her for a week while you takes the wagon in to stock up on goods. She's only a skinny little thing so won't eat much, not like that bloody dog you brought home last month.'

'He's a good watchdog, and earns his keep.'

And so the deal was struck. It wasn't much, a chunk of bread and some corn beef and dried apple, which she kept for breakfast. Sometimes there was tinned soup. Sarette found that if she swallowed the dried apple then drank some warm water, the apple would swell in her stomach and make her feel full. Grateful for the food, she worked hard to pay off her father's debt. She swept the sand away from the store, weighed dry goods, kept the shelves filled and the place as dust-free as possible.

She didn't go back to her camp at night, it was too far. Instead, she cuddled up to the dog under the flap of the tent. He seemed glad of her company.

Mrs Benstead wasn't as severe as she looked, and when Sarette's debt was paid she handed her a sack containing some provisions. 'The flour's got a few weevils, but I reckon you're not too fussy and can cope with that.'

'Thank you, Mrs Benstead.'

'You're a good girl, Sarry. You've worked hard and have nice manners. Your dad would have been proud of you. He was a decent man, right enough, not like some of the miners around here. They'd steal your eyes from your sockets before you had time to blink.'

The woman cleared her throat, which made Sarette think she had more to say.

'I can't afford to keep you on here, since we can barely make ends meet. But I'll be the first to say you're a willing worker. I've put a couple of shillings in the bag so you've got some water to take home with you. But only because you've earned it. Don't think I'm a soft touch.'

'Oh, no ... I wouldn't want you to think that I'd think that about you, Mrs Benstead.'

The woman's eyes narrowed a little, then her mouth twisted into a reluctant smile. 'You're not as daft as you look, are you? You can take the old water bag that's hanging on the back veranda. I've put the word round that you're looking for a position, and if anyone needs a reference they're to come to me for a recommendation.'

The praise was unexpected, as was her generosity. 'Thank you, Mrs Benstead.'

'Well, go on then girl,' she said gruffly. 'Get out of here. The water carrier's coming, so you'd best get in the queue.'

Sarette had forgotten how heavy water was. 'Heavier than gold and twice as precious, so don't waste a drop,' her father had often said. Usually he'd fetched it with the horse and cart. Provisions in one hand, water in the other, she made her way back to her camp under the eucalyptus trees, frequently changing hands as her shoulders began to ache.

Finally she reached the track that led to her tent. The horse and cart was nearby. 'Flynn,' she shouted, and placing her bags on the ground she hurried forward. She was brought up short when a woman emerged from the tent. She was wearing the blue dress that had once belonged to Sarette's mother. 'Who are you?' she said.

'Sarette Maitland. This is my camp, and that's my mother's dress you're wearing.'

The woman's hands went to her hips. 'Is it now? We bought this claim and everything in it from Flynn Collins. Lock, stock and barrel.'

Dismayed, Sarette stared at the woman. 'But it wasn't Flynn's to sell. He only owned half the claim. The rest belonged to my pa before he died. And the horse and cart was my pa's too. It didn't belong to Flynn. He stole it.'

'Well, that's too bad. Get off my property.'

'I'll go to the police.'

'Please yourself. You can't prove any of this is yours, and I have a receipt.'

'You're a thief and a liar.'

The woman advanced on her and slapped her several times around the head. 'Don't you call me names, you skinny little wretch.'

Sarette couldn't ward off the stinging slaps and as she staggered backwards her heel caught on a root and she tripped. The woman picked up a branch. Scrambling to her feet Sarette turned and ran, crashing wildly through the undergrowth until she was out of breath and her exposed face and arms were covered in scratches.

After a while she realized she wasn't being followed. She'd also left her precious provisions behind. She didn't intend to leave the water, she'd worked too hard for it.

18

Later in the day she sneaked back to the camp. Her provisions had gone. There was a man there, with a youth, skinning a kangaroo with a sharp-looking knife. Both of them were too big and mean-looking for her to tackle.

She had nothing now, only the clothes she stood up in. As the shadows lengthened she slowly made her way back towards town, though what she was going to do there, she couldn't imagine.

When darkness fell and she could walk no more she sank to the ground, too weary for tears. The earth beneath her still retained the heat of the day and the air was humid and balmy. Above her, the stars scattered thickly across the sky and Sarette thought she could feel the world turn.

Her stomach rattled with hunger, her face stung from the woman's slaps and her throat was parched with the need for moisture. It would be a good night to die. Sarette willed it, and the stars began to blur before her eyes and her limbs became lethargic. Darkness crept through her body and she thought she could hear an angel singing. His voice was loud and deep, and she wished he'd shut up, so she could die in peace.

'Abide with me; fast falls the eventide. The darkness deepens, Lord, with me abide—'

John Kern tripped over something soft that grunted with annoyance. 'Damn and blast, and I was in fine voice tonight too, Hercules.'

His horse, who was following a couple of lengths behind him came to a halt and gently snickered.

John crouched, felt along the bundle, then

19

announced his verdict. 'It's certainly a child,' he told his horse.

The horse nudged a wet nose at the bundle, the force of which rolled it over. It hissed with annoyance. 'Go away. I want to die in peace.'

'And a fine night for dying it is, too. I think I'll die with you. *When other helpers fail and comforts flee, help of the helpless—*'

'Do be quiet.'

He lowered his voice to a whisper and finished, *'Oh, abide with me.'* There was a moment of silence, then, 'Before you die, could you direct me to my house? I'm lost.'

A muffled sob reached his ears. 'How can I, when I don't know who you are and where you live? When I heard you singing I thought you were an angel coming to take me to heaven.'

'Don't be in too much of a hurry to get to heaven, my dear. Angels are tedious creatures who sit on clouds, flap their wings and play harps. Besides, they have to be good all the time, and I'm sure that wouldn't suit you at all. My name is John Kern. What's yours?'

She gave a watery giggle. 'Sarette Maitland.'

'Ah, just the person Hercules and I was looking for before I was lured into the grog shop by a lady with a large bottom and a thirst on her. Well, never mind. You're too young to know about such things.'

'What things?'

'Grown-up things. What were you doing way out here by yourself? I was looking for the horizon.'

'In the dark? I thought you said you were

looking for your home.'

He laughed. 'Perhaps my home is on the horizon. I lied. What's your story?'

'My father's partner sold the claim and the camp. The woman who lives there now was wearing my mother's dress, one I was keeping for myself to grow into it. And she beat me when I asked for it, so I ran away, leaving my water and provisions behind. When I went back for them they were gone. Her husband and son looked mean and I was too scared to ask for them. So I left. I was going into town but I think I took the wrong trail and it got dark. I was tired, and I decided to stop and rest. Then I got it into my head to die. I was just going to when I heard you sing, and thought you were an angel.'

'I saved your life then. Hercules was very clever to find you.'

She decided to humour him. 'Why were you looking for me, sir?'

'To employ you, of course. I'd noticed you working around the store, and you reminded me of someone. Mrs Benstead said you work hard, don't eat or talk much and never complain. I need a housekeeper if you're willing. The stars look pretty, don't they?'

'I used to sit and watch them with my pa. Sometimes one would shoot across the sky and we'd both make a wish. Pa's wish was to find enough gold so he could buy a proper house and could take me away from here and give me an education. I used to wish that Pa's wish would come true, so he'd be truly happy. He was so sad after my ma died.'

* * *

Poor girl to lose both her parents, John thought, and her looking so much like his own dead daughter that his heart had nearly stopped when he'd first set eyes on her at the store. Not that he'd ever seen Margaret covered in dirt like this ragged little waif, or wearing worn boots that were too big for her. Margaret had been bathed by her governess every day and had dressed in satin and lace. She'd worn ribbons in her hair and the softest of kid slippers on her feet.

And what was he doing, offering to take this stranger in and giving her a home when he'd made plans to dispose of his life? He was too old for children. The grief of losing Margaret had turned his mind. Like Sarette, he'd wanted to die so he'd started to drink himself to death, and he'd almost succeeded, but not quite.

He wasn't really a believer, but if God did happen to exist, what if He'd sent him this girl, who reminded him so forcefully of the child he'd lost. What if this was his opportunity to redeem himself by saving this little waif?

Claptrap! he thought uneasily. Nevertheless, she needed somebody to care for her. He placed a bottle in her hand and sighed. Conscience was a hard taskmaster. 'Here, swallow this. Then we'll go home.'

She must have smelled the liquor on his breath because she asked prissily, 'What is it?'

'Ah, a typical female. We've only just met and you're nagging me about my drinking habits.'

'My pa said only fools drink whisky in the diggings.'

'I assure you that this bottle contains only water, twice boiled to keep the typhoid at bay. I brought it along for Hercules, but I daresay he can manage without it till we get home. I reserve the whisky for myself, it dulls the brain while it quietly rots away the guts. So your pa was right, and I admit to being a fool. Now we have that settled, drink up or shut up.'

Only water, he thought, giving a wry smile as she put the bottle to her lips and tipped it. Water was life and death here, and the girl was gulping it down as though she'd decided on living after all and had a private river of water at her disposal.

When she'd emptied the bottle he lifted her on to the horse and mounted behind her. She was slight, weighing next to nothing. He clicked his tongue. 'Take us home then Hercules. And mind your manners. We have a young lady on board.'

Two

Dorset, England

My dearest Magnus,

Today I find myself on the diggings in a place that is called Coolgardie. A large amount of gold was discovered here a little while ago, in an area appropriately named, Fly Flat. So far I've sifted a little dust, enough for my day to day needs, but riches still evade me.

The area is a Godforsaken place, dusty and hot, and with sparse vegetation and no water, except what is carted in. As you can imagine the longing for the green hills of home overwhelms me from time to time.

I have pegged my claim and built a temporary shelter on it (one cannot really call it a home), a sketch of which I enclose. As you can see, I show very little promise at architecture.

Magnus Kern chuckled. His uncle John had a sense of humour, one that was evident in his sketch of the ramshackle hut. By the looks of it, the walls were made of sacks sewn together and attached to a frame. There were sheets of corrugated tin for a roof, and tacked on here and there. A veranda was built on the front supported by rough wooden poles, with branches to provide shade. Under it was a stool to sit on and a wooden barrel next to the support, either to store water, or to use as a table, he supposed. A peasant would scorn the offer of a mean hovel such as this in which to house his pigs.

His uncle's present address was quite a step down from Fierce Eagles, once his uncle's home, and now the property of himself, the last to bear the Kern family name. The house was named after the stone eagles perched atop each gatepost, which gazed fiercely down at visitors as they passed through, and those after the business the Kern family had derived its livelihood from.

His solid home was of a size easily managed by a half a dozen servants. It drew its income from land rents and the interest paid from investments. Magnus Kern had a personal fortune of fifty thousand pounds a year, a fortune inherited from his father.

I can't remember the last time I had a bath. It matters not since we all smell the same here, and are used to it. It rains very little. If it did rain I daresay I'd strip down to my skin and run about in it. Not many of the women who live here would be scandalized by such behaviour. Most are decent women who support their families through hunger and illness, and I admire them greatly. Conditions here are wretched, and they cope with such privation, and would welcome a substantial downpour, I think. It makes me realize how spoilt I have been all my life.

As had he, but it worried Magnus not at all that the fortune he'd inherited had been gathered in the first place from thievery and smuggling. Honest he might be known as, but Magnus knew when to close his eyes and look the other way.

The deeds to Fierce Eagles had been gifted to him by his uncle John before he'd left for the Antipodes. Magnus's name had been added to the deed, his uncle's signature witnessed and notarized by his solicitor.

In vain Magnus had argued, 'You're only fifty years of age, still young enough to marry and father a child again.'

'Nay, Magnus. There was only ever one woman for me, and my marriage was riches indeed. When I lost her I knew I could never love another. And when my sweet girl followed her mother to the grave just as she began to blossom into womanhood, my heart began to die inside me. Since then I've willed myself to stop breathing with each dawn that comes.'

'But the house—'

'Is yours now. Find yourself a woman you can love and live with for ever. Preferably a wicked one, who can give you as good as she gets in bed. Fill her with your children, give her your heart, smack her arse when she needs it and be content. With me leaving, this house has seen the last of its wild days.'

Magnus had laughed at that. 'I will be forever looking at things and wondering which pirate brought home that, and which smuggler risked his life with the revenue men. You must consider me tame compared with yourself and my ancestors.'

'Not tame, just honest, and there's a certain bravery in that. You enjoy life, and you have a reputation amongst the fairer sex as well as being an astute judge of mankind. You deserve a house such as this one. It wears its current reputation badly, and needs someone like you to bring it some dignity. It punished me, but it will treat you kindly if you do the same by it. I promise you, Fierce Eagles will give you a huge amount of prestige, which will attract the most deliciously naughty of the damsels to your side. They will like the reputation of your ancestry, and secretly hope you make as dangerous a husband as you look as if you might.'

Magnus had tried to hide his grin. He'd never have thought that his uncle would wax so poetic. 'You're trying to shackle me before I've finished sowing my wild oats. You should take your own advice.'

He remembered the sadness that had come into his uncle's eyes. 'I'll never be able to live at Fierce Eagles again. I'm off on my last adventure, before the final one calls me. If I grow tired of wandering I'll return and reside in the house I bought in Bournemouth. I'll gaze at the sea and the coast and dream of the time your father and grandfather, and every other Kern before us, lived a life of adventure and took on the authorities and won.'

'Except for my father.'

'Aye lad, and to my infinite sorrow, for I loved my brother dearly. But he gave me you to care

27

for, and I'm so proud of you. If he's looking down, or looking up, whichever is appropriate, he'd be extremely proud of his son, too. As for me, who would have thought that John Kern would eventually earn his living by his wits and the sweat of his brow.'

'Good luck with the venture. Keep me informed of your progress.'

Magnus had been taken in a bear hug, and his uncle's voice had been thick with the emotion of the parting. 'You'll know when I've struck it rich. I'll send you some gold. Look after my dog.'

With that John Kern had turned away and strode off. Now and again Magnus received a letter from him, but they were few. He gazed down at his uncle's elegant hand.

Life is interesting, if nothing else. Like most people here I live for the moment I discover a significant gold strike. Odd how a search for riches takes a hold of a man. But it's not the gold I want, but just to unearth it from where it hides in its bed. They call it gold fever. I keep my eyes to the ground when I walk in case I inadvertently uncover a large nugget with my big toe and cover it up again with my heel. How ironic an act that would be.

I hope you are well, Magnus. Wed yet? I think not. Time has a habit of slipping by, and there's nothing quite so sad as an ageing roué. Remind yourself that you need to get yourself an heir for Fierce Eagles. In the meantime I'll console myself with the fact that you enjoy the company of women, and will be firmly hooked by some fluttering miss one day.

At twenty-four he was hardly an ageing roué yet, Magnus thought, and he grinned. He could not imagine marrying a woman who fluttered.

If this letter arrives in time, I wish you and the staff a happy Christmas and a prosperous New Year. There's a brace of brandy bottles in the cellar that I laid down fifteen years ago. You'll know the ones. Open them for the staff with my felicitations. Yes, yes! I know the house and contents are now yours. Humour me on this occasion, and drink to my health with the staff.

If this letter doesn't arrive in time, it's bound to get there by your birthday in April, if not, the one after. So, happy birthday.

From your affectionate uncle,
John Kern.

The letter was dated a year after John's uncle had arrived in the colony, and had taken six months to get to him. Now it was February and he was a few weeks off the birthday after, when he'd be twenty-five years of age.

He crossed to the window and gazed out at the day. The grass was crisp with frost and the early morning air was blue with smoke rising from the chimneys. The sky was clear, and he doubted that it would rain. Today he had business to conduct, a meeting with Ignatious Grimble, family friend and the solicitor who'd always managed

John Kern's affairs. Together they'd inspect his uncle's house in Bournemouth, note any maintenance needed, and make sure that all was well with the tenants before the lease was renewed for a further year. He had to be careful with tenants, since as far as he knew, the rent was his uncle's only source of income now.

After that he would call on Isabelle, surprise her for her birthday, even though she wasn't expecting him. He took a small box from his desk and slipped it into his pocket.

Smiling, he strode into the hall, shrugged into the long coat and overcape that his manservant held out, then pulled on his gloves and went out to the waiting gig.

His horse was impatient for exercise. Steam snorted from his nostrils and he stamped his forelegs when Magnus approached. Stepping into the gig, Magnus settled himself and took the reins from the stable hand. 'Thanks, Robert.'

'He's frisky this morning, sir, 'tis the cold.' Robert looked as though he was about to say something else as he fussed with the bridle.

'What is it Robert? I have to get going.'

'Branston noticed that the post arrived yesterday and—'

'You want to know if I heard from John Kern?' He smiled at the loyalty still shown to John by his former staff. 'Yes, I did receive a letter from him. You can tell the staff that at the time of writing he was in an area called Coolgardie, which is situated to the west of the Australian continent. He was quite well and is looking for gold. He's built himself a ... dwelling of sorts.'

Robert grinned happily at that. 'The master was allus good with his hands, and pitched in when any maintenance was needed on the house.'

'Quite.' Magnus allowed the mistake to go by, though by now they should be thinking of himself as their master. 'My uncle also wished us all a happy Christmas for the one before last. Rather belated, I'm afraid.'

'The sentiment's the same. Thank you, sir. The staff will be relieved to hear that he's all right.'

'He's given me instructions to crack open a bottle of brandy and drink his health, so if you would all present yourself to the library this evening after dinner, we shall do that and I'll read you his letter.'

'That's right nice of him, sir. And of you, of course.' Robert tipped his cap and moved off, hugging his arms against his body to ward off the cold.

The horse nearly jerked the reins from his hands.

'Have some patience, and kindly remember you're between the shafts today.'

When they were safely past the stone eagles and on the open road, Magnus had to fight to keep the beast under his control. After a while the gelding settled into a comfortable trot and he breathed a sigh of relief. With thirty miles to cover he didn't want the animal winded when they'd hardly started out.

Later in the morning, he stopped outside Ignatious Grimble's mansion and handed his rig over to the groom. His horse could rest before the return journey. From here they would walk up the hill and along the west cliff to his uncle's house, which overlooked the sea.

Ignatious Grimble was beginning to resemble a turtle, Magnus thought as they shook hands and started walking through the town centre. He wondered how old Ignatious was, since he'd also been his grandfather's solicitor. Magnus vaguely remembered him from his childhood, but couldn't remember him looking any younger than he did now. He was sprightly enough though, and had fathered eleven children from two wives, now deceased.

'You look more like your father and uncle every time I see you,' Ignatious said. 'The Kern blood runs strongly in you. They were all imposing-looking men.'

'As long as it's only their looks I've inherited.'

A cackle of laughter came from the old man. 'You would have enjoyed the adventurous life they led, I'm sure. When he was a young man, about your age, your great-great-great-grandfather cuckolded the local magistrate and had to live abroad for a while. He ended up in Corsica. There he purchased a ship and became a pirate, building up his networks. He made himself a fortune.'

'And he married Esmerelda Rey, the daughter of one of his partners in crime, brought her back to England and set up house in Fierce Eagles.'

'Isolated, and perfect for smuggling goods into England.'

'Yes, Mr Grimble. It's certainly that, and I've been brought up on tales of the exploits of my

32

ancestry.' Not caring if he sounded prim, he added, 'I feel no urge to emulate them.'

'I'm sure you don't, Magnus. Nearly everyone got ahead by dishonest means in those days. Money meant power, and plunder and smuggling became a Kern family enterprise.'

'Which stops with me. If I ever have sons they'll be brought up to earn a decent and honest living. I don't want to risk early death from a bullet or a hangman's rope, and leave them orphaned.'

'Your father made provision for you, and your uncle did a good job of bringing you up.'

Magnus gave a faint smile. 'John told me it was too late for him, but as the last of the Kerns it was my moral duty to redeem the family name.'

'I'm sure that's something you will do admirably.'

As they began to head up the cliff road Magnus slowed his step to accommodate the older man's. He chuckled. 'Are you? Others are not quite so certain of my honesty. More often than not I manage to attract shady characters to my law business.'

'Somebody has to represent them.'

'But I rarely make any money.'

Ignatious sighed. 'You have an ample fortune in investments behind you, Magnus. You don't need to earn more money. Look at it this way. By and large, the wealth you already have was not honestly earned. You're giving a little of it back to the poor, in kind. I imagine that's what your uncle meant by moral duty and redemption of the family name.

'Magnus Kern, philanthropist?' This time he laughed. 'Considering my background, my Uncle John sets a high standard for me.'

'He does, but he was of the opinion that most men would surrender pride for a price, while you would do the opposite.'

Magnus laughed at that and his glance went to the sea. The air was fresh and bracing, the water a pewter stretch of ripples into a horizon that was almost white. The tide was on the ebb leaving a pattern of damp, ridged sand behind. Seagulls followed the foamy hem of the water, pecking up stranded baby crabs and transparent shrimps as they were uncovered. Along the water mark a man walked with his dog.

Magnus recalled that his uncle's old dog had died not long after his master had left. He'd gone to sleep on the rug in front of the fire and hadn't bothered to wake, knowing his adventuring days were over. Magnus hadn't replaced him.'

'I heard from my uncle today. The letter was written six months ago. He was in a place called Coolgardie that's situated in the west.'

'An odd name for a town.'

'I was wondering if you'd had any more recent news of him since.'

'John's not a man to be found unless he wants to be.' Grimble flicked him a look. 'But aye, he does report in to a mutual agent from time to time. There was a telegraph message from him about three months ago. He was well, and was still looking for gold.'

'Is that all he said?'

'He said he was managing quite well, and that the lack of personal comforts and the hardship and the poverty of others had changed his priorities, and...'

'And?'

'That was just about it. The house looks well from the outside doesn't it?'

'Mr Grimble. You're trying to sidetrack me.'

The man stopped at the white-painted gate. *Smuggler's View* the house was called. 'Apt ... very apt,' Grimble murmured, and turned back to him. 'May I remind you that I'm your uncle's solicitor as well as his friend. I handle John's affairs personally, while my sons manage the rest of the business. I keep confidential the business between us and carry out his wishes to the letter. Rest assured, if anything untoward happens, I will make sure you are informed and consulted with immediately.'

Magnus had to be content with that. 'Thank you, Ignatious. I understand perfectly, and his business couldn't be in better hands, though I would have wished to be trusted with it.'

'Sometimes having an executor within a family can be detrimental to both parties. Now, if you're agreeable, we will drop the matter and attend to the business at hand.'

'Yes, of course.'

Three storeys high, *Smuggler's View* overlooked the bay to the Isle of Purbeck, a view that could never be built out. The house was roomy enough to cater for a large family, but not ostentatiously so.

Ignatious told him, 'They're good tenants, and

are willing to renegotiate the rent if we'll renew the lease for the life of their relative. She's an elderly lady who resides here for the benefits of the sea air. She is not expected to live much longer.'

'Allowing the tenant to dictate the terms of the lease is not a good business practice, neither is taking a gamble on longevity. What if the lady lives longer than expected, and John returns?'

'I daresay you'll offer him a home at Fierce Eagles.'

'Offering is not the problem, but my uncle has stated he'll never live there again. I do have to think of his welfare, and not out of duty but because I love the man as if he was my own father. I suggest we renew the lease on six monthly terms, payable in advance, and at a rent that's reasonable for this area. When that time is up, we'll give them the first option on another six months. If the lady is not expected to live, then they should welcome the chance not to be encumbered with a long lease.'

Ignatious Grimble gave a faint smile as he pushed open the gate. 'You're as astute as John believed you were. You were always a studious, steady and thoughtful child – and a steadying influence on my son, Gerald, for which I'm grateful.'

'Gerald and I are the best of friends, always will be.'

The inspection didn't take long. The invalid lady managed to walk with a stick, but she ran out of breath easily and placed her hand against her chest to ease it. Having been paraded and her

36

condition witnessed, she was ushered away by a nurse. Her son was happy with the lease arrangement, and they departed.

An hour later Magnus was in Poole, knocking at the door of a smaller house situated in the lower part of Constitution Hill. A maid he'd never seen before showed him into the drawing room. 'I'll enquire if Mrs Parkhurst will see you.'

Magnus raised an eyebrow at that. He paid Isabelle's rent and expected her to be able to see him on short notice.

She came in five minutes later, looking slightly flustered, her dark hair hastily styled, and wearing a fussy, over-decorated pink gown that he didn't particularly like. She was uncorseted, for her flesh strained against the material at the waist. 'Magnus, I wasn't expecting you. You usually visit on Friday evening.'

'Yes, I do seem to be a creature of habit, don't I? I was over this way and decided to drop in. A pleasant surprise, I hope.'

'Of course. It's always a pleasure to see you, Magnus.'

She was flustered, and he was suspicious. 'You look dishevelled, Isabelle. Were you in bed?'

A blush seeped under her skin. 'I had a bad headache earlier today ... I'd been resting. then I took a bath to relax me.'

'Ah, so that's why the maid said you might not be able to see me. And is this bad headache gone now?'

She shrugged. 'It was nothing, really, and the maid's new.' Isabelle moved to the sherry decanter on the table. 'Would you like some refreshment?'

'I came to see you, Isabelle. Do you not have a kiss for me?'

She came and stood in front of him, the alarm now faded from her brown eyes. She was a beautiful woman, and he'd known her before she was widowed. Her luscious mouth showed a row of white even teeth when she smiled and surrendered her mouth to his. There was a faint smell of cigar smoke in her hair as her body pressed against him, humid, and musky with perspiration. Ringlets curled damply against her pale neck. She'd lied about the bath.

There came the sound of the door to the street stealthily closing.

He resisted the urge to cross to the window and see who was leaving. 'Were you entertaining a man when I arrived?'

She turned her head away. 'I told you, I was taking a bath.'

Taking her chin between finger and thumb he turned her face back to his. 'You smell of tobacco smoke. Are you telling me the truth? Shall I call the maid and see what she has to say?'

She shrugged. 'I told her to leave us alone together. As for the cigar smoke, my former brother-in-law visited earlier. We shared a glass of wine in the conservatory because the sun had warmed it. He smoked. It was probably that which gave me the headache.'

He didn't know whether to believe her or not. 'Strange that he felt he had to sneak out without being introduced.'

'Oh, he left much earlier. It would have been the maid leaving on an errand. Don't be so suspicious, Magnus.' She stroked her hand against his groin and her voice took on a husky, but slightly sullen note. 'Are you staying the night?'

The thought of sleeping with her when she might have come from another man's embrace was abhorrent to him. In fact, despite looking forward to his encounter with Isabelle, his need had suddenly fled. But no doubt it would be back.

'I think not, Isabelle. I'll be here as usual on Friday, and I'd be obliged if you'd change the bed sheets and take a bath.'

Anger fired in her eyes. 'Oh, don't be so stuffy about our arrangement. It's not as if we're married, and you weren't so fussy when I was wed to Henry.'

'I wasn't supporting you financially then.'

'Just cuckolding a business client. Do you think that paying my rent gives you exclusive use of my body and control over my life? I can quite afford to pay my own rent.'

'I'm well aware of your financial state. You'd be a prize for some man.' Perhaps he was taking her too much for granted.

'But not for you, obviously. If you want me exclusively you can put a ring on my finger and move me into Fierce Eagles.'

He felt genuine surprised at that. 'Marriage?'

'Does it surprise you that I might want a secure relationship, and normal things like a child of my own?'

'Yes, it does. You were an unfaithful wife to

39

Henry, and you'd be the same to me. You're a trollop. How many other men are paying your rent?'

She laughed. 'Do you really want me to tell you?'

'Yes.'

'None. Just you, Magnus Kern. You're jealous.'

He wasn't, and that bothered him. His feelings for Isabelle didn't go past the physical. He was comfortable in such an arrangement as they had, and so was she, he'd thought. He was also selfish. Like any other beautiful possession he admired certain aspects of her. But did he want to marry her?'

'I've always been honest with you Isabelle. I'm not looking to wed just yet, but if I were...' He shrugged, left himself uncommitted, because he still wouldn't want marriage with her. 'Would you rather we brought this relationship to an end?'

She moved against him again and began to loosen his cravat. 'Don't be silly, Magnus. You have spoiled me for any other man and I've been totally faithful to you. I think of nobody else.' When she pressed a kiss against the hollow of his throat his desire came back. Shrugging out of his coat, he pulled open her gown, slid it from her creamy shoulders and watched it pool around her ankles.

She was full-bodied, her breasts ripe, her hips wide and her thighs firm and heavy. He reached out with a fingertip, caressed each rosy nipple, so they sprang hard against her silky skin. The smell of soap rose from the dark apex of her thighs and he felt ashamed of himself.

'I'm sorry I was mean.'

She kissed him, released his trousers bringing him surging against her. 'Be mean to me again. Punish me. Let's go upstairs so we can play games.'

What if her room smelled of smoke? What if the bed was rumpled? He decided he didn't want to know one way or the other. 'I haven't got time, there's no moon tonight and I want to be home before dark.'

'Then let's do it here.' She pushed him gently on to the chair and straddled his lap.

Sliding his hands under each dimpled buttock he said against her ear. 'Yes, let's.'

Later, he handed her the jeweller's box he'd brought with him. 'Happy birthday, Isabelle.'

She exclaimed over the diamond brooch. 'You remembered?'

'Of course I remembered. Don't I always?'

'Just like a proper husband,' she mocked.

The hair on his neck prickled a warning. Isabelle was tightening the noose a little. From now on he must be careful not to say anything that would give her hope.

He'd stayed later than he'd meant to. His horse gave him an annoyed look and stamped its foreleg a couple of times. Soon they were heading home, at a faster pace than usual. As the light began to wane the air grew bitterly cold and the horse began to blow. One of the servants had possessed the sense to open the gates and hang a couple of lanterns on the gateposts. He gave the horse a little slack, and as the last vestige of light fled he passed under the scrutiny of the eagles.

The groom must have heard him coming and the door to the stables opened, spilling light from the lanterns across the yard. Robert stepped forward to take the lathered horse away. 'Sorry, Rob. I was held up and had to push him.'

'He's up to it. It'll take the ginger out of him a bit. He'll be all right after a good rub down and a feed.'

Magnus grinned. He was in need of a good feed too. He'd already had the rub down. As he strode towards the house he mused that he'd had both an interesting and productive day.

The house looked warm and welcoming. He'd always liked Fierce Eagles, and had been astounded when his uncle had gifted the place to him.

As he entered the hall he looked up at the portrait of the former mistress of the house. Dressed in dark red satin, her dainty, bejewelled hand held a fan. Her daughter was about eleven, and clothed in pink taffeta and lace. Margaret leaned into her mother's lap, grave-faced except for a hint of mischief in those innocent green eyes that looked straight at him.

Poor John, to lose both of the women he loved. Margaret had been lovely, delicate, and lively and she would have grown up to be like her mother. Magnus had loved his sweet little cousin. Perhaps he would have married her had she lived. John would have liked that.

He avoided the drawing room, instead heading for the cosy confines of his study, where he knew a fire would have been kept burning for his return. Pouring himself a brandy he took the chair by the fire and savoured each sip as he waited to be called to his dinner.

The staff would be waiting with some eagerness to hear the news from his uncle, and he smiled as he reached out and touched the missive.

Three

Sarette had settled into the shelter that John Kern called home.

He'd built another lean-to on the side for her, just like his own, so she could have some privacy. A wooden frame supported flour sacks sewn together for walls, and a slope of corrugated tin. He made a bed frame from branches to keep her off the ground, and stood the legs in tins of water with kerosene in them to keep the ants at bay.

Today he'd rigged up a line and said, 'That's a wardrobe to hang your clothing on.'

'Thank you, but I only have what I stand up in.'

'So you do. You can't blame those people, since they paid hard cash for the claim and the camp. It was the Irishman who robbed you. I'll go and see them. I can't carry off the whole camp and won't get a second opportunity, so what means the most to you?'

She didn't hesitate. 'There's a small tin trunk that contained personal goods that belonged to my mother. My father gave it all to me. That's where the woman got the dress from.'

John scratched his head and thought for a moment. 'Can you make me a list of what was in the trunk?'

He unfolded a polished writing case with silver hinges and mixed a small amount of ink before handing her a pen, with the advice. Don't press too hard or you'll ruin the nib.'

She began to write on a scrap of paper he gave her, concentrating on her spelling and getting all the letters even. *Hairbrush and mirror. Bible. Gloves...*

'You have been educated, I see. You have good writing skills.'

'My mother taught me. She was a governess before she married my father, and my father taught me numbers. He was a clerk in a bank. When we left here he was going to send me to a proper school.' Speaking of her mother had triggered Sarette's memory. 'Oh, yes, and there was a brooch with my mother's likeness in it.' Spitting into the inkwell she mixed the last traces of ink in and added in almost invisible lettering, *locket brooch*.

'Ladies shouldn't spit, not even to moisten inkwells. Don't do it again.'

Sarette looked up into eyes as dark as molasses. John Kern had a handsome, but rather stern face under his grey whiskers. He wasn't a man she'd deliberately disobey. 'Sorry, sir.'

'You needn't call me sir.'

'But I'm your housekeeper.'

He laughed at that, said mockingly, 'And what a grand house it is that you have to keep, Miss Sarette Maitland.'

'I like it. I have my very own room.'

'You're easily pleased. Have you ever lived in a proper house?'

'Sometimes I remember a house in England. It had a thatched roof and a garden that smelled of roses.' She closed her eyes and smiled, drawing on some distant memory. 'Everything was green, and I remember being happy there. My mother drew a picture of it in her sketching block.'

'Would you like to go back to England?'

'Oh yes. When I'm grown up. I could be a governess like my mother was.'

'Not a very worthy ambition, if I may say. Governesses are usually spinster ladies. They don't earn much and when their charges grow up they're dismissed from their positions.'

'Well, perhaps I'll find gold and be wealthy, and marry a fine lord.'

'You think a blue blood would want a scruffy little ragamuffin like you when he has the most beautiful, most wealthy and perfectly mannered young ladies in London to choose from?'

'My pa said I'm beautiful. And you'll be sorry you said that when you have to bow to me.' She opened her eyes to the sight of him pushing a revolver into the waist of his trousers. 'Are you going to dig for gold or hunt for dinner? I can help you. I know how to sift the dirt and you

45

could give me fifty per cent of what we dig up.'

He began to roar with laughter at that. 'Fifty per cent, when I'd be doing the lion's share of the work? You're more ambitious than I thought, Princess.'

She began to giggle. 'Twenty per cent then.'

'I'll think about it. After all, twenty per cent of nothing is nothing.'

'Then you could easily afford to pay me fifty per cent.'

'I could, but twenty per cent of nothing works out to the same amount, so why should you complain? All the same, I quite like your thinking process. I'm going off to retrieve your trunk, young lady. I can't promise you the dress, the woman might be wearing it.' He reflected for a moment, then his eyes filled with amusement. 'I could rip if off her body, I suppose.'

She gasped, saying, before she realized he was teasing, 'No don't. Be careful, sir, the men living there look tough.'

'They'll probably be out working the claim. If I'm lucky they won't even see me.'

'You're going to steal it? I thought you were going to see them and ask for it.'

He shrugged. 'Never you mind how I'm going to obtain it for you, but obtain it, I will.'

'But you're an honest, respectable and pious man who sings hymns when he's lost.'

He laughed. 'Respectability can be acquired along with fortune, however dubiously it's earned. As for being honest, nobody has accused me of that before. I'm not pious, though I believe there is goodness in me when the occasion arises. I sing hymns because Hercules likes them. He belonged to a preacher man.'

'What shall I do while you're away?' she called out as he mounted.

'You're a female. You could always take a wash, unless you want to be mistaken for one of the native children. Then I can see for myself whether or not you're beautiful under all that dirt. There's a tin bath in the kitchen, water in the barrel and some soap on the shelf. Use what you need as long as there's enough left to last until the cart comes tomorrow. And you could wash your clothes in it afterwards. You can wear my robe while they're drying if you like.'

'Fight the good fight with all your might...' He began to sing, and Hercules's ears pricked forward and he gave a small snicker as they moved away.

A wash! A whole bath of water for herself! First she washed her hair, which turned the water a dirty yellow. Standing, she washed herself all over with the soap. It was a crude yellow block which had been made by Mrs Benstead, then cut into chunks to be sold in the store. With her knees tucked under her chin Sarette just managed to sit in the bath. Closing her eyes she scooped water over herself with her hands and savoured the coolness of it running over her skin, which brought her out in goosebumps. When she was rich she would sit and soak in a bath every day. The feeling was delicious, but she felt guilty for wasting so much water on herself. She would make sure it was put to further use.

After her bath she plunged her skirt and bodice into the brew and scrubbed away at the dirt and stains. Wringing them out as best she could she spread the clothing over the shrubs to dry. She fetched a cloth and used the water to wash the dust from the table, chairs, storage shelves and a wooden trunk.

She was about to pour the filthy water remaining into the roots of a shrub when she remembered another use for it. Scooping up some dirt she placed it in the gold pan that was leaning against the tree, added some of the water, stirred it about then gradually allowed the silty swirling water to spill out. Amongst the traces of mud left behind she found half a dozen sparkling specks of gold. Carefully, she lifted them out and placed them in an empty match box.

An hour later her clothing was almost dry. The fabric was covered in brown stains and crinkled up. But at least she felt clean as she'd braided her long hair and tied a rag around the end.

She gazed around wondering what to do next, then hung a kettle of water over the campfire. An examination of the dwelling revealed that the wooden box with a tightly fitting lid contained dry goods, and there was some meat in a damp sack. She made a loaf of bread, cooking it in the ashes.

John had no compunction about retrieving Sarette's clothes. He was outraged by what had happened to her. If he ever ran into the cowardly Irishman who'd sold the girl's home and living from under her he'd give him a good thrashing.

No man worth his salt would make destitute and abandon a girl so young on the diggings.

He left Hercules and proceeded to the camp on foot. As he'd expected, the males were absent. But where was the woman? The campfire in its circle of stones was barely alight, and unattended.

As he listened he heard the snap of twigs and branches, of a chopper slicing into wood. He stepped forward and entered the tent, which was little more than a piece of canvas over a tree branch. It was secured with ropes tied to pegs in the ground.

The trunk was at the back and had the name Sara Maitland on it. No mistaking who that belonged to. He picked it up and made his escape, snatching up the blue dress which was thrown over a hammock.

There was a shout as he headed into the bush. The owner of the voice, a man, crashed in after him. John zigzagged back and forth, heading for his horse and keeping a tight hold on his prize. Behind him he heard a click, then an explosion. Buckshot peppered the bushes around him and a few pellets lodged in the cheeks of his arse.

A woman began to screech hysterically. A man answered her in a hectoring voice and she shut her mouth.

John cursed. His backside stung, but he wasn't about to give them the chance to reload and come after him. He made his horse in record time, mounted with the trunk in front of him, and, head down, put Hercules to the run and was out and gone. As soon as he was out of range he slowed down and began to laugh. He'd forgotten how exhilarating flirting with danger was.

Circumnavigating the main street of the town he entered his own camp from behind, leading his horse in. It was a precaution he took in case someone was lying in wait for him.

He saw Sarette at the campfire and was transfixed by what he saw. She must have sensed him, for she turned, stared at him for a moment then gave him a wide smile. 'I didn't hear you coming.'

Her father had been right. The girl was beautiful with a sweet delicacy to her movements, and her long braid had a coppery sheen, like chestnuts, which reminded him of the trees in autumn at Fierce Eagles. He experienced an ache somewhere in the region of his heart. 'What are you cooking?'

'What remains of that kangaroo in the sack. I thought I'd make a stew with it. It will last a day or two.'

He nodded and walked towards the hut carrying the small trunk and the dress. She followed after him. 'You're bleeding.'

'It's nothing,' His bravado had fled and he felt a fool when he told her, 'It's buckshot. Someone mistook me for an emu and tried to scare me off.'

Her lips twitched. 'Someone mistook you for a thief, you mean. You'd better drop your pants and let me doctor you. Wounds go rotten very quickly here.'

She wasn't telling him anything he didn't know. 'I'll do no such thing, you saucy little

50

hussy.'

She tossed him a grin. 'Suffer, if that's what you want.'

'I can see to it myself.' He placed the trunk on the floor and the dress on top of it, then went back into the living room and assembled a metal probe, a pair of tweezers and a bottle of iodine.

Sarette came through with a wooden-backed hand mirror and propped it against a jug filled with leafy twigs. 'Here, so you can see what you're doing.'

He gave the twigs in the jug a second glance. Typical of female thinking to pretty the place up in such a manner. 'Thanks.' He shooed her outside. 'Go outside and give Hercules a feed of oats and a drink while I doctor myself. The oats are in that sack hanging from the nail. If he's difficult, sing him a hymn.'

A few minutes later, as he got the first pellet out, he heard her sing:

There was a black gelding from kucamandoo who uncovered a nugget of gold with his shoe. A pretty white mare from kucamandee wore a red garter tied over her knee, and a handsome young mule from kucamandonga woke up the dawn with a sweet braying songa, while the ass who lived at kucamandaisy honked like a goose and drove everyone crazy.

'D'you like that song, Hercules? I made it up specially for you.'

John peeked out of the door and saw Hercules with his head on her shoulder and his eyes shut.

Sarette was gently rubbing his nose.

He probed for the second pellet and exclaimed, 'Bloody hell! That one's gone too deep.' He couldn't see a damned thing in the mirror without bending at the knees. Also, he was right-handed, and the pellets were embedded on the left side so he could hardly reach. And when he did locate a pellet in the mirror his hand went in the opposite direction to where he'd meant it to go, as if it had a mind of its own.

Feeling frustrated he called the girl in. 'You'll have to do it, but don't look at my backside.'

'Then how can I get the pellets out?'

'You can look without seeming to, can't you? Pretend you're a doctor.' Luckily he was able to keep himself fairly decent by holding his trousers over the rest.

The pellets were dug out with no regard for his comfort or dignity, and they were dropped on to the table he was leaning over, making little metallic thuds. Picking up the iodine she dripped a little into one of the wounds. It stung like hell. He sucked in an involuntary breath and gave a yelp.

She sighed. 'You're a grown man, John Kern. Stop making such a fuss about nothing.'

Nothing! Wait till she had a backside full of lead pellets to sit on. As it was obvious she was going to give him no quarter he proved to himself that he wasn't at all grown-up by subsiding into a heap of ursine rumbles.

When she'd finished doctoring him she turned her back modestly while he straightened himself up. 'Thank you,' he grunted.

'It's my fault. If you hadn't fetched my things ... Thank you, I appreciate it.'

'You're a surprising girl. How old are you, eleven?'

'I'm fourteen ... almost grown-up.'

She was grown-up in many ways. The gold-fields did that to children. But she was un-developed and slender, like a boy. 'Are you sure you're fourteen?'

'Yes. I had a birthday in March. That's when my pa gave me the trunk. He said I'd soon grow into a woman and would be able to use the things inside it.'

'I doubt if you're a woman yet.'

He could have kicked himself when colour raided her cheeks. She might not be a woman yet, but she thought like one. 'I'm sorry if I embarrassed you.'

She shrugged. 'Pa said it would happen to me all of a sudden.' Tears filled her eyes at the thought of her father. 'What will happen to me?'

'You can stay with me if you wish. I'm not your pa, but I'm old enough to be your grand-father. I had a daughter of my own once. You resemble her a lot. Her name was Margaret.'

'What happened to her?'

'She died.'

'I'm sorry.'

'So am I. I couldn't stay in the house where she died because everywhere I turned I imagined I saw her. And worse, I imagined she could see me, a miserable and lonely old man without her. So I came adventuring to Australia.' He gazed at her. 'You have a good mind, Sarette. I could teach you.'

'Are you a teacher then?'

'No. I came from a long line of pirates, smugglers and adventurers.'

The trill of laughter she gave was a pure delight. 'That's an awful lie. Anyone can tell you're a gentleman from the way you talk. I'll stay if you're lonely. Where else would I go?'

'I could take you to the city. You could probably find employment as a servant.'

'I'd rather stay with you and find gold.'

'I'm not as respectable as you believe. I really am what I said I was.'

'I don't care. I like you.'

That this child would take him at face value and trust herself to him was humbling.

'What would you teach me? I can already read and write and add up numbers.'

'The geography and history of the world. And I'd give you some books to read before the termites finish them off, and I'd expect you to write essays on certain subjects, as well as keeping a journal of your time here.'

'As long as I don't spit in the inkwell.'

'There's that, of course. We could work on your manners. Think about it and let me know tomorrow. Reflect on what your parents would have wanted for you, if you will.'

'Do you keep a journal?'

'Yes. It's for my nephew, Magnus Kern, and will go into the family records eventually.'

'What do you write in it?'

'I record day to day life on the goldfields, and what happens.'

'So I'll be in it for this Magnus Kern to read about. Will you allow me to read what you've written about me?'

'Certainly not. Journals are private.'

'So if I kept a journal I could write what I liked about you.'

She was certainly quick-witted. Warily he eyed her grin, then nodded. 'Journals will end up as family history for your children and grandchildren. After we're dead they will be interested in what their ancestors got up to, and how well we lived our lives.'

She made an impatient huffing noise. 'Give me time, I've hardly lived mine yet.'

'You could record the passing of your father, and what caused it.'

'A soddin' bite from a soddin' death adder, that's what killed him.' She looked sad. 'Right at the end he told me the biggest lie of all. He said he'd never leave me. I hate snakes.'

Gently he touched her cheek. 'Remember they were here first, and we're the intruders. You can't blame them for defending their territory.'

'Well, I do, and so would you if one had killed your pa. He suffered, my poor pa did.'

He didn't want to start her bawling all over again. 'Yes, I daresay I would blame them too. Now, a word about your manners, Miss. I don't approve of ladies swearing, especially in the company of gentlemen. It's a bad habit that makes them appear crude and common.'

Colour rose to her cheeks again. 'Sorry, sir.'

'You can call me Mr Kern, or John if you wish.'

55

'Mr John is nice.'

She'd misunderstood, and his mind went back to Fierce Eagles where the servants had always referred to him as Mr John.

'Would you call me Sarry, like my pa used to?' she said.

He nodded, picked up his shovel, pan and pickaxe and placed them in the wheelbarrow. 'I'm going off to do some work now. I'll be within shouting distance today if you need me. And if you go into town don't wear your mother's dress in case those people see it and come after us. I don't want any trouble.'

'Can I come with you and earn my twenty per cent? I can dry blow the dust.'

'I'm not wasting my time with dust. I'm looking for nuggets, or a quartz outcrop that contains gold veins. The man who sold me the claim said he got lost in a dust storm and saw it poking up out of the earth. Of course, that could have been outside the claim, but since nobody but he and I have come this far out yet, I'll consider anything beyond my legal boundary of fifty by one hundred feet, mine to explore ... until someone pegs it, that is.'

'So why didn't your reverend stay here and uncover it for himself?'

'He was taken ill. When he recovered he couldn't find it again.'

'A likely story.'

'As likely as not, I agree. But the man was the clergyman I bought Hercules from. His words had the ring of honesty about them, but then so do those of most good confidence tricksters, so you could be right. There's a book on the bedside table called *David Copperfield*. The author is Charles Dickens. If you have nothing better to do you can start reading that. I'll be home before dark.'

Off he went with Hercules following after.

She found the book where he'd said and opened it to the first page of the first chapter, where she read: 'I AM BORN. Whether I shall turn out to be the hero of my own life, or whether that station will be held by anyone else, these pages must show.' She read on a little more, stumbling over the more difficult words. Excitement filled her. Just what Mr John had said. This book was the journal of a man's life. She couldn't wait to start on one of her own.

True to his promise, John Kern came home just before dark, preceded by snatches of hymn singing. It was the time of day when the sun was low and the sky was a dusty molten orange melting into the trees. The heat of the day had become a bearable warmth.

She went to the door and beamed a smile at him, full of the delight of what she'd read, and eager to discuss it with him.

He dismounted and fell flat on his face. Hercules's snicker sounded suspiciously like a laugh.

When Sarette rushed to help him to his feet she smelled whisky on his breath. He stood there swaying, a wide smile on his face, but a smile that didn't make him look any the less menacing, so she began to think there might be some truth to what he'd declared his former profession to have been.

She whispered, 'Mr John ... I think you're drunk.'

He reached out and gently touched her face. 'Aye, I think I might be, my sweet little apparition. It helps me through the night, when demons stalk.'

A rush of disappointment filled her because the man she was beginning to respect was flawed. 'I'll help you inside and get you some dinner. It's stew with barley in, and I've made some bread.'

'I'll sup your stew and eat your bread, then I'll sleep. Will you guard me till daylight returns?'

'I'll name you in my prayers, after I name my parents, and I'll remember Hercules as well.'

John snorted, and so did Hercules.

Four

The following day John was back to normal. Putting Hercules between the shafts of a small cart he went into town and came back with a flitch of smoked bacon, the inevitable dried apples and two gallons of water. There were two hens in a crate.

'I thought it would be nice to have an egg to go with the bacon.'

A good thought, but one that proved impracticable. Sarette was delighted with them and named them Betty and Jean. John built them a wire run and the chickens scratched about in the dirt, their efforts uncovered a few flecks of gold to add to her matchbox. But before they'd settled in enough to lay an egg a snake got in through the wire and swallowed them both. The snake was lying on the floor of the run when they came back from town, trapped there by its own stomach, which was too distended to push through the wire again.

Her blood ran cold when she saw the lethal greyish-brown creature. She stood and stared at it, mesmerized, and trembling. Her heart was filled with loathing. She was unable to tear her eyes away.

John came between her and the chicken run. He took her by the arms and led her inside. He went out again. A minute later there came the sound of a shot. She rushed outside and caught a quick glimpse of the snake writhing about in its death throes before she turned and was sick into the undergrowth.

'So much for them being here first,' she said shakily.

'It was my fault. I should have realized that the chickens would attract snakes.'

A year passed by, the winter bringing a little relief from the heat, but no relief from the water shortage. The town began to grow and the wide streets were crowded with teams of camels and horses. People thronged in the town. There was talk of a railway being planned, of a water condenser, then of a water pipeline to Kalgoorlie from Perth. Lawbreaking became common.

Sarette wasn't allowed into town by herself.

A photographer came and took a photograph of them standing outside the hut, John with his rifle in hand. He bought them a copy each to keep inside their journals. He taught her to shoot his pistol as well as the rifle, and she proved to be a good shot.

Sarette had made her own routine. John had always politely declined to take her when he went looking for his reef of gold, so she'd stopped asking. He found a couple of small nuggets, with which he paid his bill at the store, and the next week the sound of his pick took on a feverish intensity.

'Just enough to encourage a man,' was the way he put it.

Sarette's dry panning was painstakingly slow but she made steady progress and her matchbox began to gain weight.

Inevitably, John came home the worse for drink. Far from making him abusive, it brought out the gentleman in him, though that gentleman was often melancholy, especially when he talked of his home.

'You would like Fierce Eagles, Sarry,' he said, one day when he was in a nostalgic mood. 'It has a view down a hill to a little cove, where my forebears used to bring the goods ashore. My grandfather and his father before him were both magistrates, despite their other professions. Everyone knew what they got up to. Half the town was on their payroll.'

She no longer disbelieved his tales. 'What sort of goods did you smuggle?'

'Brandy, wine, wool, tea, tobacco, anything that attracted a tax. The brandy tubs used to be sunk on a weighted line at a prearranged spot, and the boats would go out with grapnels, creep along the water channels and hook them up. Sometimes boats came into the cove if the tide was right, and whatever they carried would be taken up to the house and hidden in the cellars. Fierce Eagles has an extensive network of cellars, and there's a secret room down there. The key hangs on the wall outside.'

Her eyes widened. 'What's secret about it?'

'I promised my father I wouldn't tell anyone what was in there.'

'But surely ... when he died.'

He grinned at her. 'Sorry, my dear, but I made him a promise.'

She didn't know whether to ask him or not, but curiosity got the better of her. 'You can tell me. I'd promise not to tell anyone else.'

He gave a bit of a grin, 'It's part of the Kern family history.'

'You mean it's full of pirate treasure and ill-gotten gains,' she said, breathless with anticipation.

'It was once. And that's all you'll get out of me.'

'Did you never get caught ... or scared?'

'I had a couple of close calls. My brother was killed by a stray bullet. By that time the family had built up quite a fortune. I had a wife and children to raise and I didn't want to be parted from them, by death or other means. So I gave it up and settled down.' He was reflective for a

61

moment, then added soberly, 'I didn't imagine that fate would take the innocents and leave me to suffer their loss.'

'Was the death of your loved ones your fault?'

'No, Sarry, but it was my punishment. Magnus is my heir.'

'Tell me about Magnus Kern. Is he a smuggler and pirate, too? Is he handsome? Does he have a wife?'

He laughed. 'Magnus looks like me a little. Whether that's handsome is for you to decide, and no, in his last letter he was still unwed. Do you want to marry him? I could suggest it to him. Though he's the type of man who has a mind of his own, and as I recall he preferred ladies with a little bit more flesh on them, not a skinny little minnow like you. He would probably reject the suggestion out of hand.'

She felt herself turn a fiery red and protested, 'He sounds mean and horrible. Don't you dare suggest it. I'm too young to wed. Besides, a handsome man of fortune who lives in a big house will have many ladies sighing with love for him.'

A grin spread across his face. 'You're beginning to think like a woman.'

'I am not.'

She was subjected to a critical look. 'You're beginning to look and act like one too. You must have gained a foot in height over the past year.'

She felt discomfited and didn't know where to look. It was true that her mother's skirt fit a little better. And she filled in the bodice a little more. She hollowed her chest. Not that she was large, but her breasts were like small pointing cones, and sometimes the pink nubs became as hard as gum-nuts and she was conscious of them, and of men staring at them, and it made her want to hide away.

His expression became thoughtful and he whistled for Hercules.

'Where are you going?'

'Into town ... I won't be long.'

He came back looking pleased with himself.

The next morning he was gone again, so was the cart. He returned with Mrs Benstead from the store who, with a basket over her arm, dismounted and said, 'I can't stay long.'

'Shout, when you need me,' John said. He sat on the cart with his back to them, out of earshot, then took out a knife and began to whittle on a piece of wood.

'Let's go inside,' Mrs Benstead said. 'Yon man wants me to talk to you.'

Sarette felt mystified. 'What about?'

'About what's going to happen, and before too long by the looks of you.' Her eyes darted around the interior of the shack, lighting with approval on the sleeping arrangements. She nodded. 'You keep it clean. He's a nice man, is Mr Kern. He treats you with respect. Not many men would do that for a girl in your situation. Tell me, have you got the curse yet?'

'The curse?'

'Your monthly bleeds?'

'I'm not sure what you're talking about, Mrs Benstead.'

Mrs Benstead nodded. 'Exactly what Mr Kern

63

suggested, that you were ignorant of the womanly things because your ma had died when you were young and you had no one to tell you.'

Half an hour later Sarette was well aware of what being a woman involved. She accepted the package of hemmed linen cloths and safety pins that John had been assured she would need. Mrs Benstead demonstrated how to fold them. 'Now, dear, just you remember what I told you. You might get some cramps, but don't you worry about that too much, since it'll go after a few hours. And if you boil the cloths in a bucket with soap added, the stains will soon go away.'

'Thank you, Mrs Benstead,' she said.

'You be careful of the men from now on, Sarry. Men can be mighty persuasive when the mood's on them, and you don't want no baby planted inside you until you're married. So mark my words. Men don't marry girls who are loose with them, if you get my meaning.'

Sarette nodded. 'I won't be loose with them, I promise.'

'Good girl. Now you come and see me if you need any more advice. I won't mind.'

'Yes, I will,' she said politely as Mrs Benstead took her leave and headed for the cart.

When John came back from town the second time he had a parcel for her and a slightly embarrassed look on his face. 'I bought you a new outfit yesterday, but I had to wait for the dressmaker to shorten the hem.'

From the parcel emerged a dark blue skirt, with a puffed sleeved blouse sprigged with printed flowers. To go under it a flannel petticoat, bodice and drawers with lace around the hem and ribbons at the neck. It was all so pretty and soft to wear, and she could have died of delight at being given such a present.

'Is it all right?' he said, awkwardly.

She did something she'd never done before. She threw her arms around his neck and gave him a smacking kiss on the cheek. 'Thank you, Mr John. You're so kind.'

He was laughing now. 'Well, don't tell anyone. Go and try it on so I can see you in it and admire you.'

She felt shy when she came back dressed in her finery. She held her skirts up off the dusty ground and paraded around.

'You look lovely, Sarry. All the men will be after you soon and I'll lose you.'

After what Mrs Benstead had told her she had no intention of ever getting married. 'You won't lose me, unless you send me away, because I'll never be loose with men.'

John tried to hide his smile as he thought: Send her away? He'd never do that. Sarette's company made him happy. She prevented him from feeling sorry for himself and gave him someone to be responsible for.

As he gazed at the youthful bloom on her face and her innocent eyes, he knew he was being selfish. The climate wasn't kind to women. In ten years the dry air and the harsh sun would wreak havoc on her. By the time she was thirty her skin would be like stringy tanned leather and she'd look fifty.

John doubted if he'd be here to see it, and his

heart gave a wrench. He must put his dreams of gold aside and do something for her. After all, he had more than enough money for his needs.

He'd give himself another year. By that time she'd be fully developed. He'd grown to love Sarette. Not as a man loved a woman with body and soul, for drink had dulled his male urges. Not even as he'd loved his daughter, for that had been a tender and emotional connection. He loved Sarette for her courage and honesty, and he valued her companionship. That decided, he told her, 'Your parents would be proud of you, girl.'

'And they'd be proud of you, Mr John. They'd be pleased to know that a reformed adventurer with a heart of gold had taken charge of me.'

This time he grabbed her up and swung her round before he hugged her tight. She began to laugh and pulled on his beard. 'Your whiskers are tickling my ear. What do you look like without this beard.'

'Like the rogue I am at heart. Reformed...? Hah!'

The days had a certain routine to them. Chores didn't take them long, after which she did the reading and writing he set her, though John never bothered to check it. It was enough for him that she did what he expected of her, and to the best of her ability, so to please him.

The quartz containing the gold seam still eluded him, and he was beginning to think it didn't exist.

Out of habit he still drank regularly, but he'd cut down a little for her sake. His stomach bothered him from time to time, but not enough to allow him to see a doctor on his quarterly visits to Southern Cross, where they had a telegraph office.

Another year passed quickly. His little companion had filled out in that time. She was still slim with soft round hips and breasts that were firm and upstanding. Although she looked delicate she was strong, and breathtakingly beautiful.

He thought about her as he headed for Southern Cross on one of his trips. He'd sell the claim. He'd take Sarette to the city and pack her off to a friend in England, who ran a small establishment. There, she'd be turned into a lady.

'What then?' he said out loud.

He ignored the question his mind threw at him and sent his usual telegraph to Ignatious Grimble, to let him know he was all right. He told Grimble to stand by for further news. John wouldn't know what ship Sarry would be on until he reached the Port of Fremantle and arranged things. Grimble would meet the ship, and he'd send a letter with her for Grimble, who would tell Magnus nothing, unless John specifically instructed him too.

He supposed he ought to write to Magnus, let him know of the plans he was making. No ... perhaps not. Magnus would misconstrue his relationship with Sarry. John would prefer to explain things to Magnus when he got there himself.

It was July, and the midwinter day was warm

and humid. For a change the sky had clouded over and he could smell rain in the air. Often the clouds passed over but there were some rumbles of thunder in the distance that sounded promising.

He'd sloped a sheet of corrugated iron into the barrel to give direction to any water off the roof before he'd left. 'I'll take the rifle. Keep the loaded pistol within reach and I'll be back as soon as possible.'

She'd nodded, and smiled. 'If it rains I'm going to stand in it and wash my hair.'

'You and every other man, woman and child in the place.'

And down it came as he was heading home. How sweet it was. It beat against the dry soil, sending up puffs of dust at first, then sinking into the earth. When the earth was saturated it formed little rivers that filled up the gullies and holes, and the dusty track became sticky with mud.

John turned his face up to the shafting rain and sang at the top of his voice as it soaked through his clothing, *'Christ the Lord is risen today, a-a-a-a-a-alay-loo-oo-ya!'*

Hercules whinnied and did a little dance as the drops began to sting his hide.

'It's rain. Make the most of it, my lad.'

Taking a bottle from his saddlebag John pulled out the cork. He took a good swallow as they ambled along then waved the bottle in the air and yelled, 'Here's to rain. Without it they couldn't make whisky.'

* * *

Back at the camp Sarette stood with her petticoat plastered against her body. She'd been there for several minutes rinsing the soap from her hair and allowing the water to run over her. She'd also put a pail out to catch the fresh water for cooking. The fire had gone out, the hot ashes spitting out steam with each wet extinguishing drop. The rain had been refreshing, but now she was cooling and her body was covered in goose-bumps.

Going back into the hut, which was dripping water from the roof, she pulled on her old skirt and bodice, since she didn't want to ruin her good clothes in the mire underfoot.

Taking up the gold pan she scooped up some mud and allowed the rain to half fill the pan. She began to swirl it around, and soon became absorbed in the occupation. She'd panned enough gold dust to fill a quarter of a teaspoon when instinct told her she was being watched.

Hair rising on the nape of her neck she strolled casually back towards the hut and picked up the pistol.

Someone called out, 'Hello, the camp.'

She went outside, the pistol held at her side. Opposite the door beyond the campfire site was a ginger-haired man of about thirty. He had a sly look to him.

'What do you want?'

'My name's Jimmy. Can you spare something to eat?'

She had made a loaf and a pot of soup before it rained, but there was only enough for herself and Mr John.

He took a couple of steps towards her. 'Is your man home, missy?'

'No, he's...' She realized her mistake when he smiled, and she said hastily, 'He'll be back any minute.'

Sarette pulled up the gun when he took another step forward. 'If you come any closer I'll shoot you. Move back, and I'll give you some bread if you're hungry.'

'Thank you, miss, I didn't mean to frighten you,' Jimmy said humbly and backed off. She lowered the pistol and was about to turn back into the hut when she was seized from behind by a second man. Her heart nearly exploded from fright and she gave a loud yell before a hand was clapped over her mouth. The gun was wrenched from her hand and thrown into the bush, where it went off with a loud report that set the birds into the sky, crying out in alarm.

Dragging her into the hut they threw her on the bed and looked around. First, they helped themselves to the stew, spooning it into their mouths, then they ate the bread, washing it down with the water that ran off the roofing sheets. Afterwards they ransacked the place, throwing her mother's things into the mud and grinding them in as they tromped all over them. Jimmy slid the matchbox containing her gold into his pocket.

Sensing an opportunity, she leaped off the bed and tried to dodge through them. The dark man grabbed her by the arm and jerked it up her back. 'Where's your gold?'

She gave a loud yell when he twisted her wrist. 'Let me go, you're hurting me.'

'Let her go, Col.' When Col did as he was told, Jimmy pushed her back on the bed. 'Stay there and you won't get hurt. Where's the gold?'

Fear filled her, drying her mouth so she could hardly speak. 'I don't know what you're talking about?'

'We heard that John Camly had made a big strike.'

'This is John Kern's claim. D'you think we'd still be here if we'd found a lot of gold?'

'She has a point,' Jimmy pointed out. 'Come on, let's get out of here before her man comes back.'

Col's eyes raked down her and his eyes changed. 'Not just yet. She's a nice-looking piece. She owes me a little something for aiming that gun at me.'

A snatch of a hymn came to her ears and Sarette experienced relief. All she had to do was keep them at bay until John got here. She opened her mouth and let out a piercing scream.

Col gave a bit of a grin and punched her in the midriff. When she collapsed, gasping for breath, he threw her skirt up over her head. 'There, that shut her mouth. Look at that sweet piece of pie. Hurry up, so I can have my slice of it.'

Sarette kicked out with her remaining strength, only to have her legs seized and pulled apart. Someone grasped the front of her drawers and pulled. There came a clanging noise and the full weight of a man's body dropped on her. She shuddered, pulled down her skirt and struck out with her fists. The unconscious body was dragged off her. It hit the floor with a thud.

John handed her the rifle. 'Keep that on him, and shoot to kill if he moves.' Taking a rope down from a nail he tied the unconscious man's wrists together.

She eyed the iron skillet on the floor then gazed at the man again. 'What are you going to do to him?'

Sarette gasped when John told her, 'I thought I might hang him. After that I'm going to shoot his companion. If I bury them in the bush nobody will ever know.'

Col said, 'Without giving us a chance? That's murder.'

'So it is. You didn't give my niece much of a chance, did you?' Sarette didn't know whether John had meant what he'd said or not, until he winked at her.

'We wouldn't have killed her. Aw, come on, mister. My brother never got anywhere with her. She gave him a flirty look and he was just giving her a bit of a kiss.'

'You lying scum. I'd rather kiss a dead lizard.' She grabbed up the skillet and was about to take a swing at him when John said in a voice she didn't care to argue with, 'Put it down.'

'We was hungry that's all. She was scratching for gold over there. We asked for food and she gave us some. She looked so pretty and we thought she gave us the come on. Sorry if we upset her. We didn't mean to.'

'Is that true, Sarry?'

She shook her head and said fiercely, 'It's true that I was scratching for gold. I thought the rain might have turned some up. They stole the food.

72

But he tried to ... to force me, and he punched me in the stomach, and they turned everything over and stole my twenty per cent. It's in his pocket. It took me over eighteen months to collect it, and if I don't get it back I'll shoot his legs out from under him.'

'He'll give it back. Won't you, young man?'

'Yes, sir.' The man turned out his pockets, so did his brother when he came round. Tied together by one set of joined wrists at the back and another at the front, the pair looked like a sorry sight. Tying their ankles together John took them outside and pointed them towards town. 'Coolgardie is that way. When you scum reach there, go to Warden Finnerty's house, tell them what you've done. I'll be right behind you with my rifle in a minute or two. And if you step on my claim again you'll be shot out of hand. Is that understood?'

'Yes, sir,' they said together, and shuffled off sideways like a couple of dancing crabs.

'I doubt if we'll see them again,' John commented.

'I thought you were going to escort them in.'

'I don't see the point. They should be able to figure out a way to get those cords off. There are a lot of people coming in now the train service is here, and it won't be long before the adjoining land is pegged. It's nearly time we left.'

She just laughed. She couldn't imagine living anywhere else.

The next morning when the sun came up the air smelled fresh and clean. Sarry was busy clean-

73

ing up the mess. She'd been badly shaken and the innocence in her eyes had been replaced by sadness. John had heard her crying during the night, and hadn't known how to help her.

He'd come to a decision though. He doubted if those men would come back for Sarry. But if not them, then others would try. She had reached that age of desirability when she was peachy with innocent youth and ready for plucking. He couldn't fight them all off. He was too old. He had to get her out of here, take her to a place that was more civilized. He would tell her tonight.

The sun shifted a little in the sky. From habit he placed his pick in the wheelbarrow and set off. It was a pretty day. The trees shook off the moisture from the downpour in rainbow-coloured drops, the sun shafted beams down through the branches. In the distance John saw a patch of yellow. His eyes narrowed in on it, identified it, then mesmerized, he found himself drawn towards it, his heart pounding in his chest and hardly daring to hope.

There were several nuggets strewn about on top, and sticking out of the soil, a chunk of quartz, uncovered by the punching force of the rain. How lovely it looked.

As he drew nearer he began to shake as though he had a fever. *'The ridge! At long last!'* He couldn't leave now. He'd work it until it ran out, then he'd leave, taking Sarry with him.

He began to hack at the quartz, ignoring the pain that haunted his stomach. He'd grown used to it. By the end of the week his muscles ached, his spine seemed set to break in two, and he was suffering from extreme fatigue. To his disappointment the quartz reef hadn't contained any gold.

John hadn't drunk anything but water for a week and he felt out of sorts. He tipped the bottle up, took a swig and kicked at a chunk of quartz that seemed to be mocking him. The toe of his boot went under it, lifted it and sent it flying through the trees. Where it had rested was a pitted yellow patch. Placing one end of the pick under it, he loosened it from its bed in the earth and lifted it out.

Gold in the rough shape of a heart appeared from under the dirt, a nugget so large it must have weighed at least sixteen pounds. *This was it! More than he'd ever hoped for.* He named it Sarry's heart. It was for her, though she wouldn't know it yet. John wanted to shout out his good luck, but didn't dare in case he was overheard. He wasn't even going to register his find, though it would be breaking the law not to. But he couldn't remember ever respecting that, and was too old to do so now.

He laughed, kissed it and said, 'You beautiful, beautiful thing.'

Wrapping the nugget in his coat he placed the bundle in the wheelbarrow and trundled home with it. He handed a couple of the smaller nuggets to her. 'Here's your twenty per cent, Sarry girl. That's it. I've had enough of the diggings, so get ready to leave in the morning. Don't take anything we can't carry on the train.'

While she exclaimed over her twenty per cent he carried his coat inside and placed the nugget in his trunk. It would weigh heavy, but he didn't care.

As John knew she would, she resisted the scheme, reluctant to step out of the narrow little world she was used to.

'Then what?' she'd scoffed, looking displeased with the whole idea when he'd explained it to her. 'It's not much good being turned into an English lady unless it will help me earn a living.'

It was worse when he sold Hercules along with the claim, outside of the railway station. It was then that she realized that they really were leaving, and John knew that she was scared of losing everything that was familiar to her.

'He'll miss us.'

'Nonsense. He's a horse. As long as he gets his daily hymn along with his food, he'll be quite happy to transfer his affection to the person who feeds him.'

Bursting into tears she threw her arms around Hercules's neck and wailed, 'I don't want to leave him.'

John knew he'd have to be hard with her. 'Then stay.' Hefting his trunk on to his shoulder with some difficulty, he began to amble towards the train. He got into a carriage, leaving the door open in case he'd have to jump out again, and gazed back at her, wondering if she'd choose Hercules over him.

The young couple who'd bought the horse along with the claim gazed awkwardly at one another. 'I'd better carry your trunk to the train for you,' the man said eventually, and picked it up.

Sarette looked from one to the other, then said to the woman, 'You'll look after him, won't you? And you won't forget to sing hymns to him?'

'Of course. You'd better hurry else you'll miss the train. Your man looks right annoyed at being kept waiting.'

John kept the frown on his face and tried not to grin when Sarry glared at him and said, 'He isn't my man. I hate him.'

She gave Hercules a last hug and ran for the train when the whistle blew. Taking the seat opposite him she folded her arms over her chest and looked fierce as the train lurched forward and began to gather speed.

After a while he winked at her.

As John knew she would, she decided to forgive him.

'What's Fremantle like?' she said.

Five

The train journey had been uncomfortable, but when it was over Sarette would have been the first to admit to John's wisdom of selling Hercules, for completing the three hundred and fifty mile journey by horse and wagon would have been even more un comfortable.

John had slept. When he woke she gave him something to eat, for she'd made a loaf of bread the night before, hollowed out the middle and had filled it with sliced bacon covered in pickles. To go with it were eggs pickled in vinegar that she'd brought from Benstead's store, and to wash it down, some water.

After the rain the countryside was pretty, carpeted as it was with multicoloured wildflowers. But she knew the land would soon go back to its dry, scrubby self and the unforgiving sun would evaporate the moisture and bake the earth's skin to a crust.

The first sight of the ocean was unexpected because she couldn't remember seeing it before. So blue and so large it was, reaching to the horizon where it joined an even bluer sky, and on it

78

a ship with sails fatly puffed with wind, and another with chimney stacks blowing smoke. Yet despite that, the air was wondrously clear and fresh without the wind-blown dust from the goldfields to spoil it.

'Look at all the water,' she exclaimed. 'What a marvel it is.'

John smiled at that. 'You'll be sailing on it for several weeks.'

She laughed at that, for she thought he must be teasing. Nothing could be that big.

When they reached Fremantle John booked them rooms in a hotel that seemed to be in the thick of things. There was a public bar underneath and as the evening progressed the patrons became rowdier and rowdier. But they'd eaten a good dinner earlier, and she was tired, and the roomy bed with its soft mattress was both a novelty and inviting, since she'd never slept in a real bed before.

But Sarette found it hard to get to sleep, and she tossed and turned in its softness before she felt weary enough to give in to the novelty of it. She was worried about John Kern. He looked tired, and now and again he pressed a hand against his stomach.

The next morning she asked him, 'Are you ill, Mr John?'

'It's nothing, just something I ate that disagreed with me. Those pickles, I expect.'

'Promise me that you'll stop drinking rot-gut whisky and go and see a doctor.'

'Stop nagging, girl. You're not my wife.'

'If I was your wife I'd make you do what you

were told. If you don't see a doctor I'll find one and bring him to see you.'

'All right, I promise I'll see a doctor,' he'd grumbled.

He honoured his promise.

She was just readying herself for a walk around town when he arrived back, a wide smile on his face. 'The doctor said it's nothing serious. You were right about the rot-gut though.'

She couldn't help but give a smug smile at that, but it was wiped from her face when he chuckled and added, 'He prescribed medicinal brandy instead.'

She gave him a dark look. 'What sort of doctor did you go to ... a witch doctor?'

'One who knows the nature of men.'

She snorted. 'You're incorrigible, John Kern. Do I have to do any lessons today? I thought I might walk around town and look at the shops, so I can write about Fremantle in my journal. I thought the railway station was rather grand, and I thought I might go over to Cliff Street and make a sketch of it.'

'Better still, I'll buy you a postcard. My dear, you're seventeen, and have learned all you needed to have of a formal education months ago. You're far from stupid. Just keep your eyes and ears open and your reading and writing up, since it will broaden you even more and give you something to discuss with others. Now you need to learn to be a lady ... and don't make that ugly face at me. It makes you resemble a prune. We're not on the diggings now, and although you're not entirely devoid of manners, better

80

will be expected of you if you wish to function in polite society and marry well.'

'I could marry you. Then I wouldn't have to go to that stupid school, or learn any manners. And I wouldn't have to leave you – not ever.'

He looked taken aback for a moment, then stuttered, 'On the first score, if I ever decided to settle down I'd certainly expect my wife to be socially acceptable. Secondly...' He shrugged when he realized what she was about. 'I know that you're scared, Sarry.'

'But I'll miss you,' she wailed.

'And I'll miss you.' He took her by the shoulders and gazed into her eyes. 'I've never known you to lack courage. Do this for me, Sarry girl. It will only be for a year, then I'll join you in England.'

'Why won't you come with me now?'

His eyes flickered away, then came back to her. They had a slightly yellow tinge to them. 'I'm going to Melbourne first. I have some business to finalize. I'm sending my trunk with you to save me lugging it around.' He kissed her cheek and let her go.

'I could come with you to Melbourne, then we could go to England together.'

'Enough, girl! When I took you in I didn't give you permission to run my life. I'm going to book your ticket on a clipper, and I've found you a travelling companion who will act as your chaperone. We're to have tea with her later, so you can meet. You can practise your manners on her if you can be bothered to display that you have some ... and you can take that sulky look off your face and accept the inevitable.'

'Sorry, I was worried about you.'

'Don't be, my dear. I've lived a long time and I know what I'm about.'

Still smarting from the sharp reminder of her status, she murmured, close to tears, 'I don't need a chaperone.'

He took her by the shoulders, his voice softer. 'Remember what happened in the goldfields. A girl your age can't be too careful. But it works two ways. Mrs Kent is nervous of travelling alone. She's a mature lady, a widow who has lost her husband and is returning to live with her relatives in England. She has a pleasant nature, and you'll be doing her a favour, since having you to look after will help take her mind off her own troubles.'

It took all of John's will to hide his pain from Sarry as he escorted her around the busy little town, with its many fine buildings. Queen Victoria's Diamond Jubilee was being celebrated. Here and there they saw the occasional window display with the queen looking out at them surrounded by some dusty-looking bunting.

'Queen Victoria looks like a cross patch,' Sarette murmured.

'She wasn't much older than you when she took the throne, and has been ruling over the British Empire for sixty years.'

Sarette's eyes widened in the way they always did when she was impressed by something. And it happened often as she examined the goods displayed in every shop, and asked her questions.

'Why is there a striped pole outside the barber's shop?'

'I think it goes back to when barbers were surgeons as well, and the red and white pole signifies blood and bandages.'

She glanced with envy at a pair of button boots in a shop window, situated next to the barber's shop. Her own boots were clumsy, scuffed and worn out. The clothes she had were good enough for the few weeks she'd be on board, with the addition of a warm coat and shawl, for even here it was midwinter and cold during the night. And he'd made provision for her when she reached England. Ignatious Grimble would handle her expenses from John's private accounts.

'The tea room is just a few doors down. Go and secure us a table. I'll be there soon, I'm just going to get my beard trimmed.'

He did more than that. He had it removed, then he purchased the boots she'd been admiring, with the provision they would be exchanged if they didn't fit.

Seated near the window, Sarette was gazing out at the street. Her gaze washed over him when he entered the tea room. She frowned and looked puzzled. Then her pretty laugh rang out, causing heads to turn towards her, and smiles to appear.

'Miss Maitland, may I join you?'

'You certainly may, Mr John. How handsome you look without your whiskers.'

'Yes, I must admit I'd forgotten what I looked like.' He handed her the parcel. 'I hope they fit. If not we can change them.'

She would have tried them on then and there if he hadn't stopped her with, 'Manners, my dear. A lady does not take her shoes off in public.'

Tears trembled in her eyes. 'I'd marry you if you'd just asked me, you know. I owe you so much and I want to look after you.'

He knew she would. She was young, she was impressionable and she'd be willing to sacrifice her youth looking after an old man who could give her nothing of real value in return. Under different circumstances he might have been selfish enough to allow her to sacrifice herself, but he didn't really think it was worth it for the little time he had left.

John had always been a convincing liar, it had been part of his stock in trade. 'I know you would, Sarry. So you'll do as I ask, and I promise I'll consider it. Go to England and do your best to improve yourself. When I arrive home we'll see how we both feel about it then.'

Her eyes rounded in surprise, then he saw doubt creeping into them. Inwardly, he grinned. Now he'd let her know there was a possibility she would begin the process of balancing the good and bad of such a union, then find him lacking, no doubt, and forget it.

He rose to his feet. 'Ah, there you are, Mrs Kent. How lovely to see you again. We were just about to order tea. May I introduce you to my ... *niece*, Miss Sarette Maitland.'

Mischief flirted in her eyes as Sarette gave the woman a smile. Regally, she said, 'I've been so looking forward to meeting you, Mrs Kent.'

The following week was exhausting for John.

He took Sarette shopping to make sure she was well provisioned for the voyage. He wrote a letter to Magnus. He wrote another, much longer letter to Grimble with his instructions, then another to Iris Lawrence, who had once been an actress and who now coached young ladies in the female arts.

Parting was harder than he'd expected it to be, so he didn't encourage Sarette to be maudlin. 'You will hand the letter to Magnus if I'm not at Fierce Eagles to greet you at the end of your year with Iris Lawrence. Here is the key to my trunk. It contains my books and journals, so is heavy. I hope you'll take good care of it until it's time to hand it over to Magnus. Whatever else is in it is none of your business, so don't go poking around in it.'

An injured expression settled on her face. 'You can say really mean things sometimes, John Kern. Besides, you've nailed those metal bands around it, so how could I poke around in it? You know I wouldn't open it anyway.'

'I know. Safe journey, Sarry.' He fished his gold watch out of his pocket, cupped her hand in his, and placed it in her palm. 'Take this, and look after it. It has my name etched on it and will prove to Magnus that you are who you say you are if I happen to be delayed. If you get stranded anywhere and need extra money you have my permission to sell it.'

'I'll never sell it. I'd die first.' Her hug was as fierce as her voice as she held him tight. 'I'm going to miss you so much, Mr John.'

He found the strength to put her at arm's

length, took one last look at her sweet, upturned face and placed a kiss on her forehead. 'Be good now, Sarry girl. Go on. Mrs Kent is already in the boat, and they are waiting to row you out to the ship.'

John stood and watched the passenger boat being rowed out to the ship at anchor, his heart beginning to crack. He saw her go aboard, and lifted his hand in reply to her fluttering hand-kerchief.

He made his way to Rous Head, seated himself with his back against a sun-warmed limestone boulder and experienced the empty ache inside his pain. Reaching into his pocket he pulled out a vial and swallowed the laudanum it contained. After a while the pain subsided into a dull throb. He stayed there, watching the sails unfold and the ship turn towards the horizon. His eyes narrowed as the ship grew smaller and smaller, then he could see her no more.

Sarry had gone. Overcome by a feeling of abject loneliness he began to cry, taking great heaving gulps. What an inglorious end for an adventurer, he thought. He'd been a fool to take her in in the first place. He should have left her to die in the goldfields. She had no relatives that she knew of, and nobody would have missed her.

He said out loud, 'But no, not only did you take her in, you let her into your heart. Then you did something really noble Saint John. You swapped your own comfort to provide a future for her.'

Never mind that he already regretted sending

her away, and would give his right arm to have her back.

Darkness fell and the stars appeared. 'God, if you exist please give my Sarry a good life with someone who will love her as much as I do.'

It occurred to him that he could shorten the time he had left, find oblivion in that mythical medicinal brandy bottle he'd told Sarry about. After all, he had sod all left to live for. Painfully rising to his feet, he turned and lumbered towards the lights of the town.

Three hours later and he'd drunk just enough to keep the nagging pain at bay, when there came a burst of raucous laughter from a group of four men at the end of the bar. Someone shouted, 'Here's to Ireland and the Irish.'

'I'll second that, Flynn Collins. Just see if I don't.'

Flynn Collins? Where had he heard that name before? John remembered. Kicking his stool aside he staggered to his feet. 'Were you ever on the Coolgardie diggings, Collins?'

'To be sure. What's it to you?'

'Remember Sarry Maitland.'

The Irishman grinned round at his companions. 'One woman is the same as the rest, and I can't say her name sounds familiar. What of her?'

'You were her father's partner. When he died you stole all she had and left her destitute, that's *what of her.*'

'You're a fecking liar and so is the woman. She was a goldfields 'whore.''

'She was a child, only fourteen years old. Her

87

father died from snakebite, remember? You buried him, then sold everything out from under the girl and took off. She had to work her fingers to the bone to pay off her father's debts, and was wandering and almost dead from thirst when I found her.'

'Irish scum,' somebody in the crowd shouted.

Collins's face mottled a dull red. 'I was going to take her to the orphanage in Perth, but the girl ran off ... I thought she'd gone.'

'You bloody liar. You crept back into camp that night and while she was sleeping you stole the small amount of gold her father had left her. Not only that, she was turned away from her own claim by the people you sold it to, and the woman was wearing her dead mother's dress.'

Collins turned away. 'Aw, shut your clack. You don't know nothing.'

'Aye, I do. I was there. And I'm going to beat the living daylights out of you.'

'Go back to your brandy, old man.'

'He's a coward as well as a thief,' said the same person who'd shouted before, and this time there were mutters of agreement.

'Coward yourself. I'm leaving, I don't like the company in here.'

'Not without answering to me for what you did.'

Collins turned, pulling a gun out from under his jacket. 'Get out of my path.'

The bar owner walked between them, a shotgun aimed at the Irishman. 'We don't allow weapons in here, Collins. Put it on the bar, you can pick it up when you leave.' When it was handed over he said. 'Right, Outside, all of you. Let's make this a fair fight. I'll run the book. My money's on the big man. He looks as though he can handle hisself.'

'Mine's on the Irishman. He's younger.'

'Mine too.'

It wasn't much of a fight, lasting only five minutes before John floored Collins. That was enough to exhaust him, and it set up a dull throbbing in his stomach, so he turned and was sick into the grass. He wiped his mouth, picked up his bottle and took a pull, before walking off and leaving the man with his companions.

John saw Flynn Collins only once more. It was a month later and the bar was just about to close for the night. The Irishman was waiting for him in a doorway, a belligerent look on his face.

John's strength had deserted him rapidly over the past month, and he knew he couldn't take on the Irishman again. 'The score's settled as far as I'm concerned,' he said, and walked past the man.

West Australian Times. August 1896

At the Criminal Sittings of the Supreme Court today, the accused, Flynn Collins, was sentenced to death by hanging for the unprovoked and cowardly murder of Mr John Kern, who was unarmed at the time of the shooting. Witnesses said that Collins stepped out of a doorway and shot Mr Kern in the back. The bullet went through the victim's heart, killing him instantly. Mr Kern's goods were sold to pay for his burial, and a modest stone memorial erected to commemorate his passing. He has no known relatives.

The next day a second notice appeared.

The murderer Flynn Collins escaped from his warders and is presently at large. Collins is described as being about forty years of age, of stocky build with dark hair and eyes and an Irish accent. He wears a full beard. It's believed Collins might be heading for the goldfields of Kalgoorlie, where he has friends. Anyone found harbouring this dangerous felon will be severely dealt with by the law.

London
It was the early September when Sarette stepped ashore in Southampton. She had enjoyed every moment of the journey, and knew that if she was a man she would choose the sea as a profession. The captain had been jolly, both by name and by nature. He was a rotund, but nimble-footed man, and despite his responsibilities, had answered her questions with no hint of impatience.

'The ocean seems endless, Captain Jolly. How do you know where we are?' she'd asked, and he'd showed her how to plot a course, using the sextant and the horizon. She'd written it all down in her journal. Indeed, she'd had so many exciting things to write about and sketch, that she'd begun to run out of space towards the end of the journey.

Mrs Kent had proved to be tedious. The

woman was scared of her own shadow, and every small creak or snap of the sail served only to convince her that they were about to be shipwrecked. She also suffered from nerves, which made her physically sick, so Sarette was kept chasing back and forth with buckets and clothes. Mrs Kent's cabin began to smell unpleasant. Sarette didn't want to be mean to her though, for the woman was grieving for her husband, and Sarette knew what it was like to lose someone you loved.

'It's a fine day, you should come on deck, mingle with the other passengers and breathe in some fresh air, Mrs Kent. It will do you the world of good,' she told her.

'And be washed overboard by a wave and drowned?'

'But the swell is very gentle, and the breeze has just enough puff in it to fill the sails and move us nicely along. I'm so glad Mr John booked me on a clipper ship instead of those steam ships that need a fire burning in them to make the engines work. Captain Jolly said that the wind sailors call them steam kettles, and if the engines break down they are at the mercy of the weather and tides. And sometimes the boilers blow up.'

'Oh dear. How dreadful,' Mrs Kent said greyly. 'I'm such a bad sailor. I shall be glad when we reach dry land.'

And now she had, and was being greeted by a rather bored-looking man and a twittering woman. The two females cried on each other's shoulders then stood back and blew their noses.

Mrs Kent drew her forward and introduced them, explaining to her sister, 'Miss Maitland was placed in my charge for the duration of the trip.'

The sister twittered something at her.

Sarette smiled graciously, and wondered if she could keep up this polite talk, which was a bit of a strain. She twittered back, 'I'm sure I shall, Mrs Petty.'

The man gave a bit of a chuckle.

'It was kind of you to look after me,' Sarette added. 'Please don't wait. I'm sure I'll be met quite soon.'

'It's the least I can do, my dear. A young woman of your age needs to be looked after. Oh dear, I do hope your uncle's solicitor will not be long now.'

'Oh, I'm sure he won't, Mrs Kent. In fact, I believe this might be him now,' and she grinned slightly, for if it were indeed Ignatious Grimble then John's description of him was highly accurate, right down to the long neck. She waved at the rather reptilian-looking man, who appeared to be examining the various faces in the thinning crowd. She called out, 'Is that you, Mr Grimble? Are you looking for me?'

He quickly made his way across and a pair of hooded eyes gave her a thorough scrutiny. 'Tsk-tsk,' he said as he observed the sea-water stains on her skirt, and bowed slightly. 'If you are Miss Maitland, then yes, I am Mr Grimble. I expected you to be alone.'

'Mrs Kent chaperoned me on the voyage.' She gave the woman a quick hug. 'There, you are,

Mrs Kent. You needn't worry about me any more. I am claimed by Mr Grimble here.'

Mrs Kent's party bustled off in a flurry of final hugs, waves and twitters, eager to be rid of the responsibility of her and on their way.

Mr Grimble cleared his throat. 'Is this your luggage, Miss Maitland? The cab is not far away and will take us to the train station.'

'I forbid you to lift that trunk by yourself. It's extremely heavy and you look as though a puff of wind would blow you away.'

Faded blue eyes widened considerably and her grin faded at his outraged expression. 'Your pardon, Mr Grimble. Mr John said I must learn to be a lady.'

'Yes ... well, of course you must. After all, that is why you're here. I shall overlook the breach of etiquette this time, but shall keep an eye on your progress from time to time on John Kern's behalf and report back to him.'

'I owe Mr John so much and I'll make him proud of me, just see if I don't,' she said fiercely, and determined to look up etiquette in the dictionary her mentor had given her.

'Actually, I had no intention of lifting your luggage myself.' He beckoned to two brawny men, who came forward and accepted the coins he held out. They took an end each of John's trunk and grunted as they lifted it.

'It has books in it so is very heavy,' she said by way of explanation.

Soon they were in the train and heading out of the city. The English countryside was pretty and the land so softly green that it was a balm to her eyes.

'Even though I was born here, I had no idea that England was so beautiful.'

'It is a pretty time of year,' Mr Grimble said with a smile. 'Soon the leaves will be turning into their autumn colours, and it will be prettier still. Before then we must make sure you are properly clothed, for soon it will be winter and cold. Miss Lawrence will see to that, since she's a lady with a good eye for fashion.'

She stuck out her foot. 'Mr John bought me these new boots to wear on the journey.'

'They are ... *sturdy*.'

'Since I have never had a pair of new boots before, I feel very fine in them.'

'Yes, of course, under such circumstances one would. Miss Maitland,' he said, 'I must ask. What is John Kern to you? Why has he taken such an interest?'

She smiled. 'He took me in after my pa had died and I was left destitute. He became my friend, my teacher, my mentor and protector.' When Mr Grimble sucked in a breath she gently told him, 'Mr John was a gentleman in the true sense of the word, if that's what you wish to know. I reminded him of his daughter, Margaret, when he first came across me. You have no need to worry about my ... *morals*.'

'On this occasion, thank you for being so frank.' She was subjected to an intense scrutiny. 'I can see only a passing resemblance to Margaret.'

'I've grown from a child into a woman since then.'

94

'You've known Mr Kern that long?'

'Three years.'

'All that time, and he didn't inform me about you until I got that last telegraph from him.'

'I have a letter from him to give you. It's in my trunk.'

'What does it say?'

'It's addressed to you, so I haven't opened it. He gave me instructions, you see. And I always do exactly what he tells me. He has a ferocious frown when he's cross.'

'John is the kind of man who expects to be obeyed,' Grimble said with a wry smile. 'What do you know about John Kern? What did he tell you of his life?'

'I know he was an adventurer – though I didn't believe it at first – but he has told me many tales of his exploits. He also told me about Fierce Eagles and that his estate now belongs to his nephew, who has studied law and is a barrister. Mr John is very fond of this Magnus Kern, who he says will bring respectability to the Kern family. The man sounds like a priggish bore to me, and is probably severe and disagreeable by nature.' She clapped a hand over her mouth. 'I beg your pardon, I shouldn't have said that.'

At first she thought Ignatious Grimble was choking, then she realized he was laughing. She was unaccountably miffed. 'I didn't set out to amuse you, Mr Grimble. Mr John is the finest man I've ever met, and I admire him more than anyone I've ever known.' Which when all was said and done was not many people, though she wasn't going to tell him that. 'If he says that

95

Magnus Kern is a good man, then I should respect his words.' Her shrug was followed by a wide grin. 'Though as I remember, Mr John would be the first to admit that he was a fine, convincing liar at times.'

With difficulty the man composed himself. 'Perhaps you shouldn't be quite so quick to pass judgement on Magnus Kern, since he's someone you've never met.'

'And hope never to meet.' She turned to stare out of the window. 'What's that pretty tree over there with the big red leaves?'

'A copper beech. There are many of them in the New Forest.'

'Where's that?'

'We're passing through it.'

'If this is the New Forest, what happened to the old one?'

'Goodness me, young lady. Must you ask so many questions?'

She sighed. It was obvious that Mr Grimble didn't know the answer, so why didn't he just say so? Mr John had told her that admitting ignorance usually brought enlightenment, and you learned something new. She wondered if she should point that out to Mr Grimble, but decided against it. By trial and error she was learning that on some occasions it was better to keep her mouth firmly shut.

By the time they alighted at the station at Weymouth Sarette was hungry and tired, and the novelty of travel had well and truly worn off. 'You look weary, Mr Grimble. Do we have much further to go?'

'Luckily no. I admit, I'm a little fatigued myself, but I've arranged to meet one of my sons here and he'll take me back to Bournemouth, where I live.'

'How many sons do you have?'

'Seven ... and four daughters.'

'Goodness! So many. It must be wonderful to be part of such a large family.'

'I admit, they're a source of great pride to me.'

'I never had any siblings, except the one who died with my mother, but that one doesn't count because it was never born.'

'God works in mysterious ways.'

'He certainly does. Mr John said he couldn't fathom God, taking the innocent when there were so many villains and rogues like him around. When I told him that God might have kept him alive on purpose, so he could rescue me and redeem himself, he told me not to flatter myself. He said it was dark, he was as pi ... ckled as a python and he'd tripped over me.'

'*Miss Maitland!*'

She'd never heard a man sounding so shocked, and she grinned. 'Mr John said if it had been daylight and he'd been sober and in his right mind, he'd have run so fast in the other direction that I wouldn't have seen either him or Hercules for dust.'

'Hercules?' Grimble said faintly.

'His horse. We used to sing him hymns.'

'That sounds like John Kern,' he said, a smile appearing on his face, then quite gently, 'Miss Maitland, I should perhaps caution you against using vulgar expressions, even when quoting

97

others. John Kern had a rather colourful turn of phrase at times, which though it might sit well on a gentleman, does not add credit to a lady. We wouldn't want to give Miss Lawrence the wrong impression.'

'Sorry, Mr Grimble. From now on I won't speak a word out of place,' which would be a sacrifice on her part, since everything was so new and interesting to her.

The cab they were in came to a halt outside a terraced house overlooking the bay. Her heart began to pound. Being raised on the Australian gold diggings had not prepared her for what she was finding in the outside world. She was ill-equipped in every way to move in the circles Mr John expected of her.

She gave a quiet little groan.

'Is everything all right, Miss Maitland? Are you in pain?'

Nothing was all right. She was terrified. She wanted to find a hole, climb inside it and hide away from the world for ever.

She heard John's voice as clear as if he was sitting next to her. 'Where has your courage gone, Sarry girl?'

Where *had* it gone, her brash conviction that everything John had told her would come to pass as long as she behaved herself? She had no courage without him to lean on, had nobody to guide her without him. She must fall back on her own resources. But it was only for a year, she thought. He'd promised he'd be here for her then.

'Miss Maitland?'

She smiled. 'I was having a moment of doubt.
Mr Grimble.'

He gently patted her hand. 'John Kern had no
doubts, and neither do I.'

Six

'Is this the school?'

'It's not actually a school. It's a day academy
for young ladies. But you'll reside here for the
duration of your stay and act as a companion to
Mrs Lawrence.'

While Mr Grimble was summoned into the
presence of Mrs Lawrence herself, Sarette was
taken upstairs to a pleasant room overlooking
the bay, there to make herself presentable. Her
trunks came shortly after. The cab driver and a
man of all work staggered upstairs with the one
belonging to John, carrying it between them.

She instructed them to set her smaller trunk on
top of John's. Opening her own trunk she smiled
at the photograph of herself with John, then
stood it in pride of place. Inspecting her wardrobe, she sighed, then took out the blue dress
that had belonged to her mother. It was faded
now and the hem was stained where the woman
who'd stolen it had allowed it to drag in the dirt.
She shook as many of the creases from it as she
could before she pulled it on. Brushing out the
length of her hair she braided it.

She crossed to the window when she heard a vehicle draw up outside. A man got down from the small carriage. Mr Grimble's son perhaps, for he bore a passing resemblance of bearing, though he was certainly taller, and more handsome.

He came to the door below her, and knocked, and not long afterwards she heard the rumble of voices.

After a while the maid came for her and she was summoned to the drawing room. 'Mr Grimble said you're to bring down the papers you have for him.' The maid was more smartly dressed than she was, Sarette thought in despair as she followed her downstairs.

Mr Grimble himself was readying himself to depart.

'Mrs Lawrence, this is Sarette Maitland. I'll leave her in your capable hands. Miss Maitland, this is my third son, Gerald Grimble.'

He murmured a greeting. His eyes were bluer than his father's, and his lips twitched slightly, something that she took to be a smile. There was a quiet awareness about him that made her feel nervous, and she was annoyingly aware of his scornful gaze condemning her dress as she turned to Mrs Lawrence, so she reddened with embarrassment.

Mrs Lawrence was about fifty, elegant in grey silk, pink roses and lace. Her cool grey eyes swept over Sarette. But if the woman found her lacking – which she must, Sarette thought in despair, she didn't make comment.

Awed by her, Sarette curtsied. 'I'm pleased to

make your acquaintance, Mrs Lawrence.'

'Thank you, my dear. And I you. I'm looking forward to getting to know you better.' Her voice was low and cultured.

Sarette remembered to thank Mr Grimble for escorting her from Southampton, and handed over John's letter. It was thick, consisting of several pages folded lengthways into three and sealed with wax. The lawyer examined the seals, then nodded. 'Thank you my dear.' He gave a little bow. 'We'll see ourselves out. Mrs Lawrence. Miss Maitland, good-day to you both.'

'Mrs Lawrence.' Gerald Grimble kissed the woman's hand, then turned to her. 'Miss Maitland.' He grinned when she hastily put her hands behind her back, and gave a small bow. 'Welcome to England.'

After the men had gone Sarette handed the smaller letter to Mrs Lawrence. The maid brought them in some tea and thin slices of cake. Sarette could have eaten a loaf of bread with a pound of cheese inside it.

'While I'm reading my letter you may pour the tea, my dear.'

Sarette's hand trembled as she lifted the delicate china teapot, but she slopped only a little into the saucer. She tipped it back into the cup so it wouldn't be wasted, and handed it to the woman.

'Sarette, dear, returning spilled tea to the cup just won't do.'

'But water is precious. We can't throw it away. In the goldfields it cost us quite a lot of money to buy water from the carter and we had to reuse it.'

'You're no longer in the goldfields, Sarette. You've left that part of your life behind and are now in England, where we do things a little differently.' Her smile robbed her words of any intent to wound. 'John Kern has commanded me to turn you into a lady. He said you're clever and obliging, and quick to learn, and my husband and I knew him well enough for me to believe him.'

Sarette glowed with pleasure at the praise. 'Is your husband an adventurer too?'

'No, Sarette, he is not. My husband is deceased, but he was a physician.'

'Mr Grimble told me and I'd forgotten. I'm sorry.'

Mrs Lawrence handed the cup back to her. 'Now, you may have this one back. Perhaps you could try again, using the clean cup. This time, try not to spill it. Thank you,' she said when Sarette managed to carry out the action a second time with more success.

Mrs Lawrence placed a slice of cake on a plate and handed it over with a napkin. 'You might like to place it on your lap, to protect your skirt.'

Sarette gave a nervous giggle as she pointed out, 'The dress used to belong to my mother. It's my second best one, even though it's dirty. The best one needs washing, and the third best one is almost rags.'

'Nevertheless, as it's your second best gown, until we purchase another you will not wish to soil it further. In fact, if you'd taken care of it in the first place it wouldn't have got into such a disgusting state. It's stained beyond redemption.'

Obviously Iris Lawrence had never scratched in the dirt for a living, and although Sarette wanted to point it out to this superior lady that she was being unfair, she managed to restrain herself.

The cake was sweet and delicious. She ate it in two bites, then picked up the crumbs with the end of her forefinger and licked it clean. She sighed. 'I've never eaten cake before.'

'You may have another piece, this time leave the crumbs on the plate. When you've eaten it and have finished your tea we'll have a chat. I want to know all about you and your family, and as far back as you know.'

By the time Sarette went up to bed that night, with Mrs Lawrence's prompting, she'd remembered lots of things about her own family background. She'd also learned many things from Mrs Lawrence just by watching her, that the round spoon was to be used for soup, that the liquid was scooped away from the body, and that the bread was broken with the fingers before eating and her knife and fork placed neatly together when she'd finished her meal.

It was a nice night, cool, but slightly humid. She seated herself by the window in a chair covered in pink brocade and gazed out over the bay while she brushed out the length of her hair. The sea shushed gently against the shore and a half-moon burnished the water with silver gleams. It was a gentle bay, not like the ocean she'd crossed with its fluid glass peaks, sudden dips and living, curling waves that crashed and slapped against the ship, tossing it about in a ferment of foam.

She smiled as she remembered the rotund Captain Jolly, so calm and unflappable, his feet solid on the deck as if he'd been nailed into position and his voice bellowing commands above the din of the weather.

She unbuttoned the top of her flannel nightgown, exposing her throat to the kiss of night air. Mr John had bought the garment for her to wear on the ship, and like everything Sarette owned, it needed washing.

'Just in case you're shipwrecked in the night and have to be rescued,' he'd said.

He seemed too far away from her now. Her heart ached for him and she whispered, 'I'm here, Mr John, my dearest friend. Mrs Lawrence has been good to me, and I like your Mr Grimble, but I miss you so much. A year seems such a long time now. Look after yourself. I know you don't always believe in such things, and you've convinced me not to either, but I'll pray for you every night anyway, just in case.'

There was a soft knock. The door creaked open and Mrs Lawrence came in, carrying a candle. 'I heard voices. Are you all right, dear?' she said.

'I expect you'll think I'm foolish, but I was talking to Mr John.'

'No, I don't think you're foolish. Sometimes when I feel lonely I talk to my husband.' She picked up the photograph. 'Is this you with

John?'

'Yes. I was fourteen then, and it was taken nearly three years ago, not long after he rescued me.'

'You look younger than fourteen, and have grown into a beautiful young woman in that time. John looks much older than when we last met. I wouldn't have recognized him with that beard.'

He shaved if off just before I left, so I could see what he looked like without it. And he looked handsome, but odd, because the top of his face was tanned by the sun and the bottom was still pale.'

'What's this little hut you're standing in front of, a native dwelling?'

'No, it was our home.'

She gasped. 'You lived in such poor conditions.'

'Most people did. The town was just beginning to grow, with proper buildings, and a railway station. Miners come and go all the time, and don't want permanent houses. If they can't find gold they move on, as Mr John decided we would.'

'And I had the temerity to comment on the state of your dress. I'm so sorry.'

'There's no need to be sorry, since you couldn't have known. It was Mr John's home really, but he built me a room on the side with a hessian flap, so I could be private if I wanted to. It was kind of him.'

'I recall he was always a kind man, though tough if he had to be. I always thought it a pity that he didn't marry again.'

'He was still grieving for his lost wife and daughter when I left him. I offered to marry him so he would never feel lonely.'

Mrs Lawrence appeared shocked. 'John Kern is much too old for you.'

'But he needs to feel he has someone to look after. I think I gave him a reason for living. He drank to excess when we met, you see. He began to drink less after he took me in, though sometimes his stomach pained him and the spirits relieved the pain.'

'But he would have known that you offered to be his wife out of pity.'

'I didn't pity him. I respected him and was grateful to him. I owed him my life, and wanted him to be happy.'

'What a queer little creature you are.' Mrs Lawrence took the brush from her hand and began to pull it gently through her hair. 'How did John react when you proposed marriage to him?'

'He said he'd be home in a year and promised he would see how we felt about such an arrangement then.'

'Do you expect him to honour his promise?'

Sarette heaved a sigh. In her heart of hearts she suspected he might not. Her own thinking was maturing now and she was beginning to believe that John Kern had been sweetening the pill of parting for her. She'd swallowed his lie because she didn't want to face up to the fact that he wasn't the hero she'd always thought, but a flawed, troubled, and lonely old man. 'I think he was telling me what he thought I wanted to hear, but I believe he will honour his promise and return to England.'

'And if he doesn't come?'

'I promised I'd stay a year and try to improve myself, and that I'll do. I believe those instructions are in the letters I carried for yourself and Mr Grimble. After that year ... I have made no plans.'

Iris Lawrence took the letter from her pocket and handed it to Sarette. 'I can't speak for Mr Grimble, but you may read the one he sent to me if you wish to know what those instructions were.'

Dearest Iris,

May I introduce my dearly beloved little friend, Miss Sarette Maitland. Sarry has absorbed all the education I've been able to give her. I cannot, however, empower her with feminine ways. She has managed to get through my armour and find a soft spot in my heart. She is young for her age and has such a need to be loved. I think I will never forgive her for making me feel joy again when I was happily wallowing in my self-pity. Thus, I'm a sorry excuse for a man, and because I cannot be what she wants then I must send her away before I break her heart, or before she breaks what's left of mine. I can only think of two true and constant friends who will act on my behalf with the discretion and delicacy this matter needs, especially where Magnus is concerned. Ignatious Grimble will pay all her expenses, and there will be no need to economise.

Sarry will ask to see this letter because, not only is she curious about everything she'll need to know what I said about her.

'Hah!' she said indignantly.

Sarry dear, I lied to you. When we met I was not looking for you. I was in despair and about to set Hercules free and walk off into the desert to die. You brought a gift into my life. I might not have dug much in the way of riches from the earth, but you certainly brought gold into my heart and that enriched it. But you were more in despair than I, so you became my burden as well as my joy. I'll expect you to keep the promises you have made. You owe me that, sweet Sarry. Don't worry that I might carry out my earlier intent, since you have taught me to live.

Your friendship has always meant much to me. Your loving friend,
    John Kern

Tears filled her eyes and she said fiercely, 'If Mr John doesn't come back I shall find some way of going back to Australia, and I'll look after him and it'll be like it always was.'

'No, Sarette. It can never be the same for either of you. John has much on his conscience, and he is a man who walks his path alone. You owe him a debt that he'll expect you to honour.'

Sarette was overtaken by a sudden chill. 'D'you think I'll ever see him again?'

'It's possible, but not probable. Sometimes it's easier to put things in writing instead of say them out loud, and John was never glib. The letter was meant for you and he has said goodbye in the only way he knew.'

'Reading the letter has made me feel sad, and he has not said goodbye, else he would have said it face to face.'

'He has said much to commend you. It's obvious that he loved you.'

'Like a daughter.'

'Which was all you ever could be to him. John was never shallow, and you were privileged to occupy a special place in his heart, my dear.'

Sarette was overtaken by a yawn.

'It's polite to cover your mouth with your hand when you yawn.'

She giggled through her tears. 'Am I to be corrected at every turn? Sometimes yawns take you by surprise and fly away before you can prevent them. You don't have time to be polite.'

'And was it one of those yawns?'

'Yes. I do beg your pardon. Mr John used to tell me that the crows would fly into my mouth and pluck out my teeth if I didn't cover them.'

Mrs Lawrence gave a soft laugh and placed the hairbrush on the dressing table. 'Into bed now, else you'll be tired tomorrow, when we will have much shopping to do.' She picked up the candle. 'Goodnight, Sarette.'

'Goodnight, Mrs Lawrence. Thank you for having me. I'll try and improve myself. I promise.'

'I'm sure you will, my dear.'

'And Mr John will come. You'll see.'

'Goodnight, dear.' The door closed behind her. Sarette's pillow and sheets smelled of soap and sunshine. The moon rose higher. It gazed at her through the window and the lace curtain gently drifted in a current of air. Odd to think that while she had the moon at her feet John would have the sun at his head.

'Here I am, Mr John, lying in a bed so fine that I feel like a cuckoo in a linnet's nest,' she whispered, and smiled when she thought she heard him chuckle.

Ignatious Grimble was perturbed.

The next morning he summoned Gerald to his study, handed over the wad of papers Sarette Maitland had given him, then went to look out of the window, leaving his son to read them undisturbed while he sipped his coffee.

He rejoined his son ten minutes later. 'It's not John Kern's way to do something like this but it's definitely John's handwriting,' Ignatious told him, knowing he had Gerald's complete confidence.

'His instructions couldn't be clearer.'

'We should check that the witnesses to his signature are who they say they are.'

'You mean one of us should travel to Australia? We're looking at six months.'

'I was thinking that we should send Edgar. He yearns for adventure and it will take his mind off that innkeeper's widow he's enamoured with. He could check on John's whereabouts at the same time.'

Gerald smiled. 'Ah, so that's it. You want to get Edgar out of the widow's arms. What if the whole thing is an elaborate hoax by Miss Maitland to claim the rest of John's estate?'

'Miss Maitland is too ingenuous to take on a hornet's nest of legal gentlemen in the hope of bringing such a fraud to fruition. She struck me as being entirely naive.'

'She could have a partner who is directing her. What do we know about her background?'

'Iris Lawrence will discover anything there is to know about her. I'm tempted to place the matter before Magnus Kern. After all, it's he who will be affected by the will when John dies.'

'Since he's already been given the bulk of John's fortune, and doesn't know about his uncle's annuities it will affect him not at all. He will expect to have the Bournemouth house though.'

'The house is a good investment, but by the end of two years both house and annuities will belong to the girl, whether John dies or not. John trusts me to keep this quiet until the first year is up. Only then must I take the girl to Magnus and make him aware of John's plans for her.'

'And the part Magnus must play in it.'

'Yes ... there's that.'

Gerald smiled. 'I must admit I'll enjoy seeing the look on his face when he finds out.'

'Try not to allow your rivalry with Magnus Kern to work against you, Gerald. You were an intellectual match at Cambridge, but you always liked each other. Better have him as a friend than an enemy.'

'Lor, father. Magnus is my best friend and nothing will change that. Notwithstanding the generosity of his uncle, Magnus has done well in his life, and I do continue to wish him well. Our rivalry is a contest rather than real envy, and often serves a purpose. And we know exactly when to stop. We have the same tastes in women, the same outlook in life, and the same background to a certain extent. Except my grandfather was a dishonest revenue man who turned the other cheek for gain, while you—'

'Dishonestly turned the whole enterprise into a legitimate business interest. None will ever be able to prove that the Kern and Grimble families were less than honest purveyors of goods and legal services.'

'You have taught your sons well, father. I have a great deal of respect for you.'

'Ah, Gerald. You haven't got a crooked bone in your body. You'll never be as wealthy as Magnus, or as your elder brothers are, come to that.'

'I have sufficient for my needs. The poor need representation, and I do my best to provide it, as does Magnus. We are of one mind on that. It also gives the firm a good name. But we've discussed this before. Did you want my advice on the situation John Kern has presented you with?'

'I would welcome it. Of all my sons, you might not be the most sensible at times, but you're clever and quick-minded, and I value your advice the most.'

'Thank you father, but I don't know why

you're bothering me with this. You know you have no choice but to carry out your client's wishes to the letter, unless the situation changes.'

'Changes ... now?'

'If John Kern happens to die then Magnus will expect the estate to be settled on him, at which time he'll have to be told. Whenever he's told of the presence of this girl, he's not going to be at all happy about us keeping the information from him.'

'And he'll be none too pleased with the girl, either. I suspect she is not as biddable as she seems. Your advice on the situation then?'

'Send Edgar off adventuring, by all means. It will kill two birds with one stone where he's concerned, since it will get both widow and wanderlust out of his blood. Also, he's a bit of a terrier if he doesn't allow himself to be distracted. Once his teeth have locked into a problem nothing will shake it loose. As for the other business, you didn't need advice on that.' Gerald's eyes flicked up to his. 'The girl ... d'you think John—'

'No, I do not, otherwise he would have kept her there with him. Anyone can see she's an innocent. She hero-worships him, nothing more. Only a lesser man would take advantage of that.'

Gerald laughed. 'You needn't be so defensive of him, Pa.'

'Don't call me Pa, you know I detest it.'

'Iris Lawrence was engaged to John Kern once, wasn't she?'

'She was. It was an arranged match when Iris

113

was barely out of school, but she refused to marry him and she fell in love with an actor and joined his company. After a while he tired of her and she was disowned by her family. She turned to John for help.'

'And?'

'Nothing like that. He'd met Annie by then, and that was that. John offered Iris a country cottage he owned to live in, and Annie introduced her to the man who became her husband.'

'Did he know of her past?'

'Yes. But he loved her, and he reconciled her with her father.'

'So John Kern has a habit of saving damsels in distress.'

'He had a soft spot for children, and Sarette was a child when he came across her. It will be interesting to see how she turns out. She's an attractive little baggage, and that won't be lost on Magnus when he claps eyes on her.'

Gerald grinned to himself. It hadn't been lost on him, either. He might find an excuse to visit the delicious Miss Maitland from time to time himself, just to see how she was progressing.

'I don't like that smile, Gerald. If it's what I think you're thinking, restrain yourself. The girl has been placed in my hands for safe-keeping and John will expect her to be in one piece when he comes home. She's too young for you.'

'*If* he comes home. Intuition tells me that he's setting his house in order for a reason.'

His father gazed at him in some alarm. 'Let's hope you're wrong, Gerald.'

Seven

March 1898

'The corselette will give you a fashionable waist.'

'I don't want a fashionable waist, I just want to be comfortable.' Sarette groaned as the maid tightened it a little more, saying, 'Enough, I can't breathe as it is.'

Amy chuckled. 'Arms up.'

The white silk gown was slid over the froth of petticoats she wore, the bodice glistening with scattered beads that also decorated the wide, puff sleeves.

'Your hair looks nice in that bun with the curly fringe. You look grown-up.'

'Goodness, I am grown-up, Amy. I'm eighteen today, and I can't believe I've been here for six months already.'

'Mr Grimble won't recognize you when he arrives.'

'I hardly recognize myself.'

Winding a pale green sash around her waist Amy secured it at the hip with silk flowers that matched those in her hair. 'He's handsome, isn't he?'

'Who ... Ignatious Grimble?'

'You know very well that I meant Mr Gerald Grimble.'

'Oh, Gerald. He's a horrible tease and probably won't come with his father.' She gazed at herself in the long mirror. It was true that she hardly recognized herself, the child had gradually been replaced by a woman. She wondered what Mr John would make of her now, wondered if he ever thought of her. She picked up the photograph, now preserved behind glass in a silver-plated frame. What had he seen in that skinny child with the big eyes that he'd stumbled across by accident – a child in more pain than the despair he'd carried in his own heart?

She'd not heard one word from him since she'd left Australia, and was looking forward to Mr Grimble's visit to see if he'd received any news.

As for Gerald Grimble ... yes, he was handsome, and he flirted with her, but he never overstepped the line or gave her any reason to think that his visits were any more than friendship with Iris Lawrence. He wasn't the only gentleman Mrs Lawrence entertained, thus enabling the woman to train her few students in the art of engaging in dinner conversation with trustworthy gentlemen.

And what students. There was a shop assistant who wanted to get on in life and had made an advantageous marriage her goal in life. Then there was Celia, a girl so shy that she hung her head and stammered if anyone addressed her directly. Most interesting of all was the spinster who'd inherited a modest house and some

116

money from a relative she'd looked after. Edith Carter had a straightforward manner and was a member of the Women's Liberal Association.

'Tell me about the Australian goldfields, Miss Maitland,' she said. 'I've heard that the place abounds with poisonous snakes and spiders.'

Immediately Sarette remembered her father – recalled the fear in his eyes as the venom did its work and leached the life from him. She felt the colour drain from her face. 'I'm afraid I'd rather not talk of such creatures at the dinner table.'

'Nonsense,' she said in her hearty forthright manner. 'We'd all be interested, I'm sure.'

Sarette had exchanged a glance with Iris Lawrence, to whom she'd confided the nature of her father's passing. Iris smiled sympathetically at her and deflected Edith with, 'Perhaps you'd prefer to see some gold dust, Miss Carter.'

'I'd love to see it again,' Gerald said. 'It's fascinating stuff. It took Miss Maitland two years to sift it, fleck by fleck, from the sand. She had it in a match box. but I've given her a bottle to keep it in, so she won't lose it fleck by fleck in the same manner.'

She'd thanked Gerald later for rescuing her with, 'I have reason to hate snakes.'

'I know you do. You were as white as a sheet and I thought you were going to faint.'

'I don't know why you come to these dinners.'

'To oblige Mrs Lawrence, and because she provides an excellent dinner. Also because I have the pleasure of your company for the whole evening. If you put those in reverse order you will have your answer.'

'I like your company too, Gerald. Next to Mr John, I regard you as my best friend.'

He'd raised an eyebrow at that. 'Only second best? You certainly know how to crush the vanity of a man.'

She'd felt confused by him. 'I'm so sorry ... I didn't mean...' Noting his grin she'd punched him gently on the arm. 'You're teasing me, Gerald.'

'Am I indeed? Now there's a second slight. As punishment I shall go and talk to Miss Celia Ingleby and make her stammer, while you can be bored by Mr Taggard. I think he's sweet on Mrs Lawrence, don't you?'

The thought of which had made her giggle. All the same Mr Taggard visited often, and was a pleasant and gentle man. Sarette observed him with Iris over the following few weeks when he visited, and she thought that Gerald might be right.

She smiled and placed the photograph back on the dressing table.

'All right now, Miss Maitland?' Amy said.

'Thank you, Amy, you've made me look lovely. You'd better go and see to Mrs Lawrence.'

Gerald and his father had already arrived and were in the hall when she went down the stairs.

'Why, if it isn't Miss Maitland, all grown up at last,' Gerald drawled. 'Happy birthday, Sarette.'

'Thank you, Gerald. Don't forget that you promised to teach me to waltz when I was grown up.'

'So I did.' He came to the bottom of the stairs, placed his hands around her waist and lifted her down the last two. 'Come on then. I'll waltz you along the seafront and back again, and everyone will stare at us.'

'Oh, you.'

He kissed her on the forehead and handed her a jewellery case. 'For your birthday.'

'What is it?'

'Open it.'

Inside was a string of glowing pearls. He fastened them around her neck, said, 'My father has some earrings to match for you.'

'Oh, Mr Grimble, in my excitement I forgot to greet you. I'm so sorry, and I am pleased to see you.' She reached up and kissed his wrinkled cheek.'

His eyes crinkled. 'That was the best apology I've ever received, so it was worth waiting for.'

'Gerald told me you were suffering from a cold the last time we met. Are you fully recovered?'

'Yes, Miss Maitland. I am.' He handed her a little jeweller's box and cleared his throat. 'I do hope you like them.'

'They're beautiful.' Removing them one by one from their purple velvet bed, she moved to the hall mirror and pinned the pearl drops to her ears. 'What riches! I feel so grand, that I could be mistaken for the Queen of England.'

Gerald and his father exchanged a grin when Gerald said, 'Thankfully, you could never be mistaken for Queen Victoria.'

She linked her arms through those of the men. 'Come into the drawing room and tell me all the news. Have you heard anything from Mr John? I expected him to write, yet I've heard nothing.'

Ignatious gazed into her lustrous green eyes and noted the worry in them. As his mind composed something designed to soothe, he also tried to assuage his own worry. Apart from a telegraph to say he'd arrived safely, they hadn't heard a thing from Edgar.

Australia

Edgar Grimble was a dapper young man of medium height with an air of bustling energy about him and an inclination towards spur-of-the-moment decisions. He was the possessor of a modest fortune in the form of a legacy from his maternal grandmother, whom he'd adored, and he idolized his half-brother, Gerald, who credited him with more sense than Edgar knew he actually possessed.

Discounting the tale the girl had told his father, for he'd rather go back to the beginning and find out for himself, he'd travelled to Coolgardie. He'd found it to be a bustling town with wide streets, prosperous buildings, and plenty of dust.

There he'd found news of John Kern.

The shopkeeper remembered him well. 'A pleasant, honest gentleman was Mr Kern.'

'And the girl, Sarette Maitland?'

'A dear child. Abandoned by her father's partner. She worked off his debt to the shop. Mr Kern took her in and looked after her. Then they upped and left one day. He sold his claim and everything, and the new owners are doing quite nicely out of it, I hear. They took the train, they did. Sarry said they were going to Fremantle to get on a ship to the old country. As I recalled she was excited about it, but she didn't want to leave the horse behind. She kicked up a fuss, but Mr Kern took no notice of her tantrum. He boarded the train and told her that he was going, and if she didn't want to come she could stay behind. That brought her to heel, I can tell you. I haven't set eyes on the pair of them since. We would have knowed if he'd come back.'

So the girl's account of things had proved to be genuine. 'Thank you. You've been very helpful. You'll be pleased to know that Sarette Maitland is well and reached England safely. It's Mr Kern I'm looking for. If he comes back, would you ask him to contact Grimble and Sons.'

Edgar had travelled back to Perth, then on to the town of Fremantle, where he checked the shipping records. John Kern's name didn't appear on the passenger lists. It took time, but he did the rounds of the hotels. He was looking for a man called Angus Edwards.

He found him clerking in a lawyer's office.

'John Kern. Yes, I remember him. My employer was away on business and he wanted the will witnessed in a hurry, so I notarized the signature myself. He told me he was going to Melbourne on business. I offered to travel with him, since I was taking time off to visit my mother. However, he was vague about the sailing time and said they didn't coincide since we were booked on different steamers.'

'Did you read the will?'

'No, sir.' The man hesitated. 'As I recall, he told me he was leaving everything he had to his

121

niece. The document was sealed and notarized in the office.'

'This niece ... did you see her?'

'She wasn't with him. He said he didn't want her to know about it. He seemed like a nice man, but I thought he looked ill. I did see him around town a couple of times afterwards, but he was always alone, and inebriated.'

'Thank you. You have a good memory, and I'm obliged to you.' He repeated the request he'd made to the Coolgardie shopkeeper. 'If you ever see Mr Kern, perhaps you would ask him to contact Grimble and Sons.'

In Melbourne, a fine city which had taken his fancy at first sight, he'd discovered two men with the name of John Kern. He was in no hurry to leave his surroundings, even though neither man was the John Kern he wanted. The first one made boots, and the second one was a gentleman sheep farmer.

Invited to dinner by the latter, Edgar met a young lady called Amelia Rose Wallace. She was sweet-tempered and fair, and they fell instantly in love. Edgar was offered a position by her father, who was a wine merchant and they were married four months later.

After the honeymoon Edgar resumed his quest when he saw a notice in an old newspaper about John Kern's death, and he realized he'd been in the country for several months without word to his father. It was already June. Duty called. He contacted the coroner's office and the newspaper in Perth, in time receiving a copy of the report, plus further news about the escape of the convicted killer, Flynn Collins. The man had not been caught.

Resisting the sweet nothings his wife whispered in his ear, he sent her to bed on a promise one night, then pulled the inkwell towards him and began to write.

Melbourne Australia. June 1898

Dearest Father,

I'm sorry to have taken so long to report back to you, but my search has been as thorough as I could make it, as I will detail in the pages to come.

First I must tell you of the most pleasant and happy event. I have married the most wonderful girl in the world and have decided to settle in Melbourne, which is a fine city. Your new daughter-in-law is Amelia Rose Grimble (née Wallace). Her father is a wine exporter. I'm sure you will approve of her, and adore her as much as I do when you meet, which will be the year after next on a visit to England, if all goes well. In the meantime I have enclosed a photograph taken on our wedding day.

I intend to use the legacy from my esteemed grandmother to open a solicitors' office. I thought I might call it Son of Grimble. I do hope you approve, and will, of course be available for any soliciting business you wish to conduct in the colony.

As for that other matter. I've been thorough and checked back to the Coolgardie goldfields in the west. Sarette Maitland's story holds true in every respect. There are people there who remember them both, and the circumstances by which Miss Maitland was taken into the care of John Kern. So there is no need to doubt the young woman's story.

Now for the bad news. I'm sorry to have to tell you this father, because I know that your friendship with John Kern was dear to you. It appears that he is...

Bournemouth
'*Dead!* John Kern is dead?' Ignatious sank into a chair. 'I can't believe it.'

Gerald had been reading the coroner's report, and said gravely, 'It appears that he was shot in the heart through the back. It would have been instant and he wouldn't have seen it coming, if that's any consolation. The murderer was sentenced to death, but escaped before the deed was carried out. Good Lord! It happened while Sarette was still on the ship. No wonder we never got any correspondence from him.'

Gerald picked up the photograph of his brother with Amelia Rose and smiled to himself, even though the matter at hand was nothing to smile about. This was typical of his headstrong younger brother, but he hoped he would be happy. 'I admire Edgar's taste. She's a pretty little dove.'

'She'll need the disposition of an angel to deal with him,' Ignatious snorted. 'Son of Grimble, indeed! Typical of Edgar to think up such a ridiculous name. He hasn't even got his articles yet.'

'I'm sure you can arrange that. Edgar was a

124

quick learner and always managed to engage the finer points of law. He would make a fine barrister, one with flair.'

'Yes, I suppose he would. All my sons are well taught as well as gifted.' Ignatious Grimble couldn't quite hide the pride in his voice. 'I should have sent you, not Edgar. You've got much more common sense.' He gazed at the photograph. 'A wine merchant's daughter, eh, I suppose he could have done worse.'

'He might have married the innkeeper's widow.'

Ignatious shuddered.

'What are you going to do about John? Magnus will have to be told as soon as possible.'

Ignatious sighed. 'But not Sarette. John was adamant that she must finish her education with Iris Lawrence before she meets Magnus.'

'I wouldn't have thought she'd need any more. She's been there for nearly a year and appears to be socially acceptable to me, and thoroughly delightful.'

'Yes, I suppose she is. Oh dear ... I've been dreading this day.'

'Serves you right,' Gerald said, trying not to laugh. 'Your devious nature was bound to catch up with you sooner or later.'

'This is John Kern's deviousness, not mine.'

'The pair of you have always been like-minded. Honestly, father. Magnus might growl a bit, but he was close to his uncle and he'll understand his way of thinking over this once he gets over his shock. It might take him a while though.'

'You think so?'

His father looked so dubious that Gerald wanted to laugh. 'Would you prefer me to tackle Magnus?'

'No, it's a duty John has charged me with. We'll go together. Then we'll go on to Weymouth. You can take the girl out of the way while I inform Mrs Lawrence what has happened.'

'I'll go and tell Amos he'll be in charge of the firm for the day, then.'

Eight

Magnus Kern added a splash of brandy to the coffee he'd ordered for them. His face reflected the sorrow he felt at the news. 'I can't say this comes as a complete surprise. My last letter to my uncle was returned and I wondered.' Though he'd hoped his uncle had moved on. 'You must bill me for Edgar's expenses.'

Ignatious nodded. 'I'm sorry to be the bearer of bad news.'

'What killed him? Heart? He seemed quite healthy when he left here.'

'He was shot, Magnus.'

Magnus's hand jumped and his cup rattled on the saucer. 'Shot?'

'In the back. Death was instantaneous.' He handed over a copy of the newspaper cuttings and coroner's report.

The men were silent while he read the papers, then Magnus glanced over at father and son. 'At least he didn't go into a pauper's grave. I should have thought to look for him myself.'

'Your uncle was strong-minded, Magnus. He wouldn't have liked either of us to interfere in his life ... or oppose his will come to that.'

Magnus's eyes darkened as his glance slid over Gerald – who was examining his finger-nails – to narrow in on those of Ignatious Grimble. There was a suspicion forming in the back of his mind and he said, 'Oddly, you took it upon yourself to do both. You must have had a very good reason for that. What was it?'

Gerald cleared his throat and exchanged a glance with his father, who nodded.

'There's a girl involved,' Gerald said.

'So my uncle had a lady friend. What of her? Pay her off.'

'Not that sort of lady friend, Magnus. John Kern took a destitute child under his wing and he'd made her ... his responsibility, and he left her a bequest from his remaining estate. It was his wish that her welfare be passed over to you.'

'The devil take him! Where is this girl?'

The bland smile Gerald offered him gave nothing away. 'She's at ... *school*. We're to deliver her into your care when we decide its expedient to do so. We will need your assurance that you'll do as your uncle wishes.'

Magnus wondered if the girl was a child his uncle had fathered. John had been in Australia for long enough to have met some woman on the ship and got a child on her. She wouldn't be older than four years, at the most. Rather young to be in school.

Pushing back his chair Magnus went to the window and gazed out over the pleasant garden. But he shortened his gaze and observed the reflection of the two men in the glass. 'When *you* decide? If the child is to become my responsibility, it's I who will decide. How long have you known about this girl?'

It was Ignatious who answered. 'It's eleven months since she stepped off the boat and her female chaperone handed her over to me.'

'And you didn't do me the courtesy of informing me?' Magnus said silkily.

'I was acting under your uncle's instructions.'

'The instructions of a dead man.'

Gerald stepped in. 'According to the dates, John Kern was still alive when the girl left Australia. We sent Edgar to check on the veracity of the signatures on the will, and to seek your uncle out. As soon as we received news we brought it to you. The girl is a pretty little thing. I'm sure you'll like her.'

'Do you have a copy of John's last will and testament with you?'

'We do.' Ignatious opened the briefcase he'd brought with him, because it contained the legacies for the staff. He then took out a handkerchief and hastily mopped his brow. 'Before you read it I'd like to run through one or two points that need clearing up.'

Magnus turned. He noticed the perspiration on the old man's face and shrugged. Surely he wasn't that frightening. 'I can see from your faces that I'm not going to like the contents of the will. I'd rather you just left it on my desk. I'll call on you later in the week and we can discuss the finer points then. I might as well tell you that if he has left this girl his Bournemouth house, I intend to contest it.'

'Which might end up costing you more than the house is worth, but that will be up to you, of course,' Gerald said, and smiled, which immediately put Magnus on alert.

'I don't like that smile. Gerald. What else?'

'I thought you wanted to read the will yourself.'

Gritting his teeth, Magnus forced out. 'Stop looking so damned smug. What else, dammit!'

Throwing a wad of papers on to the desk, Gerald said, 'My condolences on the death of your uncle. A pity you didn't learn some manners from him, but like all the Kerns, you always were an arrogant bastard.'

'Enough,' Ignatious said quietly. 'A man who was a good friend of mine has died in a tragic manner at the hands of a coward. Let us at least recognize that fact and act with the dignity this deserves.'

'My apologies, gentlemen,' Magnus immediately said, and held out his hand first to Ignatious, then as the older man began to leave, to Gerald. 'You caught me at a bad moment, and I'd forgotten how good you are at needling me.'

'Any time, Magnus. I really am sorry about your uncle. The world will be a less colourful place without him.' He lowered his voice.

'How's Isabelle these days?'

Magnus gave him a dark look. 'Don't you already know?'

Gerald smiled. 'A gentleman never tells what he knows, but I'm not one of her confidants. A tip to the wise, Magnus. I do know that you'd be better off without her, and the sooner the better.'

After they took their leave Magnus poured himself a stiff brandy and opened his copy of John Kern's will. His uncle had left the servants the princely sum of two hundred guineas each, along with his profound thanks for their faithful service. The money was in the form of cash, provided by Ignatious, and placed in sealed envelopes with their names on it.

To Sarette Maitland I leave my house in Bournemouth and the income from my annuities, as listed.

Magnus whistled. He'd known nothing about the annuities, and the total was quite a staggering sum, enough to maintain the Bournemouth house with plenty left over.

To my beloved nephew Magnus Kern. The estate and monies already transferred to his name. In addition, I request that he takes responsibility for the girl named Sarette Maitland – that he should provide her with a roof over her head – keep her, and do his best to secure for her a good marriage where she can be nurtured in a safe and loving environment. To this end the management of annuities and the house in Bournemouth; known as Smuggler's View, will be placed in his hands, the income to provide for her welfare until such time as Miss Maitland reaches the age of twenty-two years, when both house and income shall revert to her, unless...

His uncle had thought of everything, including distribution of the estate should the child die. Conscience pricked, Magnus smiled. After all, there was plenty of money to go around, and it wouldn't cost him a penny. His uncle had a generous heart and it wouldn't hurt him to do as he asked with regards to the child. 'Sarette Maitland,' he murmured. 'A pretty name.'

He called the staff in and told them the bad news. The cook burst into tears, which set a couple of the maids off sobbing as well.

What was it about his uncle that commanded such loyalty? he thought grumpily, then felt ashamed of himself.

He followed it up with the good. 'John Kern has bequeathed to each of you the sum of two hundred guineas, and his thanks for your loyalty to the Kern family. He said it will be the means to escape my service, if you so wish. Naturally, I'm hoping for the opposite.'

'God love the master, where else would I go?' the cook said in a watery voice, and without his permission, the butler got a bottle of sherry out of the cupboard and they drank a toast to John's departure, followed by one to their good fortune.

Magnus left for the stables, and he supposed they'd drink half his cellar, and his dinner would be late. Saddling his horse, he sprang into the saddle and rode down to the cove. The tide

131

was in so he cantered along the cliff top, then brought the horse to a halt.

If he had a child to bring up, then she'd need a woman to look after her. Isabelle? He'd been on the brink of proposing to her once, now he shook his head. Gerald had given him good warning. He was going to London in a couple of weeks' time, leaving his partner in charge of the chambers. He'd intended to take Isabelle with him, now he decided it would be better to bring their association to an end before he left.

While he was away someone could come in and refurbish the nursery rooms, and the child could move in as soon as they were ready. The girl could go to a school nearby when she was older. He'd make his intentions known to Ignatious Grimble by letter, and leave his instructions. A woman could be hired to look after her. After all, he didn't want her running around and getting underfoot.

As for the house in Bournemouth, he must think seriously about that. He already had more than enough money for his own needs. But if he married he'd have children, he thought, and would have to consider the possibility that he'd need the house and the annuities for his own family.

But then, he argued, it was more than likely that the little girl had been fathered by John Kern. Why else would he have brought her into the family? From a moral standpoint, Sarette would be entitled to something from her father's estate, and he'd make sure that she did. After all, that's why she'd been placed in his keeping. His uncle had trusted him to do the right thing and had provided the girl with a good dowry. It was too big, and would attract all the wrong sorts, of course. Money always talked. Perhaps he would find a good woman in London, marry her and provide the child with a mother.

He grinned. No wonder Gerald had looked so smug when they'd told him about Sarette. Magnus certainly hadn't expected to have such a responsibility foisted on to him.

Idly, he wondered if Gerald was taking anyone to the Legal Association Christmas Ball. Gerald usually had good taste in women, and Magnus felt the need to give as good as he'd got ... or better.

Sarette was attached to Gerald's arm and strolling along the seafront. For August the day was cold, with a persistent wind driving the sand hard up on to the shore with a rushing sound. There were very few people about, some hardy adults and children building sandcastles and digging holes. A couple of old people struggled against the wind, their coats billowing. Others huddled in the shelters.

The bathing machines were high above the tide mark. The Queen's Jubilee clock kept watch over the Esplanade, its base rooted in the sand. One of its other two faces gazed down King Street and the other out to sea.

Sarette's carefully arranged hair soon loosened itself and went flying in the wind.

They seated themselves in a shelter and she attempted to braid it.

'Allow me.'

Gerald's hands were wonderfully gentle and she closed her eyes, shivering a little.

'Cold?' he asked, knotting his handkerchief around the end of the braid.

'A little. It doesn't feel much like summer.'

'You've been used to a warmer climate. Shall I take you back home?'

She sighed. 'What was so important that I be got out of the way for a while?'

'I thought you were so enamoured by my charm that you didn't notice.'

'Dear Gerald, I'm not in the least bit enamoured by you, though I have to admit you can be charming. You're trying to distract me. John Kern used to do that when he didn't want me to know about something.'

'It's the lawyer in us. We liked being challenged. You do know you've hurt my feelings, don't you?'

'I do know that you're a wonderful flirt. I'm sure I haven't harmed a hair on your head. Now, are you going to tell me what's going on?'

'No, I certainly am not. It's none of your business.'

'Which means it is. Have you heard from Mr John? Is he on his way home?'

His reply was unexpected, when he stooped his head and kissed her. Good Lord, what intimate feelings rioted through her. How soft and sweet a kiss it was. Alarm raced through her ... and how highly improper.

She pushed him away. *'Mr Grimble!'*

'Mr Grimble?' he mocked, his eyes alight with

134

amusement. 'Oh, don't sound so spinsterish, you know very well that you enjoyed being kissed.'

She tried not to laugh as she lied, 'I certainly did not. Your moustache tickled me.'

'God forbid that anyone should tickle you, Miss Maitland. You spent several years living with John Kern, who, as I recall, was a man who held great fascination for women, but was much too old for you. I cannot believe that you're as naive as you pretend. Isn't it about time you grew up?'

She stood, her smile fading and hurt squeezing at her chest. 'No, I'm not at all naive. But you do John Kern an injustice. I was a child when I met him, and in his heart as well as his eyes, still a child when he sent me away. He did warn me about the ways of men though. He told me how they sweet-talk a woman, and how they cheat and lie and take what they want if the opportunity arises. When you see him next, ask him about the time he fought off two men who came across me when I was alone, and were attacking me. That was when he decided what my future would be.'

'Sarette ... I'm sorry.'

She shook off his hand. 'I'm sick of being treated like a fool with your diversions. John Kern promised to come for me and he will. And I don't care if he's too old. I'll marry him so he won't feel lonely any more, and I'll look after him and he'll keep me safe.'

Turning her back on him she was about to flounce off when he said harshly, 'He'll do none of those things. John Kern is dead.'

She felt as though she'd been kicked in the back, and turned, her eyes searching his so as to see the truth in them. There was no denying it as he said a little more gently, 'John Kern was dead and in his grave before you reached England.'

The colour gradually drained from her face. 'Don't lie to me about this, Gerald ... not this. Otherwise I will never forgive you.'

He took her back into the shelter, seated her next to him. 'We were worried because we hadn't heard from him. We sent one of my brothers to try and find him. We have just had news from Edgar.'

'How ... was it his stomach? I knew it pained him sometimes, though he wouldn't admit to it. And his skin had a yellow tinge to it. He said it was his tan wearing off. I made him go to a doctor ... he prescribed brandy.'

'He was shot in the back by a coward and he died instantly.'

Tears began to trickle down her cheeks. 'Mr John took the place of my father, and he was my best friend. I've missed him so much, now I'll never see him again.'

Curiously limp, and unaware of the relief Gerald experienced at her words, she found herself in his arms and comforted against his chest.

'I'm sorry. I wasn't supposed to tell you ... not yet,' he said.

Sarette would rather have not known – would rather have gone on enjoying the life John had provided for her and living in ignorance. Gerald had used her youth as a lever to make her grow up. 'It was cruel, the way you said it.'

He gave an ashamed sort of smile. 'I know. I was envious because John raised so much passion in you, when I was so easily rejected. I wanted to hurt you.'

'And you succeeded. Why were you envious?'

'I'm not a man used to being spurned. You made me feel like a fool.'

She didn't want this level of intimacy with Gerald, there was danger in it. 'I didn't mean to spurn you. You took me by surprise, and it served you right. Can we remain friends? I'm not ready to take up a serious relationship with a man yet – not any man, if that will make you feel better.'

'Except John Kern.'

She shrugged. 'It was just words. Mr John wouldn't have allowed me to sacrifice my youth for him.'

Gerald smiled and nodded. 'You know him better than I first thought. We'd better go back to the house. No doubt I'll be chastised by my father.'

She couldn't imagine a grown man being given a dressing-down by his father. 'What will happen to me now?'

'We will follow John Kern's instructions to the letter. You will finish your year with Mrs Lawrence, after all it's only a few weeks. Then you'll become the ward of Magnus Kern until you marry.'

'Marry?'

'Well, your benefactor did suggest to Magnus that he find you a husband ... eventually. Don't worry, it will be painless. I expect you'll attend balls, and can practise those dances I taught you. Then there will be theatres and dinners, and then one day you'll meet someone and fall in love, just as John wanted. Perhaps that someone will be me. I'll ask Magnus to put a good word in for me. I've never met a female I've liked better.' Perhaps it would be Gerald. But liking was not enough. Sarette wanted to be loved before she'd contemplate marriage, and wanted a husband she could love and respect in return. But just at this moment she could only mourn the loss of Mr John. As for Magnus Kern, the nephew John had thought so much of, Sarette was not looking forward to meeting him at all.

She glanced up at him. 'Has Magnus Kern been told about this?'

'Yes. This morning. Magnus was not happy about being saddled with you, but he held his uncle in great esteem, and he'll do what was expected of him once he gets over the shock of having to be responsible for another human being. Don't allow yourself to be frightened by him. He has a good side along with the bad.'

Sarette didn't feel all that happy about being saddled with Magnus Kern either. 'He sounds perfectly horrible. Didn't he want to meet me?'

'Magnus didn't seem all that interested in meeting you. He's going to London soon, and will probably send the carriage for you when the time comes for you to move into his home. When he returns to Fierce Eagles you'll come as a complete surprise to him.'

She felt piqued. 'How rude. It's not that far to come and meet me, surely.'

138

He moved her to arm's length, took a spotless handkerchief from his pocket and gently dabbed her tears, his eyes blue and guileless. His eyes met hers. 'There.'

She was aware of him in a way she'd never been before, and it made her feel nervous. He smiled, rose to his feet and held out his hand. Hers was warm inside it. 'Come on, let's get back in time for tea.'

And he kept her hand in his all the way home.

'Are you sure you didn't drop any hints about John's will?' Ignatious said on the way home.

'Perfectly sure.'

'I'm glad you told her about John passing on though, it's over and done with now, and it will make it easier for Mrs Lawrence. She was quite upset.'

'I think I might pay court to her when all is settled.'

'Who, Mrs Lawrence?'

It was unusual for his father to make a joke and Gerald grinned. 'If I was a bit older, then I'd certainly consider giving her gentleman friend a run for his money. But it's Sarette, of course. She'll have a good dowry and I like her. She's a spirited little creature.'

'Magnus might challenge the will and win, you know. Nobody would think any of the worse of him for it. After all, the girl is no relation. It would only take the right lawyer to tie her up in knots and ruin her reputation, and the right magistrate would soon give him the nod.'

'Magnus is not that mercenary, father. He

won't challenge, I'll stake my life on it.'

'What makes you so sure?'

'I don't know if you noticed, and I don't know if it occurred to Magnus at the time, but I think not. John Kern has set a real test of his honesty. John has placed Sarette's legacy in his hands, as well as her welfare. Magnus doesn't need to challenge the will and he's accountable to nobody but himself. He could quite easily rob her blind, but that would encroach on his own sense of self-worth and the honesty he prides himself for. I think his self-discipline is stronger than his avarice. None but you and I would be any the wiser if he spent her legacy. Certainly not Sarette. And we wouldn't say a word.'

His father laughed. 'You're right. Then it will be interesting to watch developments and see if blood will out. But there's something you might not have thought of. I wouldn't put it past Magnus to do things the easy way, and marry the girl himself. He will have her under his roof.'

Gerald's frown was followed by a grin. 'That will make the courting of her into a real contest. You do know that he's got the idea in his head that Sarette is a child, don't you?'

'I noticed you didn't put him straight.'

'Neither did you.'

Ignatious cackled with laughter. 'Far be it for me to spoil your little game. Just be careful she doesn't catch you at it, Gerald.'

Mrs Lawrence's household was a sombre one that evening. It had begun to rain, a light but per-sistent drizzle that soaked through everything.

140

Mr Taggard kept them company, and the conversation was desultory.

As soon as it was polite Sarette excused herself and went up to her room, her heart weighed down with sorrow. Changing into her nightdress she sat by the window and watched the droplets chase each other down the glass. Along the seafront the street lamps came on and gave out a misty light.

Picking up the photograph of herself with John Kern she whispered, 'I'll never forget you, Mr John.' She took his watch out from the bottom of her trunk and ran her fingertip over his name, then wound it up and held it to her ear. It began to tick strongly. She placed it under her pillow when she went to bed, imagining that it was the heart of her pirate rogue beating. *Tick ... tick ... tick...*

Her mouth twitched into a smile when it chimed and she remembered him taking the timepiece from the pocket of his waistcoat and putting it to his ear, before smiling at her and saying, 'All's right with our world, Sarry girl.'

But it wasn't their world any more, it was hers. John Kern had moved on and left her behind, and she'd have to live in it without him. Gerald had been right. It was time she grew up.

She opened her eyes when Mrs Lawrence came in.

'Are you all right, Sarette.'

'Yes, thank you, Mrs Lawrence. I was thinking about John Kern.'

'Yes ... I imagined you were. It's all right to feel sad, you know. John didn't deserve to die like that.'

'I think he'd have preferred it, rather than being ill and in pain, and lingering on. The more I think of it the more I think he lied about his health. He made all these arrangements for me because he was ill, and he gave me all his treasured possessions to hand over to his nephew when the time came. They are in that big trunk.'

'Ah ... I'd wondered why you hadn't opened it. There's something I'd like to tell you, Sarette. Mr Taggard has proposed marriage to me.'

'That's wonderful.'

'You think so?'

'He's a kind gentleman, who seems to hold you in great esteem. And you get on well together.'

'So you think I should accept?'

Sarette nodded. 'You sound unsure. Do you love another then?'

Iris Lawrence smiled. 'I thought I did, but memories play tricks and sometimes you hanker after someone you can never have. We can't measure one man or his passion against another's. It wouldn't be fair to either of them. And we shouldn't allow happiness to pass us by when it's sincerely offered. Thank you, dear, I'll take your advice and accept.' She kissed her gently on the forehead. 'Goodnight.'

Iris Lawrence had just reached the door when Sarette said, 'The man you loved and hankered after ... it was John Kern, wasn't it?'

'Yes, he and my father did business together. I spurned him for another and from that learned an unhappy truth. John had never loved me. The

142

marriage would have been one of convenience.'

'Did you love your husband, Mrs Lawrence?'

A fleeting smile touched her face and she said simply, 'In my way. He was the sweetest, most gentle man I've ever known. It's to my ever-lasting sorrow that I never bore him a child.' She nodded and closed the door behind her.

Nine

When the carriage turned through the gates at Fierce Eagles Sarry stuck her head out of the window and gazed up the long curving drive to where the warm facade of the house could just be glimpsed between the trees.

She ducked back in, her carefully arranged hairstyle blown into shreds, and said to the maid who'd been sent for her, 'It's exactly as Mr John said it would be at this time of year. Look at all the leaves flying from the trees. It's so pretty. I didn't believe him when he said the leaves changed to all these colours in autumn ... not until I saw them for myself.'

'I don't know what the master will say when he comes home from London and claps his eyes on you,' her companion said, and she cackled with laughter. 'I reckon he'll get a big surprise.'

Sarette grinned at the woman. 'Have you worked for the Kern family very long?'

'I've worked at Fierce Eagles since I was

fourteen, when I started work as a housemaid for the late master and his missus. Then she upped and died, and not long after, Miss Margaret followed her. Right cut up, the master was ... right cut up. We thought he'd never recover from the loss. Then the present master came from London and stayed.'

'Mr Magnus Kern?'

'Aye. Mr Magnus we used to call him when he was younger, and when the old master was alive. He came down from London where he was trained as a barrister, and he opened an office in Dorchester. He helped his uncle to recover from his loss, right enough. He were a good companion to him and made him laugh. Mr Magnus loved his uncle like a father, since John Kern raised him after his own father died. Then one day, the master upped and offed. I'm going away to look for adventure while I still can, sez he. All that way ... fancy.'

Yes, fancy, Sarette thought, for that decision had led John Kern to her, and if it hadn't she'd now be dead, or worse. She must make the most of what his generous heart had provided for her. 'What's Mr Magnus Kern like?'

'He has a quiet way with him, just like his uncle had, and is a fair and honest man. But he's not so easy to deal with as his uncle was. He likes this house to be run well, and can't abide lateness. Sometimes he's stern, and he expects his orders to be carried out to the letter. But he gives praise where praise is due.' She shook her head, said doubtfully, 'I don't know what he'll say when he comes back from London and sees you, that I don't.'

'You've already said that once, Verna. Why should he say anything, when he's expecting me? After all, he sent the carriage.'

'He wasn't exactly expecting *you*, miss. He was expecting someone ... well, *different*.'

'Different?'

'A bit younger, like.'

'I'm not exactly old,' Sarette said in exasperation. 'When is Mr Kern expected home.'

'He didn't say, Miss. He might stay in London until after Christmas. Then again, he might come whistling through the front door tomorrow.'

The carriage drew to a halt and a man came out of the house, opened the door and let down the step. He looked past her into the carriage. 'Where's the girl, Verna?'

'There ain't no girl, Mr Branston. Nor was there any nursemaid. The agency said she got herself another position in London with a titled gentleman, and had left on the morning train.'

The man's glance wandered back to her. 'Then who—?'

'This is Miss Maitland. Miss, this is Branston, the butler.'

'Miss Maitland?' Branston exchanged a glance with Verna and said, 'Verna, perhaps you'd show the young lady to her rooms, while Robert and I bring her luggage up.'

'You want me to—'

'Mr Kern gave specific orders and he'll expect them to be carried out to the letter.'

Sarette followed Verna up three flights of

stairs, then turned left along a narrow corridor and took another left turn through a door. She found herself in a large airy room with windows that looked out over the copse. There was a fire burning in the fireplace. The wallpaper was pink and cream stripes, and sprinkled with nursery rhyme scenes.

There was a small bed with a lace cover. Sarette glanced doubtfully at it.

Verna suggested, 'You can sleep in the nursemaid's room if you'd rather.'

The nursemaid's room was stark in comparison, with an iron bedstead, a chest with drawers in, and a shelf. The window was set up high, so she couldn't see out, and was more like a skylight.

'I'd rather not sleep here at all.' Sarette turned and went back to the nursery. Her glance absorbed the cradle with a rag doll in it, a box of animal figures and a doll's house. Books were stacked neatly on a table. The place looked newly furnished and decorated, as though Magnus Kern had been expecting...? She chuckled. 'Mr Kern thought I was a child, didn't he?'

'Aye, he did. She'll be about four, he told us, which is why Robert and I were so surprised when we saw you.' She threw open a cupboard, which was filled with neatly folded children's clothing. 'See.'

'What made him think I was four years old?'

Verna avoided her eyes. 'I can't really say, Miss.'

Sarette, who'd gained considerably in confidence in the year she'd spent with Mrs Lawrence, coaxed her with a smile. 'I'm quite sure you're clever enough to take a good guess, Verna.'

Verna lowered her voice. 'Well, as long as you don't tell Mr Kern I said so ... it was like this, we've been discussing it in the kitchen. What with Mr Grimble telling the master you looked a bit like Miss Margaret, we all thought ... because Mr John Kern had been gone a long time that ... he ... Mr Magnus Kern, that is, thought that perhaps you were *related* to Mr John in some way.'

Which was a rather long-winded way to get the point across. 'Do you mean Magnus Kern thought I was a daughter Mr John fathered on a woman he'd met since he left here? Surely not.'

Verna looked mortified when Sarette began to laugh. 'If you don't mind me saying Miss ... the master won't like it, you being grown-up and all. He won't like it at all, especially since the young Mr Grimble led him to believe that...'

'Gerald Grimble told him I was four?'

'Well, not exactly. I happened to be just outside the study door polishing the hall table, and I couldn't help but overhear the conversation. Mr Gerald Grimble didn't say how old you were, and neither did his father.'

The butler came in hanging on to the largest of the trunks, with Robert on the other end. They grunted as they lowered it to the ground.

Sarette eyed it. 'I'm sorry. It will have to be moved again, Mr Branston, since we shall have to find another room for me. I'm much to old to sleep in a nursery.'

'But the master said he couldn't be bothered

147

with having a girl running underfoot, and you could live up here out of his way.'

'He wouldn't have put me here had he known my advanced age. Please be good enough to find me a room, or must I find my own?'

The servants gazed at each other in dismay, then the butler said rather stiffly to Verna, 'What about Miss Margaret's room. That's ready for occupancy, and it has an adjoining bathroom.'

Verna gave him a doubtful look. 'But the master said—'

With every word Sarette disliked Magnus Kern just a little bit more. 'Miss Margaret's room will do. Mr John told me all about her, and I feel that I know her. As for your master, I'll explain matters to him, so you needn't fear reprimand.'

'But all Miss Margaret's things are in there. It's just how Mr John Kern ordered it to be left. He said it was to be kept clean and dusted, as if she was still alive, and nobody was to use it.'

Sarette knew how much Mr John had loved his daughter and she didn't want to violate his wishes. 'Then I won't disturb it. Somewhere else?'

Verna had a mulish look on her face now. 'I'm the upstairs maid, so it's not my job to allocate rooms, it's the housekeeper's. Mrs Young is away visiting her sick mother for a week so you'll have to wait until she comes back. Could be she'll stay, what with her being old and getting her legacy, and all. Then I'll be in charge of household matters, and will be able to give you another room.'

Sarette was not going to be told what to do by one of the servants, and she needed to get the upper hand right now. Crisply, she said, 'It won't be practical for me to wait until you are promoted to housekeeper, or until Mrs Young returns. I'll find a room for myself. Branston, Robert. Bring the trunk, please.'

She headed out of the door at a fast clip, with Verna scrambling after her. Going down to the floor below she threw open a door on the sea side of the house. It was a nice room, with a view that went down the hill to the cove, exactly as Mr John had described. 'This is a perfectly good room. Does anyone sleep here?'

'No, Miss. It's the best guest room.'

'And I'm a guest, which you might kindly wish to remember from now on, so I'll use this room. Fetch the bed sheets and a duster, I'll do for myself. You can light a fire – and no arguing,' she told Verna when the woman opened her mouth.

'I don't know what the master will say,' Verna wailed.

'Of course you don't. Neither do I. We'll find out when he returns home. He can't be that much of an ogre, and if he is I'll make sure that no blame falls on you. For goodness' sake, stop making such a fuss and get on with it.'

'Yes, Miss.' With clear directions, and relieved of all responsibility for her actions, Verna's smile returned and she went off at a trot to do Sarette's bidding.

Later that afternoon, Sarette unearthed her journal and wrote in it:

149

September 1898. I have arrived at Fierce Eagles, Mr John. The house is beautiful, and everything you said about it is true. I don't know how you could bear to leave it, even though I understand why you did.

I have yet to meet your nephew, Mr Magnus Kern. He is in London I'm given to understand. I cannot say I'm looking forward to the meeting with any great pleasure. This will make you smile. I understand that he thinks that I'm a child. Thus he has furnished the nursery. He had also hired me a governess, but luckily she took another position that was offered to her.

To learn that you were dead came as a very great shock. Sometimes I cannot believe it, and wish you were here to guide me. I miss you so much and hope you discovered that God did exist, and you are now in the company of those you loved most.

Mr John, I want you to know that I feel as though I have come home at last, because everything you were is all around me.

She gazed at his travel-scarred trunk.

I am still guarding your travelling trunk, like a mangy dog with a bone. I will place it safely into the hands of your beloved nephew when he returns, as I promised. Goodbye, my dearest friend. Wherever I go in life, you will always be a smile inside my heart.

Sarette blotted the ink, closed the book, kissed it, then placed it in her trunk with the others. Tomorrow, she intended to start a new journal in the book of her life.

The next morning Sarette was served breakfast at ten in the dining room by the parlour maid. There was a huge table glowing from frequent rubs of polish. It had several chairs around it. She was seated at one end, wishing she had someone to talk to.

The dresser was covered in dish warmers with silver covers.

She imagined Magnus Kern sitting at the other end, darkly glowering at her as she ate her eggs and bacon, and crisp slices of toast. She poked her tongue out at him.

Branston gently coughed and held out a silver salver with an envelope on it.

'For me?' she said in astonishment, her face turning pink.

There was an embossed card inside. Gerald had scribbled on the back. 'I hope you'll do me the honour of allowing me to escort you to the Legal Association Christmas Ball.'

'Is there an answer, Miss?'

'You'd better give the messenger some breakfast and ask him to wait. This ball is only a few weeks away.'

'You can answer me personally if you like?' Gerald said, smiling at her from the doorway. 'The Grimble men intend to dance you off your feet if you'll come.'

A smile sped across her face. 'Gerald, you're

an answer to my prayer for company. Of course I'll come. What are you doing here so early?'

'I'm off to Dorchester on business, and thought I'd drop in on the way past to see if you'd settled in. The invitation provided me with an excuse.'

The parlour maid began to set another place while Gerald helped himself to a plate of food. He gazed about him, saying casually, 'Magnus not home from London yet, then?'

'No.'

'Good, then I won't need to ask his permission.' He smiled at her when he said, 'So ... you're living in this house and you haven't met the master yet.'

'I only arrived here myself, yesterday.'

'You look quite at home.'

'I feel at home. It's such a beautiful, welcoming house.' She grinned at him, and made sure the parlour maid was out of earshot. 'Magnus thought I was a child and decorated the nursery. He intended to confine me there, so I wouldn't get under his feet and annoy him.'

He gazed at her, wide-eyed, his fork held up in the air and dangling a sliver of bacon. 'Good Lord. Whatever gave him that idea?'

She gave a peal of laughter and wagged a finger at him. 'How do you make your eyes look so innocent, Gerald? I'm sure you already know what, or who, gave him that idea.'

Popping the bacon in his mouth Gerald chewed thoughtfully on it, then swallowed. 'You know, Sarette, my love, I'd like to be present when Magnus sets eyes on you.'

'Perhaps you will be, but the servants don't

know when he'll return. It might be tomorrow, or after Christmas. They say he never telephones to tell them.'

'Typical of Magnus.'

'I don't care if he never comes home.'

'Ah, my dear, if only Magnus could be dismissed that easily.'

They chatted about this and that while they ate, then Gerald patted his stomach and rose to his feet. 'Thank you for your hospitality, but I must be off now. No doubt my sister Olivia will be pleased to offer you the use of her guest room and the services of her maid. You really should get a maid of your own, since Magnus leads quite a social life. He likes the theatre, and is invited out everywhere. When word gets round about you, then you'll be included.'

It sounded as though life was going to be interesting, and she marvelled that it was only a week or so ago that she'd found it exciting to go for a walk along the Weymouth seafront.

'The day after the ball I'll take you to the Winter Gardens to listen to the orchestra, and there's an operatic play on at the Theatre Royal called *The Pirates of Penzance*. But perhaps you've seen it.'

Her eyes began to shine. 'I've never been to see an operatic play. Yes, I'd love to, and to stay with your sister. Thank you so much, Gerald.'

'Right, well I'll arrange that with Olivia. What are you going to do today?'

'First I'm going to explore the grounds and the cove. Then I might familiarize myself with the house. Though I might leave that till tomorrow.

Thank you for calling in, Gerald. It was nice to see you again.'

'Be careful. The path to the cove has loose scree underfoot in places.'

'Thank you for warning me.'

After Gerald had gone Sarette flew upstairs, pulled her gowns out of the boxes and heaped them higgledy-piggledy up on the bed. She had several gowns of different colours and styles for different functions, all very frilly and bright.

'One can never have enough,' she said, mimicking Iris Lawrence, then her heart fell. She'd told Verna she could do for herself, but she didn't know how to look after such delicate fabrics.

She sought advice from the butler. 'Is there anyone in the household who is able to double as a maid when I need one, Mr Branston?'

'There's Ada Price. She used to work for a dressmaker, and is clever with her hands. Mostly, she works in the laundry, but she helps everyone when she's needed. I'll ask her, Miss.'

Ada was thin, with dark hair and a pursed mouth. Her slim fingers were dextrous. Soon, Sarette's tumbled clothing was hanging in neat rows, protected by a dust sheet. 'I'll press them and do any repairs they need before lunch, Miss. With Mr Kern away, there's not much else to do anyway. Though he has his own man.'

'Thank you, Ada. Can you fashion hair?'

Ada indicated that she be seated, and picked up the brush. Her hands were firm as she drew the bristles through her hair, and soon Sarette had an elegant bun at the back of her head, at

154

just the right height to perch the back of her hat on.

'Thank you. Would you mind working for me while I'm here, if Mr Kern doesn't mind?'

Ada smiled. 'Yes, I'd like to ... thank you, Miss.'

So now she had a maid. Sarette left Ada in charge of unpacking her things, instructing her not to touch Mr John's trunk. Donning a blue velvet coat that matched her hat, she went out into the bright autumn to get some fresh air.

Life was very pleasant in England, she mused. The autumn was many shades of gold and the air was filled with drifting leaves. But she could feel a nip of cold in the air, and knew it wouldn't be long until winter arrived. The last one had come as a shock to her. This year she'd be more prepared, with some woollen shawls to wear about the house, and a warm cape for outside.

As the leaves crunched underfoot she thought of her parents, of all their hopes for a better life for her, and their dreams now lying in the dust of the goldfields with them. She felt sad that they weren't enjoying life with her, too.

With that came the thought of Flynn Collins, who had robbed a dead man of all he'd left behind.

Fiercely, she said, 'If I ever set eyes on your thieving hide again, Flynn Collins, I'll tell Gerald Grimble or Mr Kern what you did, and you'll go to prison.'

On a steamship in London, a watchkeeper turned his back to the gangplank, cupped his hands against the wind coming off the water, and put a light to a pipe cradled in his hands. Sucking in a lungful of smoke he released it slowly in a blue aromatic cloud, and gave a satisfied sigh.

Behind him, a man slipped down the gang-plank and was swallowed by a milling group of some half-a-dozen brawny dock workers who were lifting provisions from a cart on to their shoulders and carrying the goods on board.

The man with the pipe picked up his tally sheet and ticked off a basket of potatoes. 'All right, get on with it lads, we haven't got all night.' The Irish in his voice was pronounced as he shouted to the men on the shore. 'Hey you ... Paddy. What's in the sack?' He moved closer to read the label and the lumper slipped some money into his hand.

'Flour, what does it look like?' the lumper said, 'And it's heavy, so get out of my fecking way.'

Ten minutes later the lumper joined the man, who'd slipped ashore and concealed himself behind a crate. 'Flynn Collins, is it?'

'It is, but I signed on under the name of Jack Maitland.'

'Just as well. The authorities are keeping a look out for you.'

'I can't go back to Ireland, either. The polis there know what I look like, too. I thought I was going to America.'

'You will eventually. But there's work to be done for the cause right here in London.'

Flynn whined, 'I have a brother there ... he can get me a job.'

156

'That might be so, but freedom comes at a cost, *Jack Maitland*. You owe us for the journey, and that debt must be paid off first. America will have to wait, and so will you.' He spat on the ground. 'A good old Irish name, you chose, to be sure.'

'It's the best I could come up with at short notice. At least I have the papers to go with it.'

Flynn gave a bit of a laugh. 'A fine upstanding man was Jack. A snake put paid to him.'

'Did the man have any family who could identify you?'

There was a moment of hesitation, then Flynn said, 'He had a daughter, but she was a skinny scrap of a thing. The brat is probably in an orphanage by now, or starved to death ... just like the British starved the Irish. Didn't my own grandparents and my mammy get turned out of their home to starve on the streets when I was just a baby? I swore to avenge them.'

'One small girl starving to death in Australia doesn't do much to avenge something that happened over forty years ago, now does it? Talk is cheap, and it's dangerous, so keep your fecking trap shut and do as you're told. You'll prove you have some worth to us in time. If not...' He shrugged.

Fear stabbed at Flynn's guts. 'If not?'

The man gazed at him, and a smile thinned his lips to reveal a row of ratty, pointed teeth. There was no laughter in his eyes. 'We have a long reach, so let's hope you never find out,' he said. 'Follow me now, but not too close. I don't like anyone breathing down my neck, especially a man who shot another man in the back.'

'He'd threatened me.'

'The way I heard it, he was unarmed and near death from an illness.'

'Then I did the man a favour. One less Englishman on earth is better for Ireland.'

'The hell you did, Collins. The man you killed was John Kern, a magistrate from Dorset. He had friends in high places. There's a wanted notice of you in every polis station from here to Ireland.'

'Nobody will recognize me without my whiskers.'

'I've also heard that his nephew, Magnus Kern, has placed an unofficial price on your head of five hundred pounds. A man could do a lot with that kind of money.'

Flynn shrugged and fingered the knife up his sleeve as he said softly, 'Thinking of claiming it then, are you?'

'It crossed my mind. Cowardly scum like you are more trouble than they're worth. You're not fighting for the Irish cause, but as soon as you're in trouble you come running with your tail between your legs, and expect someone to risk their life to rescue you. If it was up to me they would have dropped you overboard.'

'I joined the cause years ago, and would give my life for Ireland,' Flynn lied, his hackles rising.

'Aye ... and you might be given the chance before too long.'

But not voluntarily, Flynn thought. The anarchists were dangerous, they trusted nobody, and would sacrifice him to save their own necks. He'd either be recognized and shot by the polis, or they'd kill him when he was no longer useful, or he crossed them. Long reach be damned. He wasn't going to give them the chance of seeing his face.

They were in a shadowy part of the dock. In fact, his guide kept to the shadows like a sewer rat, and they were heading towards Covent Garden. Be fecked if he was going to trust his life to this lot. As for the cause – he couldn't give a fiddler's fart about it.

A thin fog was beginning to diffuse the street lights, and it shrouded the distant buildings.

The man took a sharp left into an alley and began to descend a flight of stairs. Flynn placed the small suitcase he carried next to the wall, then silently picked up speed. Halfway down was a doorway set into a dark porch. Wrapping an arm around the man's neck, he pulled him into the alley, slid the knife between his ribs and whispered, 'Is that cowardly enough for you?'

At the bottom of the steps there was a manhole cover. He took a step back as he withdrew the knife, avoiding the initial gush of blood as the man dropped on to a pile of rotting rubbish. He stooped and went through his victim's pockets. Flynn was rewarded by a couple of pounds and a florin.

'Thanks.' Dragging the body by the feet, he lifted the manhole, lowered the body into the dark hole and let go. There was a meaty thump.

A few minutes later Flynn picked up his suitcase and walked back up the steps. Not long afterwards, he rolled a drunken gentleman coming out of a brothel, not far from Covent Garden. He earned himself a bankroll and a silver watch, but left the man alive. He'd get away with killing a navvy Irishman, but a dead toff would warrant a more thorough investigation.

The opera house was coming alive. Tightly corseted ladies in evening gowns and glistening jewels paraded on the arms of gentlemen in black suits, bow ties and cloaks. Hackney cabs and carriages were lined up, the horses stamping forelegs, whinnying and dropping steaming crap underfoot. There were several flower sellers holding up posies.

He knew the city quite well, he'd spent two years here working for a hire coach company, and was tempted to stay.

'Stay or go?' He had an English cousin working on the quay in Poole, who might take him in. Perhaps he should head for the coast and go to ground? Taking the silver shilling from his pocket he spun it in the air, smiling as it came down heads. As much as he liked London, Flynn didn't really want to put himself in the position of being recognized by lingering here. He would head south. A lawyer who'd risk his reputation and living to put a price on his head, would be dishonest himself. Nobody would expect Flynn to be living in the lion's mouth. With Magnus Kern gone the reward would no longer be available, and the matter of revenge would go to the grave with him. He'd then pick up a berth on a ship from Poole or Bridport, and make his way to America.

'Dorset it is.' Whistling softly, he headed towards the railway station named after Waterloo Bridge, his glance darting furtively from one fogbound shadow to the other as he walked.

He'd find a boarding house and lie low until morning, then take the first train out.

Flynn had been a fugitive who lived on his wits for as long has he could remember. He wasn't about to become a victim.

Ten

Magnus had been invited to Mrs Carradine's house for Christmas dinner. The widow was not wealthy, but had three daughters she was eager to see married off. Their ages ranged from sixteen to twenty-six. All were pleasant creatures with pretty blue eyes, dimples and brown glossy hair. The younger pair resembled dolls as they fluttered their eyelashes at him, giggled behind their hands, and sighed on cue. The elder sister was called Alice. She was quiet and intelligent, and resigned to spinsterhood.

They were nice girls. Magnus liked Alice a lot, and had considered her carefully, since as far as he could tell she possessed everything he desired in a woman. But there was no spark between them, and he couldn't see himself married to Alice. In fact, he still couldn't see himself married to anyone.

He had a sudden urge to be at Fierce Eagles for Christmas, and he still hadn't cleared his business up with Isabelle yet. She'd been absent when he'd called in on her just before he was about to depart for London.

'The mistress had gone to Italy a few days ago, and that's all I'm at liberty to say,' the maid had told him with a smirk. He'd been annoyed that Isabelle had gone off without a word, but had come to the conclusion that she'd sensed that all was over between them. It was not as though he'd met anyone to replace her, but he hadn't been to see her for several weeks, and she was no fool. Magnus liked his life to be tidy and without loose ends – a fault he'd long recognized in himself.

He wrote to Mrs Carradine, thanking her for her hospitality and expressing his regret at not being able to be there to celebrate Christmas with them. He offered family commitments as an excuse and invited them to Fierce Eagles for New Year festivities, if they happened to be in the district. The next morning his valet had his bags packed and he checked out of his club.

It was mid-afternoon before the train reached Dorchester. The weather had turned and the October sky was filled with churning clouds. The air smelled of rain. He stepped into his office to let his partner know he was back.

Clive Farrington's languid facade hid a brilliant mind. He offered Magnus a smile. 'I thought you'd be staying until after Christmas.'

'So did I, but I got a yearning for home. Has anything happened I should know about?'

'I've been rushed off my feet, so I'm glad you're back. Routine stuff, though. A couple of your pro bono publico clients are in trouble again, and won't have anyone but you represent them – though it would be more to the public good, and purse, if some of them were locked up.'

Magnus laughed. 'You've got to admit that they're not all villains, Clive. For those who are in genuine need we have the victim's fund. It's the women and children who suffer when their men are imprisoned.'

'You should harden your heart.'

'It's hard enough when the occasion warrants.'

'There's a package on your desk, too. It was brought in by someone called Lady Carsurina. She said I was to give it to you as soon as you came home.'

Magnus extracted the note from the package. He could smell Isabelle's perfume. She advised him that she'd married a count, was about to depart for Venice and hoped that the next time they met it would be as friends at some social occasion.

I'm sorry that I was unable to tell you in person, but really, you didn't deserve to be told, Magnus. However, you promised me nothing right from the start. I think I am with child, so there was need for haste.

His heart thumped against his ribs. With child ... whose child?

I've been seeing Georgio for some time on his visits to England. Yes, Magnus, you were right in your suspicions. I had been unfaithful to you often, and on several occasions. The count was a delightful companion. He proposed marriage to me some time ago, and recently it became imperative for me to wed. In case you are wondering, the infant is definitely not yours. You will perhaps recall that you and I have not met in any significant way for some time. He's delighted, since he's nearing fifty-five and has need of an heir. I do hope you'll congratulate us, Magnus, since I've long wished for a legal union with a man who loves me enough to give me the children I so yearned for.

I do feel it is an appropriate time to return your gifts, which have never been worn. Perhaps one day you will meet a woman you can offer them to with sincere love in your heart, rather than as a reward for services rendered. I know you to be an honourable man, and you have always been discreet where I was concerned. I would therefore be most obliged if you would burn this letter.

Until we meet again, affectionately yours, Isabelle.

Magnus smiled. Trust Isabelle to rub it in. He wished her only happiness.

'Good news, Magnus?' Clive said.

'It is.' He knew how damaging the letter could be to Isabelle now. He fed it into the coals glowing in the little black fireplace, watched the paper blacken, then burst into flames. The relief he felt was like a breeze blowing over him, though it wasn't without a modicum of guilt and regret. He'd treated Isabelle badly. But she'd been a married woman when he'd met her, and she'd made herself available. He was a man like any other where love was concerned, led by his balls, but he preferred not to frequent prostitutes for relief. Perhaps he'd never meet a woman he'd wish to share his life and children with.

He slid the package into his coat pocket. He'd keep the jewellery for little Sarette when she grew up. He was pleased she'd been trusted to his safe keeping. She was a gift, and an obligation that would keep him on the straight and narrow. Suddenly he was eager to see the child, and he didn't intend to arrive empty-handed.

Magnus visited the nearest toy shop. In the window was a black horse on wooden rockers. It was a splendid mount for a child, with flaring nostrils, a flowing tail and mane and a red leather saddle and reins. Just the thing, he thought, and went inside. The toy cost him a small fortune.

His valet had hired a cab while he'd been talking to Clive. They found room in it for the horse and set off for Fierce Eagles, the carriage rocking in the wind.

Sarette was in the hallway gazing at the picture of John Kern's wife and child. He'd said she'd reminded him of Margaret, and she gazed at them often trying to see the resemblance. Except for the clear green eyes, she could see none.

'I wish you could speak,' she said, though if they'd both lived John Kern wouldn't have left the memory of them behind, and he wouldn't have gone to the goldfields and found her. Thus, she wouldn't be here now, enjoying this lovely house. He'd probably still be alive, and she'd be dead, which was a frightening thought, so it would be better if she stopped thinking.

She heard a carriage stop outside and went to peer through the glass in the door panel. A man descended and her heart gave such a jolt she thought it might fly through the top of her head. This must be Magnus Kern. He was tall and had his back towards her, but even that was so much like Mr John to look at that she almost took fright. She backed away when he slowly turned to gaze at the door, as if he sensed her there. She had a quick glimpse of a young, grave face devoid of whiskers and topped by unruly dark curls. His eyes shone like black coals. She retreated to the back of the hall, where she tried to make herself invisible in the shadows at the side of the staircase.

The handle turned, then the door was snatched from his hand by the wind and crashed open. He struggled through the opening with a black rocking horse in his arms and set it down on the floor. Behind him came a man with a travelling bag in either hand, who disappeared up the stairway like he knew where he was going.

He closed the door, picked up the rocking horse again and headed towards the stairs. His eyes met hers, moved on then came back. He halted in his stride, stared at her again, then up at the portrait. His eyes came back to her, and this time they impaled her.

'Who the devil are you? Come out of there.'

Magnus Kern was larger than life, and twice as menacing.

Sarette began to tremble as she sidled across the hall to where he stood, drawn there by the invisible thread of his dark, steady gaze.

He wasn't quite as in command as he had first appeared to be, for there was the beginnings of bewilderment in his eyes as he said harshly, 'Are you the governess I hired? I thought you'd be older.'

She sucked in a trembling breath, whispered, 'I think you know that I am not, sir.'

'Then who—'

Sarette managed only a shaky squeak before her voice dried up.

Branston came in. 'Sir, the young lady's name is—'

'Enough, Mr Branston. She can answer for herself. Speak up, girl.'

Sarette's ears began to glow and her hands went to her hips. How dare he speak like this to her? Her annoyance gave her some courage and she found her voice. 'My name is Sarette Maitland. In future I'd be obliged if you didn't try and ... *intimidate* me.' Pushing past him she started up the stairs.

Obviously taken aback, he said, 'Come back down. I haven't dismissed you yet.'

She went back down a few steps, where she was at eye level with him. Her voice was wobbly with nerves when she said, 'But I've dismissed you, Magnus Kern. I know this is your home, but I wasn't given to believe that you would be so ill-mannered towards a guest.'

He put a hand on her wrist when she was about to turn away. 'You're right. Will you accept my apology? For a moment I thought I was confronted by a ghost.'

She shook her head and a tear trickled down her cheeks. 'I'm too upset. Release my wrist, please.'

He dismissed Branston with, 'Go and tell cook I'll be home for dinner,' then he took a handkerchief from his pocket and dried her tears. 'I'm sorry, Sarette ... Miss Maitland. I'd expected ... was led to expect ... Damn Gerald, I'll wring his scrawny neck when I next see him.'

She gave a watery laugh. 'I do hope not, when he's such pleasant company.'

A frown appeared between his eyebrows. 'Gerald Grimble has been keeping you company?'

'He's been a regular visitor with his father to Mrs Lawrence's home, where I've been living over the past year. And he called in for breakfast two weeks ago, as your staff will tell you if you interrogate them.'

'Interrogate them? What the devil do you mean by that?'

'Nothing. You have me rattled.' She tugged at her hand. 'May I go now, please?'

He released her wrist. 'I'm sorry I detained you. We'll talk later when I've thought things through.' This time it was him who walked past her.

'You've left your horse in the hall, Mr Kern,' she reminded him.

He turned, a dark eyebrow raised and a reluctant smile cracking his lips. 'It's your horse. I bought it for you so you'd feel welcome in my home.'

'It's a handsome beast. Your uncle had a horse just like him. His name was Hercules and he had a contrary nature. Sometimes Hercules refused to move until we sang hymns to him.'

Now he looked frankly disbelieving. 'My uncle sang hymns to a horse called Hercules?'

'He had a loud, deep voice, too. The horse belonged to a reverend before Mr John bought him, that's why he liked hymns. You resemble him.'

'The horse, the reverend or my uncle?'

So he did have a sense of humour. 'Hercules, except you have two legs and he had four, plus a much longer nose. I expect he could run faster, too.'

'I expect he could.'

The brief smile that lit his face settled back into his grave expression and her nerves fluttered, so she knew she'd have to control them, otherwise she'd prattle. Mrs Lawrence had told her that men didn't like women who prattled. 'Even though Mr John told me to expect you to look like him, you gave me quite a shock when you got out of the carriage. Close up you are not so similar.'

'So it was you looking through the door at me. I imagine you gave me a bigger shock. I thought you'd stepped out of the portrait of my cousin,

Margaret Kern.'

'I don't see any strong similarity. Do you mind that I'm not a child? Gerald told me to grow up because I objected when he—' She bit down on her tongue, but too late.

'When he what?'

Colour rose in her cheeks and she pressed her lips together for a moment before saying vaguely, 'Oh, nothing really ... I expect I was being facetious, I quite often am.' She felt quite desperate under his scrutiny. 'Mrs Lawrence told me not to prattle. Am I prattling? You have that effect on me. You must tell me if I am.'

A nerve at the corner of his mouth twitched. 'I thought you changed the subject quite adroitly, and yes, you are prattling.'

Her face heated even more, but she refused to back away from what seemed to have developed into a battle of wills. 'A gentleman wouldn't have said so, Mr Kern.'

'What sort of rubbish has Iris Lawrence been teaching you? You accuse me of making you prattle, then asked for my opinion and demand an answer. Now you chastise me for providing one. Must I be censured the moment I walk into my own home?'

Her mouth opened, then shut again when he didn't give her time to apologize and stated, 'Let me make one thing clear. I'm the master here, and you are my ward – but only if I choose to take responsibility for you. You must be aware that your position here is tenuous, since it relies entirely on the goodwill I felt towards my uncle. As far as I understand, my uncle took you in, merely on a whim. Whether or not I will honour his request has not yet been determined, and I'll certainly take advice on it before it is. As things stand you can consider yourself my temporary house guest.'

Her heart fell into a chasm. What would she do if he threw her out? 'I'm sorry, Mr Kern.'

'I'd prefer to be called Magnus.' His gazed drifted over her, missing nothing. He sighed. 'Like you said, you're not a child, but I shall have a word with Gerald about his inappropriate behaviour. If I decide you can stay, I imagine I shall have to adjust my way of thinking considerably to cope with a young woman's presence in my home.'

'I'll try and keep out of your way...'

'I'd appreciate it.' Going past her again, he hefted the horse up into his arms. 'Where would you like your horse stabled, Miss Maitland?'

'I'll show you ... *Magnus*.'

Magnus thought, as he followed her bobbing backside up the stairs, that his name had sounded distasteful to her, like slime dripping down a rock.

He'd never had a reaction like this from a young woman before. She was no simpering miss, that was certain, but had tackled him head on. But what was he to do with her? He needed time to think through the problem.

She'd also settled herself into his best guest bedroom. His nose twitched as he inhaled the perfumed feminine smell. It was not cloying like Isabelle's perfume had been, but a lighter, fresh fragrance. Rose water most likely.

He decided he would have his cousin's room refurbished for her to use. It caught the sun all year round. In deference to his uncle Margaret's room had not been touched while he lived, but one couldn't enshrine the dead indefinitely.

Something cream and silky with a delicate lace edging and ribbons was draped over the back of a chair. He had not overlooked the fact that Sarette Maitland was of average height for a woman. Her figure was neatly in proportion and curved in all the right places. And there was a faint chestnut shine to her hair that was altogether pleasing. Clad in that silk undergarment she would be exquisite, like a porcelain figurine. He tore his eyes away from her and grunted, feigning annoyance at being kept waiting.

Hurriedly she looked around for a place to put the horse and said, her voice thick with tears, 'Perhaps the horse should go into the nursery, since you expected to give it to a child. It was a kind gesture.'

Kind, be damned. It had been a means to an end. Still was. Her eyes were teary when she turned to him. Guilt raced through him. Lord, had he been too hard on her? He lowered the horse to the floor. 'We can move that big trunk to the attic if it's been emptied.'

'It's not my trunk, it's Mr John's. See, it has his name on it. He asked me to guard it with my life, and trust it to nobody but you. I have the key in the dresser drawer. The trunk is heavy, and it will require two men to carry it.'

'What's in it?'

'All of Mr John's worldly goods I imagine. His

journals in particular. He wanted them to come home and form part of the Kern history of the house. He said it would give continuity to the family history and his great nieces and nephews would enjoy reading them.'

His uncle had worked it all out, and Magnus suddenly grinned. At least John wouldn't know that his plans had come to nothing.

'All he kept were his guns and a change of clothing,' she said. 'He said he would be here when I arrived.'

When she sniffed he handed her his handkerchief again. 'It's hardly his fault that he couldn't be. Please don't start weeping over my uncle. He wouldn't like it.'

She didn't take his offering, but pulled an embroidered, lace-edged scrap from her sleeve. Her translucent green eyes flicked up to his, stormy with her youthful defiance. Despite her year with Mrs Lawrence learning her airs and graces, it came hard to her. He reminded himself that, underneath, Sarette Maitland was a feral child his uncle had rescued, taught and partly tamed on the goldfields in a distant land. Like a wild pony, she still wanted to run free.

The difference between Sarette Maitland and the Carradine sisters was marked. Good manners had been bred into Alice and her sisters.

'I'll never forget Mr John. He was always so kind to me, and I'll cry over him if I feel like it,' she said.

Of course she would. Her loyalty to the memory of his uncle was all too apparent, and he warmed to her because of it. But John was gone and she hadn't yet learned he was no longer there to protect her, and she had to let him go.

As for exactly how kind his uncle had been to her, the girl was as yet unaware. Magnus thought he might leave her in ignorance of that particular fortune until she was a little older and wiser, and had more sense in her exquisite little head. Gerald had been right ... she did need to grow up.

He wasn't looking for an argument, so he said evenly, 'As you wish, Miss Maitland. I'll see you at dinner, and would be obliged if you'd finished crying by then.' Turning the trunk up on end he tested his strength against it. It was heavy. Too heavy for comfort, but not impossible. He crouched, and, lifting it to his shoulder, straightened up, feeling his thigh muscles tighten to take the strain. He widened his stance for balance and departed.

Magnus was enjoying his small triumph of his physical strength over her caution when she flung her final words after him with a soft, 'Hah! Your uncle could lift it with one hand.'

He didn't believe it for one second, and pretended he didn't hear her final taunt. He carried the trunk along the corridor to where his own room was situated, then was obliged to ask his valet to help him lower it to the floor. 'Have it taken to the library when you've got a minute, and get someone to help you,' he told George, when the man looked askance at it.

The trunk was dirty and scuffed, the brass work dull. It was secured by metal straps. Magnus ran a finger over his uncle's name and said,

'Welcome home, John Kern. Your adventuring days are finally over, but your spirit lives on. I think my adventures are just about to begin. But don't expect me to thank you for this creature you've foisted on me, for I'm set in my ways.'

Sarette Maitland joined him for dinner, demure in a cream, high-collared gown with puffed sleeves. Her bun was made less severe by a cluster of pink silk roses that were entirely youthful. The style revealed her delicate bone structure and exquisite features. She was as pretty as a peach.

She seated herself at the other end of the table, where he'd instructed her place to be set, as far away from himself as possible, for he didn't want to hear her slurp her soup.

When Branston was serving the soup she slipped something into his hand and whispered a few words. She didn't slurp, and the missive was duly delivered to his end of the table when Branston served the main course. Magnus slipped it into his waistcoat pocket. Nothing was going to spoil his enjoyment of his favourite dinner of roast lamb and vegetables. It was followed by a delicious tart containing stewed apples and rhubarb, and floating in a creamy custard.

'Congratulate the cook on the meal please, Branston.'

Branston gazed at the girl, who smiled at him. 'Miss Maitland ordered it, sir. She said it was your favourite meal and should be served as a welcome home.'

He sent her a cool glance. How dare the damned creature attempt to take over his household?

'Will you read your note please, Magnus?' she almost pleaded.

It was a note of apology for her earlier behaviour. She had a good hand. Her sentences were clearly constructed, her letter formation steady and without too much embellishment. He made no comment as he read the prettily worded appeal, then finding nothing to criticize, slipped the missive into his waistcoat pocket.

Her composure slipped a little and her eyes became anxious. 'Do you not wish to comment?'

'I don't really feel the need.'

'Have I apologized for nothing?' she said, her voice wounded.

'Ah ... and I thought it was an apology for your earlier rudeness.'

Colour drained from her face and she whispered, 'It was, and it was one that came sincerely from my heart. But it seems to me as though your heart is made of stone, for your manner is so surly. Excuse me please.' Her chair scraped across the floorboards as she stood, and she turned and walked away.

Magnus sighed. How could he have been so churlish? 'Come back here, Sarette.'

She kept going, her back as stiff as a ramrod. The door closed behind her. Branston clattered the plates on the dresser, and he couldn't keep his disapproval from clouding his voice. 'Do you want coffee, sir?'

'No ... dammit, Branston. Send somebody up to Miss Maitland, tell her to come back down here at once.'

176

'The young lady is upset. I don't think she will appreciate being disturbed.'

He decided to take Branston's advice. He could only add fuel to the flame now. 'It was my fault, wasn't it?'

'Since you ask, yes, sir, it was. Miss Maitland is just a sweet young girl who goes out of her way to try and please people.'

To Magnus she appeared to be a provocative little minx sent here by his uncle to plague him. 'What do you suggest I do to make amends?'

'A small gesture like a posy of flowers would probably please her. She is very appreciative of the nature of her surroundings.'

'I'll personally pick one in the morning and give them to her at breakfast, so stop looking so long-faced at me. I'll have that coffee now, Branston, thank you. Take Miss Maitland's up to her, and don't stay and gossip about what took place here. How the devil did she know what my favourite dinner is?'

'Your uncle told her, I believe.'

His uncle had told her a lot of things ... how close had these two been, that he should leave her such a fortune? It seemed disloyal that he could even think it, but his uncle wouldn't be the first ageing man who'd fallen under the spell of a young girl. Perhaps there would be a clue in his journals as to what had taken place between John and the girl. He would open the trunk tomorrow and see if he could make sense of it.

Flynn Collins had secured employment in a coal yard in Poole, courtesy of his cousin, who'd preferred to deny any connection between them in public. That bastard didn't want to know him, but all the same, he'd promised to help him get away when the time came.

The job consisted of shovelling coal into sacks, then weighing them and sewing up the tops. He'd also found accommodation, a back room in a mean house in Smuggler's Lane. His landlady wasn't too fussy, but she wasn't a bad cook and she didn't ask questions.

The job was worse than working down a mine, what with the dust, and all, and he'd done some of that in his time. But it meant that for most of the day his face would be black with coal dust, so if by chance someone looked for him here, the chance of him being recognized had lessened.

He could do nothing about his Irish accent, but it was common. He frequented the bars at night, keeping his ears open and his trap shut. He'd befriended an Irish engineer off a cargo carrier who sailed on the American route.

'Jack Maitland?' he said when Flynn offered his assumed name. 'It doesn't sound like an Irish name to me.'

'It's my mammy who was Irish, God bless her. Ireland is where I was born and raised. America is where I'll end up when I can get signed on. I have a brother there, and my mammy has gone to live with him.'

The engineer downed his pot of ale. 'I might have a job as a stoker opening up. You'd have to be signed on as crew, but I'd need surety money. Half up front and the rest when we're under way.' While Flynn fumbled in his pocket, he said, 'You have legitimate papers?'

'Aye, I have. Got to get some money first, though. My father used to work for someone called John Kern. He died in my father's arms in foreign parts. My old man followed after him still being owed his wage, and my mammy asked me to collect it from the heir before I join them. But I've lost the letter and I don't know where the Kerns live.'

A sceptical expression came into the engineer's eyes. 'What's this man called?'

'Magnus Kern.'

'Odd sort of name. He shouldn't be too hard to find. Can't say I've heard of him m'self, but then, we're only here for a few days' turnaround to unload cargo and load coal.'

He downed his ale, wiped his mouth on his sleeve and stood, holding out his hand. 'I hope you'll be able to finish your business with this Kern fellow as soon as possible. I'll be back now and again, and no questions asked. I'll keep our mutual acquaintance informed.'

Flynn palmed some money into the engineer's hand. His bankroll was being reduced rapidly. He'd have to find another randy toff to roll before he left.

An old man sitting at a beer-stained table said, as he was about to leave, 'The Kern family made their wealth from smuggling hereabouts. Magnus is the last of the Kerns. Nothing dishonest about him though. If the family owes you money, he'll pay up.'

Flynn nodded. You bet he will, he thought,

179

then said out loud, 'You know where he lives, then?'

'I might do. It will cost you a pint of ale though.'

Flynn nodded to the barman.

Eleven

Magnus woke at dawn, dressed and went out into the garden to look for wild flowers. The mist drifted across like curtains of drizzle and soon his hair and coat were damp. There weren't many wildflowers left. She might have to wait until spring for an apology from him, he thought grumpily.

He found some blue speedwell, mayweed and campion, and going back through the orchard, a leafy bough hung with crab apples. Then there was a branch covered in hazelnuts, and some small feathery branches of the yew tree with sticky red berries. His glance was drawn to a splash of scarlet in the hedge where the berries of the black bryony shone, jewel bright. And the bramble leaves, red like wine. He reached out to snap the bract off, and sucked in a swift breath when a thorn ripped through his skin.

'No perhaps not,' he said, sucking the blood from his finger. He didn't want the girl to accuse him of plotting her downfall.

It had been a long time since he'd taken time

to observe his surroundings, and he was reluctant to go inside. But it looked like it might rain, and he'd promised himself that he'd go through his uncle's belongings.

His arms full of late autumn glory, Magnus carried his booty through to the kitchen, and ignoring the knowing looks and grins his staff exchanged, asked for a pewter jug. He shoved the branches into it and went upstairs to bang at Sarette's door.

Nobody answered. He opened the door and gazed inside. The room was empty. 'Where the devil is she?' he said.

Behind him, a woman gently coughed, and he spun round, encountering one of the maids, who had a gown over her arm.

'Miss Maitland is at breakfast, sir.'

He recalled that her name was Ada, and gazed at the gown in her arms. 'Are you acting as maid to Miss Maitland?'

'Yes, sir, but only when she needs me to fashion her hair or tighten her ... well, never mind. She does for herself mostly.'

'Miss Maitland is my guest, and shouldn't need to fend for herself. Ask Mrs Young to see me after breakfast.'

'Mrs Young went to see her mother and she never came back. We reckon she's not going to now she's got that legacy. She sent a letter to you but you haven't had time to go through your letters yet. Branston has put Verna in charge of the housekeeping, pending your permission. Would you like me to take those ... branches?'

'No. They're for Miss Maitland.'

'Well, you'll find her in the dining room, sir. Though she said she was going for a long walk after breakfast.'

He found Sarette there. Her face took on a wary look when she set eyes on him and she whispered, 'Good morning.'

'Good morning.' He plonked his offering in front of her. 'They're for you.'

He blinked when a wide smile sped across her face. 'The colours are lovely, and you've arranged them so beautifully. Thank you so much. What are these sticky berries? Can I eat them?'

He wondered if she was teasing him, then realized she wasn't. 'They're from the yew tree. The only fruits safe to eat, apart from the crab apples which will pucker your mouth up and are too sour to enjoy anyway, are those round hazelnuts.' Plucking a couple from the branch he cracked them together in his palm, shucked the shell from them and offered her the nuts.

She ate them both, said, 'They're delicious.'

'Yes, they are ... I believe you intend to take a walk after breakfast.'

'The countryside is so pretty.'

'I think it will rain before too long, so take an umbrella from the big vase in the hall. Can you ride?'

'I used to ride Hercules, but I had to sit behind your uncle and hang on to him, so I could never see where we were going to or coming from. I could drive my father's horse and cart, but the horse was a plodder.'

Magnus helped himself to some breakfast. 'Tell me about your father.'

Her smile faded. 'He was a nice man with a big laugh. I loved him, and he died after a snake bit him. It was only a scratch, and he laughed, and then ... it was a cruel, relentless death that robbed him of strength and the will to resist it. I'd never seen fear in his eyes before that day. Three hours later he was dead.'

'I'm sorry, that must have been hard for you to bear. And your mother?'

'Typhoid, I believe. She was expecting a child. I can't really remember her, but I have a brooch with her picture painted on it.'

'Do you have any living relatives?'

'None that I know of. My father was a clerk and my mother a governess.'

'Where were they employed?'

'I don't know.' Her face began to close up, obviously her memories were painful. 'Is there anything else you want to know, Magnus?'

'My uncle—'

'Was the kindest man I've ever met, even though he was tough. I adored him, and can put no measure on that. I'm sorry you are put to such trouble on my behalf. It was wrong of Mr John to take advantage of your kind nature by imposing my presence upon you.'

He felt all types of a rogue and squirmed on a self-created, but imaginary, devil's roasting fork as he stumbled over the words... 'My kind nature?'

'I've been thinking of my position here. No wonder you were angry with me. I'll move as soon as I can make plans. Perhaps Mrs Lawrence will take me as a paying guest, or perhaps

183

Mr Ignatious Grimble will help me find employment where I can live on the premises. I would very much like to look after children. I thought I might be a governess, but Mr John advised against it. He said they're dried-up old spinsters.'

She should marry and have children of her own, which, after all, was what his uncle had planned for her, Magnus thought.

She rose, and her smile wasn't quite so spontaneous now. 'I will take these upstairs to my room, and will try and stay out of your way when I return. I promise.'

'Sarette,' he said when she reached the door, and she stopped her flight, but she didn't turn. 'My offering is by way of apology for the way I treated you yesterday. I should have accepted your note. As for staying out of my way, my home is yours and you may use it as you will while you're here. Also, I don't want you to leave. I'm used to solitude here, so your presence will be good for me. Perhaps you'll make me more human.'

'It takes a brave man to bury his pride and admit he's wrong. I shouldn't have expected you to measure up to your uncle. Thank you, Magnus.' She departed, her nose buried in the fruity bouquet. His smile fled when he suddenly thought: What was it she'd said? She shouldn't have expected him to measure up to his uncle? What the devil was that supposed to mean?

The downpour sent a satisfying rattle of rain down on Sarette's black umbrella. She loved the rain after living in a place where it was a rarity, loved the way it turned the soil to mud beneath her feet and the way the raindrops raced each other down the window pane. When it was heavy it made the boughs downcast, dripped off everything, then turned into glittering icicles when the wind was at its coldest.

Happiness was bursting from her like flowers opening to spring sunshine. The only reason she could think of for this feeling was that the argument with Magnus Kern had been resolved, and they had reached a point from which they could progress. It had taken a considerable sacrifice on her part.

She heard the yelp of a dog, and stopped. Along one side of the path a small brook headed towards the sea. With the rain, the water in the brook had become a rush. In the middle of it was the limb of a tree, and hanging from a woody twig, a sack, partly submerged, as if it had been washed there by the force of the water. The sack moved and a desperate yelping came from its innards.

Folding the umbrella, she laid it on the ground and attempted to crawl along the tree limb. She was hampered by her skirt and she squealed as the limb tipped sideways, sending her tumbling into the water. She managed to grab the sack as she went down, but the tree snagged her skirt and pulled her under with it. Holding the heavy sack above her head she fought to hold her breath and tried to pull her skirt free with the other hand.

It had just occurred to her that she might be

about to drown when the sack was taken from her hand. Someone entered the water beside her and her skirt was ripped apart. Borne to the bank she was flopped on her face in the mud, where she coughed the water from her mouth and swooped in a few gasping breaths.

She sat up and found herself gazing at Gerald, who was covered in mud, along with other debris. He still wore his hat, which had gone out of shape, had a leafy twig on top and resembled a soggy Christmas pudding. She giggled, more from nerves than anything, said, 'Sorry,' then giggled again.

'Hang on till we get you home. I don't want a hysterical woman on my hands,' he said. 'What the hell were you doing in the creek, panning for gold?'

The cold had seeped into her bones and she'd begun to shiver. 'There was a bag on the log and I could hear a dog yapping. I tried to rescue it and the branch moved and I slipped.'

The yelp came again. Reaching for the sack Gerald opened it and pulled out a shivering brown puppy with dark legs. He gazed into the sack, poked at the remainder of the contents, then said, 'The other one is dead. I'll leave it here for now.'

'How could anyone be so cruel?' She cuddled the puppy protect ively against her and its heart beat against her cold stomach. Good God, her bottom half was clad only in a ripped petticoat! The puppy whined and licked at her hand, then it peed warmly in her lap. Not that it would be noticed amongst the drips and mud stains.

Gerald pulled her upright. 'Come on, let's get you home. I'm frozen, I'll have to borrow some dry clothing from Magnus.' He bundled her into the gig, wrapped the horse blanket round her and they headed for Fierce Eagles.

'Thank you for saving my life, Gerald.'

'My pleasure, but only if I don't have to make a habit of it.'

'Stop being so horrid.' The energy seemed to be draining out of her.

'You were lucky it was only your skirt that was pinned under the log, otherwise I'd never have got you out. How are you getting along with Magnus?'

He was trying to take her mind off her plight. When she shrugged and made a face, he laughed. 'Magnus has always been a bit of a law unto himself. His bark is worse than his bite, you know.'

'Perhaps I should call the dog after him then.'

'I wouldn't if I were you. Call the dog "Boots", since he seems to be wearing them.'

'Good name.' She yawned. 'I feel fatigued, and my strength is fading.'

'It's because you're cold and the shock is beginning to set in. Hold on, Sarry love. Don't go to sleep, because I can't handle both you and the horse. We'll be home soon and I'll let the big bad wolf take over. He'll probably give you a blast that will singe your eyebrows off.'

'At least I'll be warm.'

Magnus didn't chastise her. He called for his man to tend to Gerald, then carried her upstairs and stripped the clothes from her body. Wrapping her in a soft blanket he tossed her face first on the bed like a sack of potatoes, and began to vigorously rub her cold body and limbs through the blanket.'

'Mr Kern!' Ada said in a shocked voice from the doorway, 'What are you doing to her?'

'Massaging some life back into her, what does it look like? Go to the kitchen and warm some milk. Tell Branston to put a good dollop of brandy in it. And take that animal with you. It stinks, and is probably jumping with fleas.'

Through chattering teeth, Sarette got out, 'Give Boots something warm to eat, Ada.'

'Boots? Good God, that's an odd name for a mongrel. Throw it into the stables, Ada. Tell Robert to shoot him.'

'No don't! The poor creature has been through enough. If you do that to him I'll never speak to you again, Magnus Kern.'

'That would be a definite improvement in my life, I'd imagine.'

Ada giggled.

Magnus smiled in a manner that knocked the breath from her body. 'All right, Ada, I'll let her have her own way this one time. Feed the damned mongrel and find it a basket to sleep in.'

His massage was relentless, and soon Sarette began to glow. 'Stop it, Magnus, I'm too warm and I'll have no skin left on my body,' she protested.

'That would be messy.' He gazed at her flushed cheeks, then threw her nightdress at her and turned his back. 'Put that on.'

She scrambled into it, was wrapped in the

blanket again and seated in front of the fire. He took the poker to the coals and soon the flames were roaring up the chimney. Magnus arranged himself at the other end of the fireplace. He gazed at her for a few seconds then picked up her hairbrush. 'Lean forward, I'll brush that mane before it dries into tangles.'

He had a gentle touch with the hairbrush, and it was calming against her scalp. After a while she grew sleepy and began to lean sideways. She jerked herself up and a few seconds later began to lean in the other direction. He set her back against the cushions. She was wonderfully relaxed. When Ada came in with the milk Magnus put the glass to her mouth. 'Drink it.'

She took a sip then shook her head. 'It tastes awful.'

'I don't give a damn what it tastes like, since it's not me who has to swallow the muck. Now, get it down, or I'll hold your nose and pour it down your throat.'

She wanted to giggle. 'You're oozing with charm, Magnus.'

'I'm pleased that you've finally recognized a positive quality in me. Drink!'

Sarette did as she was told, then gently belched. She muttered an apology and added, 'Go away now, I want to die in peace.'

He chuckled as he tucked her under the covers. 'You're too feisty to die. Look after her, Ada. She's to stay in bed for the rest of the day, else she might end up with a lung infection. I'll have her dinner sent up on a tray. Call me if she causes you any trouble and I'll take a horse whip to her.'

Magnus had a few words with his valet, then went downstairs to the drawing room. Gerald was sipping on his best brandy, a satisfied expression on his face.

'How's the hero of the hour feeling?' he asked.

'Envious ... where did you get this brandy from?'

'The cellar. According to the date on the label it's the ill-gotten gains of my grandfather.'

'We should have taken up the profession, Magnus. We'd have made good adventurers, you and I.'

'The world has become much too moral, and you and I with it. That's what comes of having a woman on the throne. Besides, you look as though you've had all the adventure you can take. My man thinks he can rescue your clothes, though.'

'Good. It was a brand new suit. How's Sarry?'

Magnus smiled in satisfaction. 'Totally defeated. She's asleep.'

'She's quite a woman, isn't she?'

'Sarette Maitland is a damned pest.' He glowered at Gerald. 'And don't get any ideas. You can keep both your eyes and your hands off her. She's not old enough for men like you.'

'But older than you first thought, eh?'

'Thanks to you I furnished the nursery and filled the cupboard full of children's clothes. And I bought her a rocking horse to win her round with. She said it was like the horse my uncle rode.'

'Your uncle rode a rocking horse?'

Magnus laughed and threw a cushion at him. A gust of wind rattled the windows, and he was filled with a sense of security to be here at Fierce Eagles, safe and sound in this solid house his ancestors had provided for him. He should have children to inherit. He put the unwanted notion aside. 'There's a storm brewing. Stay for dinner ... stay the night. We can have a game of chess and drink each other under the table.'

'We haven't finished the game we played when last we did that. I believe I was winning at the time.'

'The devil you were, the board's still set up in the library, though some of the pieces have been moved during the maids' dusting excursions. Use the telephone if you need to let anyone know. I take it you were on your way to somewhere.'

'I'd heard you were home and was on my way to visit Sarry, to make sure she was surviving you.'

Magnus's eyes narrowed. 'My dear, Gerald, you had only to pick up the telephone and enquire.'

Gerald shuddered and said soberly. 'If I'd done that Sarette Maitland would now be dead. She was trapped. I saw her fall in as I rounded the bend, saw the branch shift. Then her arm came out of the water and held the sack up with the dog. She was determined to rescue it, and it crossed my mind that she might be able to breathe under water – she was under for quite a while, holding it up out of the water.'

'You don't surprise me. I thought she was

191

going to scratch my eyes out when I suggested that the animal be ... humanely disposed of.'

'D'you mean, shot?'

'Something like that. I wasn't serious, of course, but it certainly got her dander up.'

'Sarette wouldn't have known that you're as accomplished a liar as your uncle was. She's a young lady with a tender heart. I was never so relieved as when I saw her arm. At first I thought the tree had rolled on her. It would have, except there was a stumpy branch sticking out that acted as a prop to prevent it. Extraordinary luck, really. But she was pinned to the bottom by her skirt, with her head under water. All I could do was rip her skirt from her body to free her.' He gazed at the leaping fire through his brandy bowl and reflected with a grin. 'She had shapely legs, I thought.'

The girl was shapely all over. Her body had been firmly moulded under the blanket – that much Magnus had noticed, even though she'd wriggled and protested. But he'd had her arms pinned to her side by the blanket. He grinned as he remembered her indignation at his treatment of her, and one green eye glaring at him from a gap in the wild tangle of her hair. However, he wasn't about to tell Gerald that. 'I didn't notice.'

Gerald's glance slid his way. 'I know you better than that, Magnus. You wouldn't have missed a thing about her, and you always play things close to your chest. Tell me, what have you planned for her?'

'Nothing as yet. I haven't had time. If I'm to follow my uncle's instructions, a suitable marriage – in time.'

'And will you follow them?'

'Uncle John was a man of good sense. I want to know more about her first. She might have living relatives. I'm going to set an investigator on to that.'

'Family will come crawling out of the woodwork when they learn of her fortune.'

'Which is one reason why I'm keeping quiet about its existence. It's not as if it originated from her own kith and kin. Also, I need a better insight as to my uncle's motivation for this generous bequest. He has sent his journals home and I intend to read them over the next couple of weeks. The nature of their relationship bothers me a little. It all sounds too simple when she relates it.'

'The truth often is. I must admit it bothered my father a little, too. But he carried out John's wishes to the letter, even after he knew he was dead. I'm sorry we were unable to inform you, Magnus.'

'I'm surprised John insisted on secrecy, and to be honest, a little hurt.'

'I don't think it was a reflection on you. Sarette has grown up a lot since she arrived in England. Both her behaviour and thinking have matured. She wouldn't have been able to cope with you then.'

Magnus sighed. 'Perhaps not. Sarette's a sharp-minded little thing. I don't know what my uncle's state of mind was at the time of signing that will. She could have manipulated him. It could all be an elaborate plot to get her hands on the fortune, and she might even have an accomplice.'

'You think she might have been acquainted with the man who shot him in the back?'

'I can only hope not, because I wouldn't like to see her hang. I've heard a whisper that there's a price on Flynn Collins's head. D'you know anything about that, Gerald?'

'I'd heard that you'd offered five hundred pounds to the man who brought Collins to justice.'

Magnus gazed at him, perplexed. 'It's not something I'd do.'

Gerald shrugged. 'My father perhaps. John was his friend, and father was upset when he learned the nature of John's death. He has a wide network of acquaintances and a long reach. It wouldn't be beyond reason for him to have the man hunted down and made to pay in kind for such an offence. But he'd never admit to it. Unlike your uncle, my father leaves no record of his journey through life.'

'A pity since he'd have some interesting tales to relate.'

'Yes, I daresay he would. You know, I doubt if Sarry is involved in any way. She has an early memory of a thatched cottage with roses. The memory of her mother is faded, but the death of her father is sharp and upsetting. Then there was her father's partner, who sold everything from under her and took off with the proceeds. Your uncle appeared on the scene at the very moment when she had nowhere else to turn.'

'Then perhaps her father's partner will know if

she has any relatives in England. Do we know his name?'

Gerald looked blank. 'I must admit, we completely overlooked that thread of possibility.'

'Then I'll ask her in the morning.'

The afternoon passed quickly as the two men talked companionably. The storm came in with a fresh ferocity as evening drew in, buffeting the house.

'It will blow itself out by morning, I imagine,' Magnus commented.

The clock chimed seven. The last chime had barely faded away when there was a knock on the door and Branston appeared.

'Dinner is served, gentlemen.'

'Good, we're both ravenous,' Magnus said.

'Cook wants to know what to do with the puppy. It's getting under her feet.'

'Has it been washed and fed?'

'Yes, sir.'

'Good. Tell cook she can either make a stew out of it, or ask Miss Maitland what to do with it. It's her dog, after all.'

Branston grinned. 'We're keeping Boots then, sir.'

'Under protest, Branston. Miss Maitland caught me at a weak moment.'

'Yes, sir. I'll tell everyone. They'll be pleased.'

Gerald laughed after Branston had gone. 'Does Sarette know you have these weak moments?'

'Not yet. I've got the girl completely flummoxed.'

The men grinned at each other.

195

Twelve

Sarette hurried down to breakfast, so she could see Gerald and thank him properly before he left.

The men stood when she walked in. 'Can I get you some breakfast?' Magnus said.

'Don't let your own get cold. I'll help myself. Please sit, both of you.' She frowned as she gazed at Gerald. 'You look pale, Gerald. You haven't caught a cold from your dunking, have you? You deserve better than that after your gallant rescue. I'm very grateful you came along when you did.'

Magnus answered for him. 'Your sympathy is misplaced. Gerald guzzled down my brandy without applying any caution, and he's suffering from a hangover. He shouldn't try to out-drink me.'

'That's true,' Gerald croaked. 'But he forgot to tell you that I beat him at chess.'

'Only because I allowed you to.'

'I'll never drink again.'

Sarette laughed. 'Mr John used to drink a lot. I bought him a bottle of Eucrasy from a travelling salesman to help him stop.'

Seemingly mystified, the men gazed at one other.

'Eucrasy?' Gerald said.

'It's medicine that takes away the urge to drink.'

Magnus asked her. 'Did it work?'

'No. Mr John spat it out and gave the rest to his horse.'

'What happened to the horse?'

'Hercules spat it out too.'

They began to laugh as she helped herself to a piece of toast. She wasn't very hungry, but poured herself a cup of tea, then spread a thin layer of gooseberry conserve on the toast.

Magnus gazed at her plate. 'Is that all you're eating?'

'I'm not very hungry this morning. Please don't decide to be overbearing and threaten to force-feed me, after your efforts at doctoring yesterday. I'm much stronger this morning, and I'll bite your damned fingers off if you so much as look at me the wrong way.'

A grin curled his lips, and he nodded. 'Gerald and I were discussing you last night.'

'Me?'

'You don't have to look so surprised. You're bound to pique our interest. We only know about you from what you've told us. With your permission we intend to make enquiries, and find out if you have any relatives. Will you mind?'

She shook her head. 'I think I would like to belong to someone again. You must feel the same, Magnus. Gerald belongs to a large family and his father is so very proud of them all.'

Magnus knew exactly what she meant. 'There is something we forgot to ask. What was the name of your father's partner? We thought that if we could find him, then he might be able to tell us if you have any relatives we can contact.'

'If I had, he would have already contacted them and stolen the teeth out of their mouths. That no good Irishman was called Flynn Collins, and if I ever see him again I want him arrested for what he did.'

Magnus made a strangled sound and Gerald's cup clattered in his saucer as they gazed in dismay at one another.

Sarette gazed from one to the other. 'What is it? Have I said something wrong?' She sighed. 'Of course I have ... I said damn, didn't I. Sorry.'

Gerald cut in smoothly, 'Tell us about this Flynn Collins. Anything you know about him. Where he came from? How did he meet your parents? Had he known them before you went to the goldfields? How did you get on with him?'

'Goodness, Gerald, all those questions. Surely he isn't all that interesting, besides, I was a child and don't know the answer to any of those things ... no wait! He joined us when my father broke his arm. It was shortly after my mother died. They came to a business arrangement.'

'How did he seem to you?'

'He wasn't unfriendly, all the same I didn't like him much. He didn't speak much as I recall, and kept himself to himself. My father trusted him. I suppose it was naive of me to expect him to take over where my father left off. It wasn't until he robbed me that I realized he was a bad lot.'

Magnus raised an eyebrow. 'But you expected

my uncle, who was a wealthy man, to take you in and treat you like his own.'

A yawning hole appeared in her stomach. 'Expected him to? No ... no, it wasn't that. I didn't know he was wealthy. He seemed the same as everyone else, perhaps a little better off. He used to go into Southern Cross every once in a while and come back with money. He said I could be his housekeeper when we first met.'

'His housekeeper? How much did he pay you?'

'Nothing. We came to an arrangement. The housekeeping was a joke between us.' She gave a faint smile at the thought of the hovel they'd occupied. 'Mr John gave me twenty per cent of any gold he found. He didn't find much, though. I have a few small nuggets, and some gold dust I sifted from the sand. I cooked his meals, did his washing and kept our home clean.'

'Are you referring to that shack?'

Her blood rose. 'It was more than a lot of people had to shelter in. Of course Mr John didn't want a housekeeper. He called me that to leave me with some pride. But you've never been there, have you? You've never experienced the relentless heat every day and the lack of water to drink when you're so parched that your skin cracks open.' Gerald put a hand on her arm but she ignored it. 'When did you ever dig for anything? You sit here in a house that was supplied to you free of charge, and bought by money earned through illegal means, and you pass judgement on everyone, like a spider in his lair, Magnus Kern.'

'Spiders have webs.'

'Not all of them,' she argued. 'In the goldfields they'd fry in the sun if they hung around in webs all day. Some live underground ... in *lairs*. They run like the devil's after them, too.'

'Interesting,' he said mildly. 'You'll have to tell me all about them.'

She remembered she was mad at him. 'Oh, don't pretend you're interested in spiders. Why are you saying such horrible things? Why do you want to know about Collins?'

'Flynn Collins killed my uncle,' Magnus said.

The breath nearly left her body at such a staggering revelation. 'And you think I might have had something to do with it, that I was in league with that ... scum?'

'It's crossed my mind.'

Sarette shot to her feet, feeling the colour drain from her cheeks. 'Consider yourself released from any commitment you thought you were under, you utter ... *scurrilous worm*,' she scorned, and headed for the door. Halfway there her knees began to buckle.

It was Magnus who caught her. She struggled weakly against the arm that bound her to his side for support. 'Stop struggling else I'll drop you,' he said, and she drooped limply against him.

Magnus relinquished her when Gerald slid a chair under her and said, 'Sit there until you recover, my dear. I do hope you're satisfied, Magnus.'

'That she had nothing to do with the murder ... yes, but I didn't expect her to become hysterical over such a simple question.'

'Hysterical ... simple question?' She was hot and trembling with rage. 'How dare you suggest I was in league with the killer of your uncle.'

'But I didn't. The suggestion came from you.'

'Enough, Magnus. You know it was an interrogation. In a courtroom it would have been a questioning technique to trap a witness. You should have remembered that you're at home and that Sarette is your guest and so am I. That was not worthy of you.'

Magnus spread his hands and looked suitably ashamed. 'My manners obviously left a lot to be desired. My apologies to you both. My impatience got the better of me.'

Both men looked at her, obviously expecting her to forgive him.

When she glared at the man who was reluctantly responsible for her welfare, his dark eyes lightened in amusement and his skin crinkled at the corners, in exactly the same way that Mr John's used to, Magnus reminded her so much of him that her heart ached. He took her hands in his, pulled her upright and kissed her knuckles. 'Now you've roasted this low-bred scurrilous worm to a crisp, will you please forgive him?'

Magnus possessed a great deal of charm, though he wasn't obvious like Gerald, and he was sparing with it. Against her will she softened towards him. 'You're forgiven. I imagine I jumped to the wrong conclusion.'

'Not at all. Now, you'll sit down and have some breakfast with us.'

Any appetite she'd had, had fled. 'No, I'm really not all that hungry. I just wanted to say goodbye to Gerald and thank him before he left. I wish I had seen a little more of you yesterday, Gerald.'

Magnus gave a huff of laughter. 'You wouldn't have got any sense out of him.'

'I'm afraid he's right. His ancestor smuggled some really good brandy into his cellars, and I have the feeling I'm going to pay for it over the rest of the day.'

When the door closed behind her, Gerald gave Magnus a sharp look. 'What was that little charade about?'

'Sometimes when she looks at me I remind her of my uncle. She wants me to be him.'

'Is that so bad?'

'It is when she's living under my roof. I can't afford to become involved with her.'

'Why ever not? She's exquisite, a peach ripe for the plucking, and you're unmarried.'

'I'm well aware of her charms, and I'm just as aware of my single status. I enjoy being unencumbered. Enjoyed, I should say, I nearly proposed to Alice Carradine, just to have a mother for the child I was expecting to bring up. Nice trick, Gerald.'

'I've not yet met Miss Carradine.'

'You'll like her when you do. She's calm and level-headed. She's the type of woman who wouldn't give a man any trouble. The Carradines will be down here after Christmas, and I've invited the family for New Year. I intend to invite your family and make a party out of it. I thought Alice might stay on afterwards and be a good influence on Sarette.'

Gerald choked out a laugh. 'You're scared that you might fall in love with Sarette, aren't you?'

'Why should I be scared? I'm not the falling in love type. I'm too self-centred and enjoy my own company.'

'You're certainly not Sarette's type, Magnus.'

'And you are, I suppose?'

Head to one side, Gerald met the challenge in his friend's eyes. 'I wager I could succeed where you would fail. I have a year's start on you, thus Sarette knows me really well and feels safe with me. I've already become her hero by saving her life. But you, my friend have raised her ire considerably, and on at least two occasions in as many days to my knowledge.'

'She has the makings of a shrew.'

'She's defensive because you challenge her all the time. Try being nice to her and see how she responds. You could have her eating out of your hand in no time.'

'Don't you mean biting it?' Magnus thought for a moment, then he grinned. 'It wouldn't be the first time we'd competed for the favour of the same woman, would it?'

'Or bet on the outcome.'

'I admit the odds are against me at the moment, but never mind. So I'll take you up on the wager, my friend. Just remember that Sarette is my ward and I'll not allow you to ruin her. So let's make this more interesting. The winner will actually be the loser, because he'll have to lose his freedom to gain a wife and fortune. Before she's bedded, it's marriage or nothing, and we play it straight down the line.'

Sucking in a breath Gerald considered it for a moment, then held out his hand and grinned. 'Sarette's pretty, she's pert, and she'll have a fortune at her disposal. The fortune alone would compensate for the loss of my freedom. Would you be able to bring yourself to part with the cash?'

'Of course I'd part with it ... should the occasion warrant. It is hers, after all. And as she kindly pointed out, I didn't earn it.'

'You asked for that. In all honesty, Sarette has everything a man could desire. She's beautiful, intelligent, and ... passionate by nature. What more could a man want in a wife?'

'Nothing.' Magnus smiled and shook Gerald's hand, knowing the agreement would be honoured in the way it always had. 'Winner takes all, then, Gerald. May the best man win.'

'You asked me to arrange a suitable marriage for your little friend. That will be Gerald, and I know you'll approve,' Magnus said to his uncle's portrait a little later in the evening. Nobody was more suitable than Gerald, and it was obvious that Sarette liked him. Personally, he'd do nothing to encourage her affection, and would allow nature to take its course. 'Now, let me discover what you got up to in your absence.'

He'd already removed the metal straps from the trunk now he fitted the key in the lock. It turned with a satisfying clunk. Opening the lid he lifted a note from the top and read it. Apart from his journals everything in his uncle's travelling trunk was to be given to Sarette. There were several books, all well-thumbed and a little worse for wear, plus his writing desk. His journals were layered in the middle, leather bound and bulging with drawings, pressed flowers and leaf samples. He placed them reverently on the desk. It would take several evenings to read them properly. There was a lined tray for guns ... empty except for a dead cockroach. Magnus remembered the newspaper cutting stating that his uncle's guns had been sold to pay for his burial. When he lifted the tray to gaze at what lay beneath, his eyes widened.

'Oh ... my God,' he whispered. 'Look at that.'

Sarette saw very little of Magnus. He breakfasted early and went off to his office, arriving home before it was dark. After dinner he disappeared into the library. Sometimes he slept in Dorchester, and she learned from the staff that he retained a room in a boarding house, in case he needed it. Sarette didn't know whether to be sad or sorry that she didn't see so much of him. She had Boots for company, and he was growing fat.

One day the following week, the staff began to remove items from Miss Margaret's room and the adjoining one, which had belonged to the late Annie Kern.

'We're to pack everything up and take it to the attic,' Ada said. 'The master said you're to move in here. It's very convenient, the rooms are connected by a proper bathroom.'

A team of men arrived and soon the rooms

were completely refurbished with a pretty ivory wallpaper dotted in flowers, and new furniture and fittings.

Sarette's things were moved into Margaret Kern's room the next day. 'On the master's orders,' Ada said, and that was that.

He came up to inspect it, Mr John's little writing desk in his arms. 'My uncle wanted you to have this. There's a little note in the inkwell for you.'

She chuckled. 'I imagine it will say, "Ladies don't spit in inkwells."'

'Something like that.' He smiled and placed it on the desk. 'He'd had the name plate changed.'

It said: 'To Sarette Maitland from John Kern'. She would think of him every time she wrote in her journal. Gently, she ran a fingertip over their names etched in the silver. 'That was kind of him, but I don't need to be reminded of him. He's in my heart.'

'I know. My uncle also wants you to have his books.' He turned her round. 'You're not going to cry are you?'

'Mr John never quite knew what to do when I cried.' Nevertheless, there was a tear trembling on her lashes.

'Not many men do know.' He changed the subject. 'Do you like your new room?'

'The wallpaper has got all my favourite colours. The lilac beneath the window will be fragrant when it's in bloom, and the large bay window lets a lot of light in. Yes, I like it. It's a lovely room.'

'I thought you'd rather sleep this side of the

house. It's warmer, and although it hasn't got a view of the sea, it's also sheltered from the wind that comes off it.'

'That was thoughtful of you.'

He picked up the photograph of herself with John. 'There was one of these in his journal. You look very young ... and small and thin.'

'The photograph was taken not long after your uncle took me in. The man who took it had a camel, and it smelled awful.'

Magnus smiled at that. 'He looks happy, more contented than before he left.'

'Taking responsibility for me stopped him from grieving so much for his daughter.' She hesitated, then confided. 'In a private letter to me, he said that on the day we met he was going to free his horse then walk off into the bush to die.'

'Tell me about it.'

Her voice thickened. 'My father had died a few days before. I'd had nothing to eat or drink all day, and had nowhere to go. I was lying on the bare earth willing myself to die, my throat so parched I could hardly croak. It was nearly dark and he stumbled over me. At the time he told me he'd been looking for me to offer me a job as his housekeeper.'

'My uncle was always a convincing liar.'

'Yes, he warned me of that. Now I know that I saved his life by being in his path. I do know that he saved mine. I think we could sense each other's sadness, and that was a special bond between us. He said ... he said the stars were pretty. And they were. Silly isn't it? We were both hurting, and he noticed the beauty of the stars.'

When she gulped and her tears spilled over and sped down her cheeks he awkwardly patted her hand. 'I'll go and get your books while you compose yourself.'

Here was a man who guarded his emotions carefully, she thought as he walked away. She wished he was softer.

Boots came out of his basket and gave a little yelp. She picked him up and cuddled him close. 'You've got a fat stomach.'

'He needs to go outside,' Verna said, bustling in. 'You have to train dogs right from the beginning otherwise they think it's all right to squat on the carpets and ruin them. And the males cock their legs up on the furniture. That dog might look cuddly and helpless, now, but he's going to be a big dog, and he needs showing who's the boss right from the beginning, so he'll have respect for you.'

'How do you know he's going to be big?'

'By the size of his feet.'

She gazed at the soft pads of his feet. They did appear too large in proportion to the rest of him. 'I'll take him down to the garden every hour then, until he gets used to it.'

She passed Magnus on the stair. He was coming up with an armful of books. He raised an eyebrow when he saw the dog. 'That's not going to grow into a lapdog. I'd prefer it to be kept in the kitchen, especially at night.'

'Boots will get lonely and he'll yelp.'

'If nobody gives him any attention he'll get used to it,' he said.

* * *

Magnus hadn't been able to sleep, and clad in his robe was nursing a brandy in the library. He'd reached the last journal, and his concentration was being ruined by the constant yelping of the dog. The last entry in the journal could wait until tomorrow, he thought. He went through to the kitchen and turned up the gas light.

'What's all this noise?' he said sternly.

Boots gave a series of yips and galloped towards him, his legs splaying out. Rolling on to his back with his tail between his legs he writhed back and forth, displaying his belly. When Magnus patted it the dog stood and pressed, quivering against his legs. 'You know that you're keeping everyone awake, don't you?'

The dog whined.

He sighed. 'Sarette was right. You are lonely. I'll have to do something about it. In the meantime, you can come and sleep in my room. But don't tell anyone.'

His valet had gone to bed long since. The dog settled against his back like a furnace. And it snored, scratched, farted and jerked in its sleep. The damned creature needed a companion all right, but it was not going to be him.

At breakfast the next morning he was tired and incommunicative. Sarette's broad smile of welcome faded at the sight of him. She ate her breakfast in silence, then made an excuse. He left for his office feeling as though he was a leper.

It was market day in Dorchester. In court he disputed the last will and testament made by a wealthy man. He was representing the man's two sisters – women who had looked after him all their lives, and who were now left destitute and without accommodation. The will had been fraudulently altered by a male cousin. Magnus was able to prove it and won the case for them.

Feeling more cheerful he strolled through the market. There was a ragged-looking boy with a terrier for sale. It was black and white, small, handsome and intelligent-looking, everything that Boots was not, in fact.

'How much?' he said.

'Five shillings, sir. Patch is a good ratter.'

'Half a crown.'

'He's worth more than that, sir. My father trained him well.'

'Where's your father now.'

'In prison, sir. Four shillings would be a fair price,' the lad suggested.

'Four then. You're a good salesman.' He fished two florins out of his pocket and exchanged them for the string with the dog attached. He handed the boy his card. 'If you need work come and see me next week at my rooms. We need someone to clean the windows and sweep the yard.' After the boy had gone, the dog wagged its tail at him and licked his hand.

'Don't try and get too friendly,' he said. 'I've bought you to keep Boots under control and teach him his manners.'

That night the silence was blissful as the two dogs settled down together in front of the crackling fire. Magnus opened the last entry in the journal.

I had never thought I'd fall in love with a young girl who could be my granddaughter. Sarry would wed me if I asked her. Her eyes shine when she looks at me. It's hero worship, of course. I was there when she needed someone, and she was there when I needed someone.

Exactly what Sarette had said. They had been attuned to each other, Magnus thought.

I cannot allow her to love me, then break her heart. It's been many years since I was able to be a husband to any woman.

Today, I was given a death sentence by a doctor. I lied to Sarry. I gave her hope, something to cling to. Go, I said. Improve yourself. I'll see you at Fierce Eagles. I couldn't tell her I was dying and watch her pity me. She would have stayed with me until the bitter end, cared for me, scolded me and wasted her tears on me. It would have broken her brave heart and mine, because she would have taken my pain and suffering upon her shoulders.

I'm an old dog who must die alone so as not to hurt the one who loves me most. I hope the end will come quickly, and without too much suffering. Magnus, I looked for gold and found it in the most unexpected place ... in my heart. Be gentle with my dear Sarry.

A tear fell on the page and smudged the ink. Then another. Magnus couldn't remember the last time he'd cried.

211

Thirteen

Life settled down for Sarette. Magnus came and went, and sometimes they passed on the stairs, Magnus looking dashing in his evening clothes as he went out to some function or another.

She felt invisible, and lonely, and wished she had someone to talk to apart from the dogs. She'd explored the many rooms of the house. Then she remembered that Gerald had invited her to a ball, and she was to be a guest of his sister. She checked her invitation, discovered it was the coming weekend and went into a flurry of preparation before she realized that Gerald had not mentioned it since.

She said to Branston, 'Will you show me how to operate the telephone?'

'You put the trumpet to your ear, and you talk into the body of the telephone. Everyone has a number, and you give that to the telephone operator, who puts you through to that person. Do you have the number of the person you wish to speak to?'

'I don't know any numbers. How can you talk to people if they're somewhere else?'

'I don't know, Miss. It's all to do with wires and electrical currents, and it depends on the person you wish to talk to. Not everyone has a telephone.'

'I'd like to talk to Mr Gerald Grimble. He invited me to a ball, and told me I could stay with his sister the night before. The function is this coming weekend. I think he's forgotten about it.'

Dubiously, the butler said, 'I think you'd better ask Mr Kern for permission, Miss. He might not like you telephoning his friends and acquaintances. Or he might want to do it for you.'

She nodded. 'Then I'll telephone him.'

'Mr Kern won't be in his chambers yet. He has a court appearance shortly after he reaches Dorchester. I'll telephone him later in the morning on your behalf, if you wish. About eleven thirty?'

'How exciting. May I speak to him myself?'

Branston smiled. 'I'll ask him if he'll speak to you direct, Miss.'

The morning went slowly. It was a dull day, but she took the dogs for a walk. Boots's behaviour had improved considerably since Patch had arrived. Both dogs had begun to favour the presence of Magnus over her though, which was a little annoying. They looked funny together. Boots, whose legs and ears seemed to be growing rapidly, lolloped along, and the neat little terrier trotted powerfully, its belly not far off the ground and his eyes on the foliage along the bottom of the hedges. Patch was a relentless ratter. A quick dart and snap of his jaws and a hapless rodent going innocently about its business would give a surprised squeak as it was efficiently disposed of.

After they returned she went through her gowns, trying to decide on which one to wear. When the clock struck the half hour she was already waiting for Branston outside the study, feeling jumpy with anticipation.

The telephone grew out of the desk like a shining black daffodil. She watched as the butler took the ear trumpet from its rest and talked into the instrument, then Branston said, 'Miss Maitland wishes to talk to you, sir.' It was handed to her with instructions on how to end the call before he left the room.

'Magnus, is that you?' she said loudly.

'You don't have to shout, Sarry, just use your normal voice,' he said against her ear.

It was so close that she turned towards the sound. 'Sorry, I've never talked on a telephone before. It sounds as you're standing right next to me, but hidden inside a tin can. It's very clever.'

'Yes it is ... what did you want to talk to me about that couldn't have waited until I got home?'

'A little while ago Gerald invited me to partner him at a ball, and said I should stay with his sister, Olivia. I've just remembered that the function is this coming weekend. He's not mentioned it since, and I wondered if I should telephone him.'

'On no account should you remind Gerald. He may have forgotten, and it would embarrass him. Also, Olivia would have contacted you with a personal invitation to stay in her home if she'd been able to cater for you.'

Disappointment filled her. 'Oh, I see. Thank

you, Magnus.'

He lowered his voice. 'Are you very upset?'

'I've never been to a ball. Gerald taught me to waltz when I lived with Mrs Lawrence, though. I enjoyed it.'

'Gerald's an excellent dancer. A pity he's let you down. You'll have to come with me instead. I'll book an extra room for the night at the hotel, if one's available. Will you be bored with my company as a substitute for Gerald's.'

Her spirits lifted. 'I won't be bored at all. Thank you, Magnus. You're so kind. I've been feeling so ... aimless lately.'

'Aimless? Why didn't you tell me? I'll have to find you something to do, learn to play the piano, or paint pretty pictures, or start a beetle collection.'

'I refuse to stick pins in poor little beetles.' She laughed. 'Actually, I'm totally lacking in artistic talent, and not used to a life of leisure. Perhaps I should find employment and earn myself some money, so I don't feel so...'

'Sorry for yourself? Most young women would like to be in your position.'

'I know. I'm very grateful, and I'm not—'

'Complaining? Of course you are. You only have to ask if you need money or entertainment. My uncle provided an *allowance* for you, after all. Do you have a ball gown?'

'Yes, I—'

'We'll buy you a new one.'

'I don't need a new one. You're not listening. I haven't worn—'

'We'll buy one anyway. Something elegant

and without silly little bobbing bustles at the back and fussy bows and frills. You have no fashion sense.'

'Mrs Lawrence chose my clothes.'

'Then she has no fashion sense either. Tomorrow I'll take the day off and we'll go into Dorchester. I know a woman there who used to dress royalty. In fact, she claims to have royal blood in her veins.'

'Magnus, I—'

'Magnus I, nothing.'

'You won't let me get a word in edgewise, will you?'

'I haven't got time to argue, we can do that tonight over dinner.' He chuckled. 'We haven't had a decent set to for a long time, have we? Try and think of something controversial we can converse about.'

'She gave an exasperated cry and stamped her foot on the thick carpet. 'I already have. His name is Magnus Kern. You're constantly *controversial*.'

He chuckled, as if he was pleased with her remark, and the line went dead. Smiling, she put the trumpet back in its cradle. He was impossible, overbearing, and exhilarating, and she felt so alive when she had his attention. She was glad he was taking her to the ball instead of Gerald. Picking up the edge of her skirt she waltzed about the room, stopping dead when the door opened and Branston came in.

He took a polishing cloth out of his apron pocket and fussily rubbed it over the telephone before giving a sneeze and admonishing her with, 'Really, Miss, you're making the dust fly about.'

'Sorry, Mr Branston. Is there anything I can do to help?'

He smiled. 'You're a guest, Miss.'

'I don't want to be a trouble to anyone, and I'm perfectly capable of doing some house-work.'

'Was your telephone call to Mr Kern satisfactory, Miss?' Which was a polite way of satisfying his curiosity, she supposed.

'Mr Kern has offered to take me to the ball himself. I was practising my dancing when you came in.'

He gave her one of his rare smiles. 'So I noticed. You looked very graceful. Mr Kern is an excellent dancer, I believe.'

'Oh dear ... Can you dance, Mr Branston?'

'I'm known to be light on my feet on the odd occasion.'

'I feel this occasion to be decidedly odd, don't you? You can help me practise if you're of a mind.'

Branston gazed around him, then managed a small, mischievous grin before holding out his arms and saying, 'As long as you don't tell anyone.'

He was adroit at guiding her round the furniture as he swung her about the room. Sarette got into the spirit of the moment by singing, lah-lah-lah in lieu of music, and soon Branston joined in.

The telephone shrilled loudly and they came to a sudden stop. Branston picked up the telephone, said breathlessly, 'Mr Kern's residence. Oh, it's you, Mr Kern.'

Sarette heard Magnus's voice clearly. 'You sound out of breath, Branston.'

'Yes, sir. I was on the stairs.'

'You must have run fast then, for the telephone had hardly rung.'

'I was referring to the library stairs, sir. I was dusting the top shelf.'

'Good Lord, does the top shelf get dusted very often?'

'Very rarely in fact, sir.'

'I see. Miss Maitland told me she was bored. Think of something to keep her amused, will you? Find her a jigsaw puzzle, or dance for her.'

'Yes, sir ... I will. Which dance would you suggest?'

'How the devil would I know? The request wasn't to be taken literally, and you're far from being as dense as you're making out.'

'If you say so, sir.' Branston hung the earpiece up, turned to her and raised an eyebrow. 'Shall we try the waltz next, Miss?'

Sarette giggled.

Magnus had hardly finished speaking to Branston when he telephoned Gerald. 'I believe you invited my ward to the ball, Gerald.'

'Did I? Oh yes, so I did. I'd forgotten. Damn! I've just been manoeuvred into asking Jessica Fenwick, who is some sort of cousin. She's a house guest of Olivia's, and rather dreary.' He groaned. 'I can't get out of it now. Look, can you give Sarette my apologies. Tell her I'm

218

indisposed, or something similar. I'll make up for it by taking her roller-skating on the pier sometime. She'll like that. Who are you bringing now Isabelle's no longer available?'

Uncharitably, Magnus doubted if Isabelle would ever be that. 'I'd made up my mind not to attend. I'm not making excuses for you either. You should honour your commitments. The girl will be disappointed. Still, it will give me the edge on our wager when I tell her you forgot. I suppose I could bring her myself.'

Gerald laughed. 'In which case she'll know that you escorted her out of duty.'

'There's that, of course.'

'Look, Magnus. I'd cancel Jessica if I could. But Olivia's house is stuffed to the gills, anyway, so there wouldn't be room for Sarette. If you don't want to tell Sarette I'm dying, which would at least get me some sympathy, tell her that family duty dictated this.'

'Damn you, Gerald. I've been out and about too much these last few days, and wanted a quiet weekend at home.'

'Then have one. There's always next weekend. I'll make it up to her then.'

Gerald sounded slightly desperate, and Magnus knew he had him on the run. He smiled. 'Yes ... I think I might do that. I'm looking forward to the festive season though. Christmas at the Grimbles is always a pleasure, but it's not somewhere a man could find the opportunity to pay court to a woman. Too crowded, and too many Grimble eyes watching what you get up to. How many of you are there now?'

219

'I've lost count. Which reminds me. We had news from Edgar, yesterday. He's to become a father. Pa's pleased, of course. He now refers to Edgar as the founder member of the Australian branch of Grimble and Sons, and is enormously proud of him. Edgar has gone through with his plan to register his business as Son of Grimble though. Father is a bit put out about that. He said it's undignified.'

'It certainly has a dashing feel to it. Long may the Grimbles prosper.' Magnus decided to let Gerald off the hook, and sighed. 'Don't worry, Gerald. I'll make up some plausible excuse for you. Sarette believes everything I tell her.'

'You should tell her what a liar you are then. By the way, rumour has it that Isabelle will be at the ball. She was discouraged by the damp in Venice and the expected event turned out to be a non-event. She left her count in Venice and has returned for the Christmas and New Year season. Shall I give her your ... love?'

'I'd prefer it if you didn't. Enjoy yourself at the ball. A pity that Sarette will be disappointed, but it can't be helped. She'll recover.'

With that final turn of the screw he hung up and began to laugh. Perhaps it was Gerald who should remember what a plausible liar he could be – a family trait he'd inherited.

Sarette had wondered what relationship Magnus had enjoyed with this French woman on the way to Dorchester. But Marie Renouf turned out to be wrinkled and old. Her crabbed hands were covered in rings and she wore a tiara in her hair.

Her salon in High West Street was furnished in peeling gilt, damp-spotted mirrors and fading velvet.

Magnus kissed her on both cheeks. 'Madame Renouf. This is my ward, Sarette Maitland, and a friend of my late uncle, John Kern. She's in desperate need of a ball gown.'

'Ah, yes. I had heard that the son of my old ... *friend* of many years ago had died,' and she rolled her rrrrs like a cat purring. 'So, you thought of me for *theess ... theess'* – eyes like brown berries darted from Sarette's waist to her breasts and she shrugged and almost spat out the words – *'theess precocious child?'*

Precocious? What on earth did she mean by calling her that? Sarette was about to ask her when Magnus gave a chuckle. 'You misunderstand, Madame. Miss Maitland was my uncle's ward. Now she's become my responsibility.' His tone of voice was rather dry and unflattering.

'You don't have to make me sound like a burden. Nobody asked my opinion of whether or not I agreed to your guardianship.'

'What is it?'

'What is what?'

Those dark eyes of his were at their most quelling. 'Your opinion?'

She allowed herself to be quelled. After all, she couldn't kick up a fuss in a public dressmaking salon, even one so exclusive and specialist that it didn't seem to have any clients except her. She grinned at him. 'I surrender myself to your *responsibility* under protest.'

He laughed. 'I can survive a protest or two.'

Madame was gazing one to the another, a thin smile on her face. 'I have two gowns in Miss Maitland's size.' She clapped her hands and a girl came through.

Madame said something to her in French, then told Sarette, 'Go with her ... Mr Kern, you would like a glass of wine while we wait, *oui!*'

'*Oui*, Madame.'

The assistant quickly undressed her, then settled a pastel green brocade gown patterned with gold and silver thread over her petticoat. Instead of a bustle the gown was fuller at the back and draped over a small horsehair pad, so it gave an illusion of a short, graceful train to the skirt. The girl arranged the puff sleeves, and adjusted the delicate cream lace over the square-cut bodice. Her bun received a cursory glance, a toss of the head and a scornful snort. The assistant tied a green velvet ribbon around it.

Sarette watched Magnus's eyes narrow when she came out from behind the curtain. Then his smile came. 'It's perfect for you.'

Not quite. It seemed that there was a delicate net cape in cream, embroidered, and decorated with crystals. 'And accessories, of course.'

'Of course,' said Magnus.

There was a beaded net and flower arrangement for the hair, plus a small bag.

The second gown was a two piece, made of delicate pink taffeta, with a beaded open bodice over a sheer printed chiffon blouse collared with lace. Again there were accessories.

Magnus said nothing as his scrutiny went from her neck down to her toes.

'Which gown pleases you most?' she said, torn between the two of them, and trying not to blush, because she was well aware of the impression they'd created.

His eyes came up to hers and he surprised her by saying, 'The gowns merely complement the woman inside them. It's you who pleases me the most.'

Her face warmed with a vengeance and she spread a little ivory fan and hid behind it, looking at him over the top.

His mouth twitched into a grin. 'Stop flirting, Sarette. I refuse to be used for target practice by a chit of a girl who's hardly out of the nursery.'

'I'm not. I wouldn't dare flirt with you. You deliberately made me blush, and I'm trying to hide it.'

'Am I that much the ogre, then?'

'Sometimes ... often, I think that you don't like me.'

'Sometimes, but not often, I think I'm beginning to like you too much for my own good.' He turned to the Frenchwoman. 'The gowns are exquisite, and you are a genius, Marie. We'll take them both. And something appropriate to wear under them.'

Madame Renouf's smile was simpering. 'But of course. It will be my pleasure to be of service to you, Mr Kern. A lady who wishes to please a gentleman should always dress from the skin out, so she can tantalize him as he unwraps her silks, satins and lace to reveal what perfection she has to offer underneath.'

'I quite agree, Madame,' Magnus said with a

grin in her direction.

Sarette gasped and placed her hands over her ears, but although she felt quite shocked by the intimate talk, she also wanted to laugh, because the conversation was so unlike the Magnus she'd grown used to. But then, she conceded, he had never allowed her to get close enough to really know him.

'See if there's any daywear you have that will fit her, while I take care of some business. I need some extra staff for over the New Year. No bustles and nothing from your special stock. Is that understood. She's pert enough.'

Sarette was pushed and pulled into a dazzling array of outfits, and soon there was a pile of silks, satins, velvet, chiffons and lace. She'd never seen anything quite so pretty, or worn anything quite so pleasing against her skin.

'Madame makes lovely clothes, but the salon looks so shabby,' she said to the assistant.

'She has a small clientele, and her prices are outrageous, but she's mean with money. There's a workroom upstairs and Madame's a stickler for good work. I've learned a lot from her. One day I'm going to open my own salon. I've not seen your gentleman in here before.'

Something lodged in the corner of Sarette's mind. 'Do many gentlemen bring their wives shopping?'

The girl giggled. 'But you're not Mr Kern's wife, you're his *ward*,' she pointed out. 'Your gentleman is very handsome. Usually it's older men who come in here with their young ladies. Madame does a saucy line in undergarments.'

Sarette blushed as she caught on, then she gasped. 'I'm exactly what Mr Kern said I am. His ward.'

'Sorry, I'm sure, Miss.'

The curtain was pushed aside by Madame Marie's stick. 'Fanny, you're being indiscreet, and I won't have you gossiping to my clients. Fetch some tea for us. The young lady and I will converse while we're waiting for Mr Kern to return.'

Sarette was simmering with curiosity when she finally left the salon. 'You should have warned me about Madame Marie's curiosity.'

'As a dressmaker, she's a genius. I don't know much about the other side of her business, apart from her reputation.'

'She and her assistant assumed that I was your mistress.'

He grinned. 'Did they? I hope you weren't embarrassed by it.'

'A little. Do you *have* a mistress?'

For a moment he looked taken aback, then he gave an easy smile. 'It's not a question you should ask a man, but no,' he said quite truthfully, because wasn't Isabelle part of his past now? 'Have you finished prying into the private life of the Kern family?'

'Not quite. Was Madame Marie really your grandfather's lover?'

'I believe she was one of them. He brought her over from France after my grandmother died. Marie pretends to be an illegitimate daughter of an illegitimate daughter of the French royal family. Actually, she was apprenticed to a seam-

225

stress at the time.'

'Had he known her before his wife died?'

'I have no idea. Starting with Alexander Kern and Esmerelda Rey, the Kern men were adventurers, but they had a reputation of marrying for love, and remaining faithful to their wives.'

'Esmerelda Rey? That's the pirate's daughter from Corsica, isn't it? Mr John said that's where the dark eyes and hair came from. He said they were all bald except for a pigtail before that.'

'And you believed him?' Magnus began to laugh.

'Of course I didn't. He teased me a lot. Is there really a secret room in the cellars at Fierce Eagles?'

He cast a long look her way. 'Did John tell you about it?'

'He told me there was one, but he wouldn't tell me what's in it, and I didn't know whether to believe him or not, because he made up such wonderful and outrageous stories.'

'It's true, there is such a room. My uncle said that what it contains is best left undisturbed, and he wouldn't allow me to see it when I was a child.'

'How could you bear not to know what was there?'

He shrugged. 'Oh, I've been down there since, and was surprised at what I found. I can see that he wouldn't have wanted it to stimulate my childish imagination, since he had other plans for me. And in case you're hatching a plan, I'd rather you didn't wander around the cellars looking for the room. It's quite dark down there.

There used to be tunnels down to the cove, but my uncle had them filled in.'

She shivered. 'What's in the secret room, is it full of treasure?'

Her smiled at her fancy. 'My ancestors preferred to convert their ill-gotten gains into cash. One day, when the right time presents itself, we'll arm ourselves with lanterns and I'll take you down there to have a look, if I can find the door key.'

'The key is hanging on a nail next to the door.'

'Is it, by God?' He gave a huff of laughter.

They were in a crowd of people and heading towards the gig, which they'd left to be minded by a young lad not far from the Antelope Hotel. When the crowd thinned she noticed a man talking to the lad.

'Did you want something?' Magnus said when they got closer.

'No, sir,' the man mumbled. 'I was admiring your horse, that's all.' Sarette only got a glimpse of his dirty face before the man turned away and hurried off, but something about him seemed slightly familiar.

'Is everything all right? What did that man want?' Magnus asked the boy.

'He said he thought he recognized the horse, and did it belong to Dr Scotter from Midbrook House.'

'I've never heard of him, or of Midbrook House.'

'That's what I said to him, too. I think he was going to steal the rig if I let him get near enough. The horse belongs to Mr Magnus Kern of Fierce

Eagles, says I, slapping the whip against my thigh so he knew I meant business if he fancied his chances. And a right fine legal gentleman he is – very generous when the occasion demands.' The boy grinned widely and held out his grubby hand.

'Am I to take it the occasion demands it now?'

'Reckon I can tell you something else if I've a mind to, and I've got a fancy to buy my ma a warm scarf for Christmas.'

'A worthy reason.' Magnus laughed and put an extra coin in his hand.

'Thank you, sir. Fact is, he didn't sound like he was from these parts, more like a northerner or a Scot, but not exactly. And when I asked who was taking the liberty of asking after the gentleman's horse, he said his name was Jack Maitland.'

Sarette gave a tiny, distressed gasp.

Magnus dismissed the lad, placed the parcels in the gig and helped her up next to them, his hands warm around her waist, his hair ruffling in the breeze. He tucked the rug over her knees. She squashed a sudden urge to kiss the tender curve of his ear, but Magnus didn't encourage familiarity. She smiled at it instead, before he straightened up, climbed up next to her and jammed his hat on his head. 'It's a coincidence, that's all.'

'It certainly wasn't my father's ghost, of that I'm sure. It was odd, though. It gave me a bit of a start. His face seemed slightly familiar, as if I'd seen him before.'

Putting the horse in motion they headed out of town on the Bridport Road. 'You can have a go at driving the gig when the traffic has thinned out if you like. Then you can get out and about by yourself, as long as you have someone with you. Ada perhaps.'

It wasn't too hard to keep control of the horse. It was a black gelding, not as big as Hercules had been, but it had a much glossier coat. She wondered where Hercules was now, and whether he missed John as much as she still did. She began to softly sing:

There was a black gelding from kucamandoo who uncovered a nugget of gold with his shoe. A pretty white mare from kucamandee, wore a red garter tied over her knee, and a handsome young mule from kucamandonga woke up the dawn with a sweet braying songa, while the silly old Jenny from kucamandaisy honked like a goose and sent everyone crazy.

When Magnus laughed she was brought back to the present, and she grinned.

'I made it up for Hercules, but it was such a long time ago that I can't quite remember the words. It's a silly song, but he liked it, and I was thinking of him.'

'You're a young lady, you should think of what the future holds, not what's gone past.' He pulled on the reins and brought the carriage to a halt. Taking her face between his hands he unexpectedly kissed her on the mouth.

It seemed as though the world came to a standstill around her. His lips were as silky as warm satin, as sweet as honey and as hot as fire.

She felt herself melt, felt the womanly parts of her body eagerly absorb the message they were being sent. How could she bring herself to be shocked by his action when she'd enjoyed it so much?

She smiled when he withdrew, opened her eyes and found herself gazing into the dark depths of his.

He seemed more surprised by his action than she was. 'Don't look at me with eyes as round as dinner plates. I suppose I should apologize.'

'Why?'

'Because you're a young, impressionable girl.'

She decided to keep it light. 'And you don't want to impress me in case I swoon in your arms and declare my everlasting love for you?'

'No ... yes.' He sounded alarmed, then he laughed. 'You wouldn't do that, would you? You're much too sensible. I'm sorry I kissed you. You looked so sweet, and so innocent and I gave in to a whim. It won't happen again.'

'Oh, Magnus, of course I wouldn't swoon over you. It was only a kiss, after all, and not a very good one at that,' she lied. 'Also, I should point out that I've been kissed before.'

'Gerald, I suppose. Is that who I'm being compared to?'

She wanted to giggle at his annoyed expression. 'Is that so bad, when he's a friend of yours? Surely you trust him with me. I do so enjoy his company.'

'Like hell I trust him, I know him too well. I've already informed him that I'm responsible for your welfare. Now I'm reminding you.'

'So why make it sound like you're warning me?'

He was still gazing into her eyes, and he said softly, 'You have the damnedest long eyelashes.'

She wasn't in love with Gerald, and she didn't want to fall in love with Magnus Kern, it would make life too complicated. She sighed. 'Now who's flirting? You might be responsible for me, but who takes responsibility for your behaviour, Magnus?'

He thought about it for a moment. 'You're right, of course. I shall try and be more fatherly towards you, like my uncle was.'

His voice was almost mocking and she gazed at him, puzzled. 'Mr John wasn't all that fatherly. He was more like a friend and mentor to me.'

'Yes, I know. Do you think you can get through the gateposts of Fierce Eagles without knocking a wheel off?'

'If you'd just stick your insufferable head out a little it will be my pleasure to knock that off with it.' She flicked the reins, picking up speed and watched his knuckles tighten. A few moments later they were bowling through the gates with plenty of room to spare.

'Nicely judged.'

Now she'd rattled him a bit she felt better. 'You don't have to sound so surprised. I'm not the imbecile you seem to think I am.' She grinned at him. 'By the way, your kiss was better than Gerald's. You kissed me as though you wanted too, not because you thought you ought to. I enjoyed it, so don't insult me again by saying you are sorry you did it, and making me feel that it was my fault. I shall now go off and swoon in private, so I don't embarrass you further.'

She walked off without another word, leaving him staring after her.

Flynn Collins was pleased with himself. He now knew Magnus Kern by sight, and where he lived. He grinned to himself. He could have killed that man there and then, 'cepting he only had his knife with him, and that could be messy. His gun was in the sack he carried. Better a bullet fired from behind. It was much quicker.

He went to the marketplace and stood with those looking to be hired.

'Name?' A beefy farmer asked, walking round him and pinching the muscles in his arm.

He remembered he'd used the Maitland name with the lad holding Kern's horse. He'd been caught off guard, and couldn't risk using it again. 'Doyle ... Jimmy Doyle.'

'There's eight weeks drainage work, ploughing in stubble, stable work and muck-spreading to be done, as well as seeing to the stock. Eight shillings a week, and all found. You can sleep snug in the stable loft, and if you prove satisfactory I'll keep you on through the spring planting.'

The man wanted a lot for his eight miserable shillings. 'The wage isn't much.'

'Beggars can't be choosers, and it's all found. Take it or leave it, Doyle.'

Flynn remembered to tug at his forelock. It would do, though there was easier ways of earn-ing money than toiling in the fields, and he already had a good bankroll to take to America with him. He'd found good pickings on market day amongst the jostling crowds. 'Thank you, sir.'

'You can come with me on the cart then. I have to drop by the mill to pick up a sack of flour for my wife.' He patted his stout stomach and smiled, trying to make up for his meanness with money by being jocular. 'I hope you've got an appetite on you, because Mrs Perkins serves a good-sized dinner. You won't go hungry while you're with me.'

Flynn smiled. 'That's nice to know, sir. I haven't eaten all day.' He didn't draw attention to his purpose by asking the whereabouts of Fierce Eagles. Which was just as well, because they passed the gates on the way to the farm, which proved to be in an isolated position.

Perfect, he thought. Nobody would look for him here.

He thought about the five hundred pounds bounty on his head. A pity he couldn't turn himself in and claim it. It would set him up for life. There was a niggle of resentment in him too. If it hadn't been for that little bit of business to take care of he would have been in America by now. Still, at least his cousin in Poole didn't know about the price on his head. The man didn't have much, but hadn't done a dishonest act in his life, and although he didn't approve of Flynn he'd agreed to help him, just to get rid of him.

Well, Magnus Kern, he thought. When I get rid of you there will be nobody to pay the bounty

233

out of your estate, and I'll be long gone. He gazed at the broad back of the farmer, and smiled. The man would hand him over like a shot if he knew about the reward.

Luckily, nobody around here had seen his face, or could connect him to Flynn Collins, wanted murderer – and he had one contact he could still trust, though he intended to tell him nothing.

Fourteen

Up to her neck in water, Sarette sighed as she gazed around the bathroom. It was pretty, with a flowered bathtub, matching pedestal, tank and sink.

It was more convenient than having to use the bathroom in the hall, which catered for the rest of the rooms on this floor, with the exception of the one Magnus called his own. The bathroom she luxuriated in had been installed for the use of Mr John's wife and daughter. They'd bathed in the very tub in which she now soaked.

'I wish you'd both lived for him, but you didn't and now I hope you're all together and enjoying the reunion. He missed you both so much,' she whispered.

Coals glowed in a little black fireplace set into the wall, and around that was a fireguard with towels hanging over it to warm. Steam glazed the walls. Feeling drowsy, she closed her eyes and thought about Mr John. She tried to imagine him as the master here, living a happy life with his wife and child and not expecting it to end, then ... *tragedy!* Her mind moved on to the goldfields, to the privation they'd suffered. Had he blamed himself for this loss, and chosen to deprive himself of luxury as punishment?

Ada bustled in just as she was about to fall asleep. 'Mr Kern said I'm to accompany you to the hotel, and look after you. Fancy that ... me in a posh hotel being a proper maid. Verna's upset. She said the master should've asked her because she's the senior maidservant. But you wanted the housekeeper's job, I says to her. Be content, you can't have everything. Here, bend forward, let me get that hair washed, Miss. You're going to be the prettiest girl there by the time I've finished with you, you wait and see.'

'You know, Ada, I still feel guilty when I soak in this big bath of water. Where I lived in Australia we used to bathe in a small tin tub, then use the water many times over. I could only wedge myself in it with my knees pulled under my chin.'

'Well, I never. Don't you worry, this water won't be wasted. With your permission, as soon as I've got you out and wrapped up warm, I'm going to hop in it and have a quick bath and wash my hair too. You can be drying your hair in front of the fire in the meantime. I don't want to go to some posh hotel looking scruffy, and having the master's valet looking down his long, superior nose at me, and it won't take me long.'

Sarette liked it when Ada was acting as her

maid instead of working in the laundry. She learned a lot about what was going on in the household, and at least she had someone to talk to.

'That valet of his likes everything neat and tidy. Thinks he's something special, George does. He dashes around, and issues orders to everyone as though he owns the place. Branston gets fed up with him because George tittle-tats to the master.'

Exactly as Ada was doing to her, though Sarette didn't want to be unkind and point it out to her.

'All the same, George is good at his job. You never see Mr Kern go out with dirty shoes, or unshaved. Those curls of his are difficult to keep tidy, George said. They've got to be exactly the right length. Mr Kern always looks really handsome, though.'

Sarette smiled under the foamy curtain of her hair and brought an image of Magnus to her mind. 'He certainly does.' She liked his curly hair and the way it ruffled in the breeze. Sometimes she felt like winding a curl round her finger or running her hands through—

A deluge of rinsing water cascaded over her head and she spluttered.

'Stay there a minute or two, Miss. I'm going to put some rose water in the next rinse. George gave me that tip. He told me it will make your hair shine, and it will smell nice when you're in the bedroom and let your hair down. Men like it, apparently.'

'Ada. You're shocking! I'm not married, so

I'm hardly going to have a man in my bedroom when I let my hair down.'

Ada giggled. 'Well, you never know. Men have a way with them that's wickedly persuasive when the mood's on them, and perhaps the master will take a fancy to you, or perhaps Mr Gerald Grimble will. Both of them give you the eye from time to time.'

The kiss Magnus had stolen from her came into her mind. That had been very persuasive. She'd wanted more. 'How do you know about such things?'

'Cook told me, and she was nearly married to a French smuggler who worked for Mr Kern's grandfather.'

'Why didn't she marry him?'

'She discovered he had a wife and family back in France, but don't tell her I told you because it fair broke her heart. Close your eyes, now, Miss.'

The second deluge nearly drowned her and she was surrounded by fragrance.

'Out you come now, Miss, else you'll turn all wrinkly.' Sarette's hair was rubbed vigorously with the towel against Ada's chest and she had a sudden, poignant reminder of making a noise in her throat while her mother did the same to her, and of her mother laughing. Lord, it was ages since she'd remembered her mother, or what she looked like.

Stepping from the bath she found herself enveloped in the warm fluffy towel Ada held out. A hair brush was placed in her hand. 'You brush your hair and dry yourself off while I hop in the tub. It won't take me long.'

'You're spoiling me, Ada. Have a good old soak. I'm quite capable of drying my own hair. It's lovely and warm by the fire.'

'Well, I can't be too long. Mr Kern wants to leave by noon, and he gets impatient if he's made to wait. He's always ahead of time, and wants you to rest after the journey, and before you need to get ready.'

The time flew by, and soon they found themselves almost out of it. 'Just braid my hair, Ada. That will do for now.' Pulling on the jacket of her blue velvet suit, she buttoned it while Ada fixed her hat in place.

The hall clock began to chime the hour. 'Hurry, Miss.' Ada pulled on her coat, grabbed up Sarette's vanity case and headed off.

Sarette waited until the ninth chime had sounded, then made her way down the corridor.

Bong...

She reached the top of the staircase and headed down, her feet sinking into the carpeting.

Bong...

From the bend in the stairs she could see Magnus gazing at the clock then back at his watch, a frown on his face.

Bong...

'I do hope I haven't kept you waiting, Magnus,' she said, descending the last few steps.

His glance swept over her, then he laughed, and, as the twelfth chime quivered into silence, said, 'Perfectly timed, but as it happens, my watch seems to have stopped.'

She returned his smile, absorbing the warmth

of it. 'It probably died from being glared at so often. I do my best to conform to your exacting standards.'

'You're intent on rubbing my nose in them you mean,' he growled. 'I just happen to like things to run on time.'

'What if I hadn't run on your time, but on my own?'

'I would have looked pointedly at my useless watch and growled and grumbled a lot, and you would have taken no notice and laughed at me, just as you're doing now. That's what would have happened.'

'Just like Mr John, only he'd have walked off with long strides and smoke coming from his heels, so I'd have to run to catch up with him. At least you don't do that.'

'There's always a first time.' He took her hand in his. 'Come along. Let's be off.'

She recalled something and came to a halt. 'I've forgotten something. I won't be long,' and she scurried off up the stairs again, followed by an exaggerated sigh.

He was tapping his fingers on the ornate silver top of his cane when she came down, but said nothing.

The gig was waiting behind the carriage, and shafted to the black gelding, who tossed his head, snorted steam and stamped his foreleg, as if eager to be off. There were two horses to pull the carriage, sturdy, well-behaved chestnuts. Swathed in a warm coat, top hat and boots Robert beamed at them from the driver's seat. 'Good morning, sir ... Miss Maitland.'

239

She waved to him. 'You look splendid, Robert. Don't forget to wear your gloves, else your hands will get chapped.'

'I've got them here, thank you, Miss.'

George held the door open. Magnus assisted her in, then took the seat opposite her. 'Ada and George will be coming separately in the gig. We have too many packages and not enough horsepower to make the journey comfortably otherwise. He leaned forward to tuck a rug around her knees, then tapped his cane against the roof. The carriage lurched forward.

The day was cold, but bright. Most of the trees had been stripped bare by winter, and the branches scratched against the pale blue roof of the sky with bony fingers. A barn was painted green with moss, against which a naked apple tree splayed its limbs. One apple, brown and rotten, clung to a branch. Holly berries were startling scarlet clusters nestled in spikes and the brown earth was crumbled into ridges.

The English landscape, and the unpredictable weather was a constant source of fascination to Sarette. She had a strong sense of belonging to the place. Her gaze shifted to where Magnus sat, his dark head relaxed against the corner cushions, the expression in his eyes far away, as if he was exploring his thoughts, as she'd been doing. She belonged to *him*, too, but in some intangible way, as though they'd been meant to cross paths at some time in their lives.

He didn't move, but his eyes had narrowed in on her, as if he'd become aware of her scrutiny. They gazed at each other without saying anything, but there was communication of sorts, as if she'd touched him at a deeper level of awareness. The faint, wry smile he offered set her stomach fluttering skyways. Something significant had happened between them, but she didn't know what.

'What are you thinking, Sarry?'

'That your uncle filled my mind with this place that he loved, and that was his gift to me.'

'You think of him a lot, don't you?'

'Yes. I don't mean to, but every so often I see something that Mr John told me about, and I remember his passion in the telling of it.'

'I know what you mean. I've been reading his journals.'

'What did he say about me?'

'He said you'd ask, and I was to tell you that what he wrote in his journal was none of your damned business.'

She burst into laughter. 'As if I'd listen. Tell me anyway.'

'You tell me about the time you removed buckshot from his rear end.'

'He told me not to look at his arse. So I said how could I remove the buckshot if I didn't and he said to pretend I wasn't looking. So I did that. What did Mr John say happened?'

'He said you laughed and dug the buckshot out with no thought for his comfort. Then you poured iodine into the wounds, and told him not to be a baby when he winced. So he did what he was told.'

It wasn't a wince, it was a yelp, and Mr John never, *ever* did what he was told. He was a rebel through and through, and I think that's why I liked him so much.' Her smile faded. 'I do hope he didn't suffer.'

'He never saw the bullet coming and it was instant, straight through the heart. No, he didn't suffer.'

She said. 'I wonder if it was a coincidence, his killer being Flynn Collins.'

'Why should it be?'

'When I'd told him what Flynn had done, your uncle said if he ever ran into him, he'd take him to task over it on my behalf.'

'So you think he ran into Collins after you left, and he had it out with him, then Collins lay in wait for him and shot him in the back.'

She nodded.

'It's quite possible, I suppose. There must have been a reason behind the shooting. I hope you're not about to blame yourself.'

She shrugged as something else niggled at the back of her mind. 'That man in Dorchester the other day, the one who called himself Jack Maitland. He reminded me of Flynn Collins. The boy said his accent might have been a Scot ... but then, he might have been Irish.'

He smiled at that. 'Sarry, my love, I think your imagination is running away with you a little and that would be just too much of a coincidence.'

'Yes ... yes, I suppose it is.'

'Then let's drop this morbid subject.'

She smiled at him, trying to keep her excitement under control. 'I'm so looking forward to this ball.'

'I'm looking forward to it myself. I'm sure you'll enjoy it.'

'Will there be an orchestra playing music?'

He looked slightly pained. 'Of course there will. It's a ball.'

Alarm filled her. 'What if nobody wants to dance with me?'

'I daresay I'll manage to swing you round and crush your toes for you now and again. You're far too excited, Sarry. Stop this, else I'll take you back home and leave you there.'

'I feel sort of breathless.'

'If you faint I'll throw you out of the carriage into the bushes.' He moved across to sit beside her. 'Tell me you're not going to faint. I never know what to do with fainting women.'

'Do women faint often when they're with you, then?'

'Luckily, no.'

'When one does, you should loosen their corsets,' she suggested, and poked him in the ribs. 'Don't worry, I'm not about to faint. I told you, I prattle when I'm nervous.'

'So you do.' When he tipped up her chin and kissed her she stopped prattling.

Sarette had rested all afternoon. Now she wore the pale green gown Magnus had bought her from Madame Maria's salon. She also wore the pearl set that Gerald and Ignatious Grimble had given her. In fact, her outfit had been provided by three men.

'There, you can look in the mirror now.'

A knock came at the door before she could,

243

and Ada wailed, 'It can't be Mr Kern. It's too early.'

It was a messenger with a small box from Magnus. Inside, in a bed of pink velvet was a sparkling brooch in the shape of a crescent moon with a trembling star hanging from the bottom point.

She turned it this way and that, watching it sparkle. 'How pretty it is.'

Ada pinned it to one side of her waist, then helped her hands and arms into long kid gloves. She placed the loop of a fan over her wrist, then turned her to face the mirror and said with satisfaction, 'There.'

The image that gazed back at her was that of an elegant woman, and she felt more grown-up than she ever had in her life before. Was this the dusty urchin that had been abandoned on goldfields? Look at me now, Mr John, she thought. I'm going to make Magnus proud of me tonight, just you wait and see.

He came for her shortly afterwards, his smile reminding her of the small intimacy between them in the carriage. She wished he'd kiss her again, only longer and harder.

'You're exquisite. Well done, Ada,' he said. 'Go down to the servant's dining room and get yourself some dinner. George will show you where it is.'

After Ada had gone, Sarette smiled. 'Thank you for the brooch, that was sweet of you. I have something for you, too.'

She picked up the object, which she'd wrapped in her lace handkerchief and handed it to him.

After he'd uncovered it he said with some astonishment, 'My uncle's watch? I'd wondered what had happened to it.'

'He gave it to me just as I was leaving. He said it would prove to you that I was genuine. He also told me to sell it if I ran out of money. It's gold, you see. And it has his name in it. I know he would have wanted you to have it. I was going to give it to you for Christmas. It's just a little early.'

Magnus was staring down at it.

'You do like it, don't you? I'd never have sold it, and I always intended to give it to you. You're not cross with me for not handing it over sooner?'

'This was one of my uncle's most treasured possessions. I bought it for him, for his fiftieth birthday.' Magnus fitted the case into the pocket of his waistcoat, and the chain through the aperture made for it. Her handkerchief went into another pocket. 'I'm pleased it wasn't lost. I'll treasure it, too.'

When she reached up to kiss his cheek he turned his head and claimed her mouth. It was soft and warm, and this time he took her bottom lip between his teeth and gently sucked it into his mouth before letting it go. She could have sworn that her toes curled.

'Don't you dare kiss me like that again,' she scolded.

'Why? Are you frightened you'll faint and I'll have to loosen your corset.'

'To be honest ... yes!'

He laughed, and held out his arm to her. 'May

I remind you that it was you who kissed me. All I did was respond. Shall we go? I don't want to be late.'

She grinned at him, feeling the excitement of attending her first ball quivering inside her. 'No, that wouldn't do at all.'

Gerald was standing with his brothers when Magnus came down the stairs with Sarry on his arm.

He hadn't been expecting to see Magnus, and could have kicked himself. He'd had no idea that Magnus had been pulling the wool over his eyes. My God, what has he done to the girl? he thought. She's glowing. So was Magnus come to that. Gerald was suspicious, but admiring of his friend's ability to outwit him on this occasion.

They were shown to their table, where Magnus greeted his partner Clive Farrington and his wife. Seated at his friend's table was a fatuous old magistrate called James Huff, who was as deaf as a post, and his rotund wife, who was dressed in green satin frills, and weighed down with so many diamonds she appeared to be wearing a chandelier. Poor old Magnus getting stuck on a table with those two, he thought. Thank goodness he personally had a large family to hide amongst.

'Who's that with Magnus Kern?' Jessica Fenwick asked his sister Olivia.

'Her name's Sarette Maitland. She's Magnus's ward, I believe.'

'The woman who's living with him at Fierce Eagles?' Jessica sounded shocked. 'They say the late Mr Kern found her in the Australian countryside living with a tribe of natives, and sent her here to be tamed and educated.'

'Ah ... so the ubiquitous *they* have singled her out, have they?' Gerald said. 'Poor Sarette. She and Magnus will be joining us for Christmas, so you'll be able to form your own opinion of whether she can use a knife and fork properly. Perhaps we should cook up a dish of snakes for her to eat.'

'Gerald, don't be so churlish,' Olivia said sharply. 'Jessica wasn't to know that Sarette Maitland is a particular friend of yours.'

Jessica sniffed. 'The gown she's wearing must have cost a fortune. Miss Maitland is lucky she has such a wealthy patron.'

Olivia said sharply, 'Shush, please keep your voice down, Jessica.'

Before I stuff a tablecloth in your mouth, Gerald thought uncharitably, because it had just occurred to him that he'd have to apologize to Sarette for withdrawing his invitation, and without being armed with the excuse Magnus had used on his behalf. But first he was placed in the position of needing to defend her. 'Miss Maitland is a respectable and charming young woman who has been left a fortune in her own right—' He clamped his mouth over his slip of the tongue.

Olivia grinned. 'I know all about it, Gerald dear. You men don't realize how indiscreet you can be at the family dinner table.'

'Then I hope you keep anything you hear private, Olivia. Now, I must go and fill in Sarette's dance card. This is her first ball, I understand.'

'Then I do hope it turns out to be a memorable one for her,' Olivia said, and exchanged a sly glance with Jessica.

At that moment Sarette caught sight of him. She tugged gently at Magnus's sleeve, something that spoke of a new familiarity between them. Magnus was not usually the type of man to encourage such familiarity.

Gerald found himself warmed by her smile, then she whispered something to Magnus.

His friend glanced over, his eyes as unfathomable as his smile, except for the challenge in them. They bowed slightly to each other, like a couple of fencers about to joust.

Gerald excused himself and crossed to their table. 'I thought you didn't intend to come, Magnus.'

Magnus smiled blandly. 'I decided I didn't want to disappoint Sarette since she'd never been to a ball before.'

'And this one is full of old legal gentlemen with not much sap left in them to expend on dance.' Picking up her hand he kissed her knuckles. 'My profound apologies for letting you down, Sarry. The pressures of work.'

'A headache wasn't it?' she said, and when Gerald heard Magnus stifle a laugh he knew that Sarette was aware of the truth.

'You know it wasn't. I simply forgot after family pressure persuaded me to escort someone else. They are eager to marry me off. I can only hope that you'll forgive me the insult and allow me the honour to be the first to fill out your

248

dance card.'

'Thank you, Gerald, but Judge Huff has already done that by claiming the second dance.'

'Commiserations,' he whispered in her ear, and she giggled and handed him her card. He filled in three spaces. 'I hope to dance you off your feet tonight, which will also give me the opportunity to grovel all evening and redeem myself.'

'Thank you, Gerald. You don't have to redeem yourself. I quite understand that you must put your family's wishes first.'

'You're an angel, and the most beautiful woman here, Sarry,' he said sincerely.

Magnus gave a faint smile. 'Your loss was my gain, Gerald.'

Mrs Huff gently coughed and Gerald's eyes went to her overpowering greenness. Best to get it over with early, before she began to perspire, he supposed.

'Except for you of course, Mrs Huff. You look magnificent, but then, you always do. Perhaps you'd honour me with the second dance.'

His father came over to greet Sarette with old-fashioned courtliness. 'My dear, how lovely you look. Can I book you for the last dance before supper?'

'Thank you, Mr Grimble. I would be honoured to dance with you.'

'Good, then perhaps you'd allow me to escort you in to supper, as well.'

Her glance went to Magnus, who gave a faint smile and nodded.

Gerald's eyes narrowed. Magnus seemed to

have her on a long rein at the moment. Her shoulders were as smooth and creamy as ivory, he thought, looking down at them. There was something about her now. She was less the child and more the woman in her thinking and ways, and she had Magnus eating out of her hand.

Or had she? Perhaps it was the other way round because he'd never known Magnus to allow anyone to lead him by the nose. But the last time he'd seen the two of them together they'd been at loggerheads. He teased himself with the infuriating thought that Magnus was better positioned to take advantage of the girl. But his friend had long resisted the pressure to wed anyone, and Gerald was surprised he'd suggested a scheme where marriage was the outcome.

When Gerald met Magnus's eyes, dark and implacable, he didn't know whether he wanted to lose this wager, or win it. His mouth twitched into a smile. The winner of this would be the loser, Magnus had said. Hah! Trust him to come up with something complicated like this, though it had seemed like a good idea at the time.

The music started and he made his excuses, remembering he had to dance with Jessica first. Her mouth had a mean, thin look to it when she gossiped.

'...and Felicia Fowler said her mother saw them coming out of Madame Marie's salon together ... and we all know what type of women *she* designs for,' Jessica was saying to Olivia as he approached.

He hid his distaste and smiled at her. 'Our

dance, I believe.'

Her smile changed from spiteful to simpering. 'Oh, Gerald, there you are. I thought you'd forgotten about poor little me.'

Gerald could only wish *poor little her* would allow him to as he led her out on the floor and she almost manacled herself to his arm.

Fifteen

The dancing opened with a quadrille, and they squared up with the Farringtons, Judge Huff and his wife, and another couple.

Sarette's heart was beating fast because she wasn't sure of the steps, but by following the other women's moves she soon gained in confidence. Magnus winked at her as they met in the middle and she took heart.

As the evening progressed it became obvious to Sarette that she lacked practised dancing skills. Just as obvious, her partners didn't seem to mind her inexperience, as a polonaise was followed by a country dance, which was followed by a waltz. She certainly didn't lack for partners as the evening progressed.

She found herself partnered by Ignatious Grimble, who gazed ruefully at her when a polka was announced. 'Oh, dear, I was hoping for something far less vigorous.'

'So was I,' she said, and smiled. 'I'm quite out

of breath, Mr Grimble. Let's go and get some refreshment, then sit and talk instead.'

They skirted the mêleé of swiftly revolving couples and went through to the supper room. A little later they were ensconced on a couch in the corner, and Sarette was gratefully sipping on a lemonade. A maid brought a plate of savouries for them to enjoy.

'Are you enjoying yourself, Sarette?'

'Enormously, though I'm not a very good dancer, despite Gerald's best efforts to teach me.'

'The more you dance, the easier it will become. I thought you danced gracefully, and were light on your feet.'

'Thank you, Mr Grimble, you are a gentleman, and your kindness always makes me feel better about myself.'

He patted her hand. 'I'm pleased Magnus brought you along. It was about time you were launched into society. People have long been curious about you.'

Magnus was talking to a rather beautiful-looking woman on the other side of the room. Her face was animated. As he was about to depart she flirtatiously placed her fan on his arm to detain him, and he shrugged it off.

Ignatious gently coughed to attract her attention. What had they been talking about before she'd set eyes on Magnus with the woman? She tore her glance away. Ah ... yes. 'They are curious about me, but why?'

'They all knew John Kern, and most of them know Magnus. Did you imagine his colleagues

252

wouldn't be curious, when he took a complete stranger into his house?'

'I never really thought about it. Fierce Eagles is isolated, and not many people visit.'

'That will change over New Year. Everyone will want to meet you.'

The music stopped and a crush of people headed for the supper tables, talking and laughing.'

'Ah, there you are, father.'

'Olivia ... and Miss Fenwick. Have you been introduced to Miss Maitland yet?'

'No, we have not, and I'm quite cross about it since both you and Gerald have known her for over a year and said not one word.'

'Neither Gerald nor I are in the habit of discussing our clients or their business interests with you, Olivia. You should know that.'

Olivia's face reddened a little. 'How do you do, Miss Maitland.'

'It's a pleasure to meet you, Miss...' Sarette gazed at Ignatious with an enquiry in her eyes.

'Mrs Crossly,' Olivia said.

Ignatious rose. 'Olivia is married to Miss Fenwick's cousin. You will excuse me, won't you? There is someone I need to speak to, so I'll leave you with the ladies.'

Sarette smiled at Olivia after her father had gone. 'Gerald has only ever referred to you by your first name.'

'As he would, since Gerald is my brother.'

Obviously they were not to be on first name terms. Sarette coloured a little at the put down, then turned to the other woman with her friendliest smile, even though she could sense some hostility in her manner. 'How do you do, Miss Fenwick.'

Jessica Fenwick looked her up and down. 'I do very well. That's a beautiful gown, and expensive-looking. I'm quite crawling with curiosity. May I ask where you purchased it?'

Something told Sarette to be wary. 'I have several gowns, and I can't quite recall where this particular one was purchased.'

'I understand you were a friend of Mr John Kern.' Jessica laughed. 'They're saying he found you living with a tribe of naked natives in the desert and he rescued you, civilized you, and taught you some manners.'

Jessica Fenwick could do with being taught some herself, but Sarette wasn't going to be the one to do it, so she laughed. 'Oh, how quaint. You must point these people out and I'll endeavour to correct that assumption.'

'Is it true that John Kern took up highway robbery and was shot by police?'

Anger raced through her, so she trembled with the effort to control it. 'Do you find pleasure in repeating such scurrilous gossip, Miss Fenwick?'

A hand closed around her elbow and she felt relief when Magnus said, 'Sarette, there's someone I'd like you to meet. You will excuse us, won't you, ladies?' He steered her away, past the woman he'd been talking to, who gave her a prolonged stare.

'Who's that woman?' she asked.

'An acquaintance. She's married to an Italian count. Should I know what Olivia and Jessica

254

were saying to you?'

'No, they were scratching like cats and I scratched back. You stopped me from strangling Miss Fenwick with my bare hands, you know.'

He chuckled. 'Something I would have enjoyed immensely, but which is not quite socially acceptable. Can you manage them?'

'Yes, and I promise there won't be any bodies strewn about on the floor when I leave. You don't have to worry about me letting you down, Magnus. I'm not going to prove to anyone that I'm the savage they all imagine I am.'

'I'm not worrying. From what I've seen and heard tonight you put most of the other women to shame. I don't want you to become upset.'

'I promise not to embarrass you,' she said stiffly.

'That's not what I meant.'

She gave him a smile, knowing he was thinking only of her feelings on this occasion. 'You'll have to excuse me, Magnus. My hair decoration is coming loose.'

In public view, he touched a finger against a stray wisp of hair to tuck it gently behind her ear. She shivered, and only just stopped herself from turning her face against his hand and purring like a cat. 'I'm going to seek Ada out and ask her to secure it for me. The dancing is very energetic, and I'm enjoying the music.'

'I'll wait for you at the bottom of the staircase.'

Sarette took the opportunity to use the cloakroom on the way back down. When she came out the woman she'd seen talking to Magnus

was standing in front of the mirror. She smiled. 'You must be Sarette Maitland.'

'Yes, I am'

'I'm Isabelle, Contessa Carsurina.' Her glance fell on the brooch at Sarette's waist and she smiled and said casually, 'Isn't that the brooch that Magnus gave me as a birthday gift? I wouldn't have thought of wearing it in such a manner. It looks so pretty.'

'Thank you,' Sarette said in as cool a voice as possible, though she was churning with embarrassment.

'I returned it when I married, of course. I'm glad Magnus found a use for it. I wanted no reminder of a man who led me to believe...' A tear trembled on the woman's lashes and Sarette nearly recoiled when she grabbed her hands. 'You are so young, and I really must warn you, dear. Magnus Kern will not allow you to keep the legacy that his uncle left you.'

Taken aback, and her heart beginning to pound Sarette gazed at the woman and whispered, 'Legacy?'

'The house on the cliff and the income from the remainder of John Kern's investments.'

'I don't know what you're talking about.'

'Oh, my dear. You don't know? Perhaps you should ask Ignatious Grimble. He handled the Kern estate.' Drying her hands, Isabelle gently touched her cheek. 'I assume ... but yes, you would be involved. You're beautiful and Magnus adores having beautiful things around him. Even so, he must think highly of you to take you under his roof after you ... *knew* his uncle. Per-

256

haps I should warn you. In my experience, what Magnus gets he keeps, until he tires of it and decides to discard it. But still, you are envied by every woman here.'

'You're mistaken in your assumption, Contessa. I was John Kern's ward, nothing more, nothing less. Now I am Magnus Kern's ward. Why would you presume to suggest otherwise?'

'My pardon, but I understood...?' Isabelle raised a haughty eyebrow and swept away.

Sarette discovered that her fingers were curled into fists, and she felt like ripping the basin from the wall and throwing it down the stairs after the woman.

Envy was such an ugly word, she thought. Why should anyone envy her for living under Magnus Kern's roof? She flattened her hands against her warm cheeks as she realized that most women would find him attractive – that she did herself on occasion, and that Isabelle must have been Magnus's mistress. As for John Kern ... how dare they sully the memory of such a wonderful man?

She hadn't imagined that either man had been celibate all their lives. And she had no reason to chide him for his past, or present behaviour. For all she knew he could have another woman he visited. He often stayed out until the early hours. Still, it was really none of her business what he did.

And the gossipmongers thought that John Kern had left her a house and a fortune? She laughed out loud, if without mirth, amazed by such a notion. How silly they all were. Magnus

wouldn't have kept that from her, neither would Gerald.

She stood there a while, waiting for her anger to subside while trying to sort things out in her mind. She realized she was avoiding going back down to him. Her chin came up. She'd promised not to embarrass Magnus, so she'd endure these gossiping creatures, even though it was more than they deserved.

Magnus watched her sweep down the stairs, and took her hand in his when she reached the bottom. 'Is everything all right?'

It wasn't, because she was now feeling un-settled. But she couldn't go running to him every time somebody upset her. Mrs Lawrence had told her that a lady should rise above petty annoyances. 'Everything is fine.' But she couldn't quite meet his eyes.

'You were gone longer than I expected.'

'My hair took a while to fix.'

His smile expanded, his eyes gazed into hers. They were honest, guileless eyes. No, he'd never cheat her, neither would Mr Grimble or Gerald. They were well-respected lawyers, the three of them would have had to conspire to do such a thing.

'You don't lie very well. Was it Isabelle?' he said. 'I saw her coming down the stairs with a smug look on her face.'

'Yes, it was. She seemed intent on letting me know she used to be a particular friend of yours.' Her fingers touched against the brooch. 'She said it was a birthday gift to her that she'd returned to you.'

His mouth twisted into a wry smile. 'She did return some jewellery I gave her, but that brooch wasn't amongst it. I purchased that especially for you as a reminder of your first ball. Would you have minded very much if it had been Isabelle's?' he said, his gaze intent on her face.

She made her smile as natural as possible. 'I'd lie and tell you I didn't mind, when secretly I would mind.'

He laughed. 'Your honesty is refreshing and your reasoning ... soundly female.'

She looked up at him then. 'She thinks we are lovers. Everyone does.'

Light flickered in the depths of his eyes. 'There's bound to be some speculation. Take no notice of it.'

'There's a rumour that Mr John discovered me living with a naked tribe in the desert, and Isabelle imagines I was involved with him, as well as you,' she said indignantly.

He chuckled. 'I've heard it. My uncle didn't give a damn about what anyone thought.'

'Do you?'

'No. Only small-minded people find pleasure in making such unsubstantiated statements. Dance the next waltz with me.'

'I promised it to Gerald.'

'Disappoint him.'

She grinned as she looked past his shoulder. 'All right, but he's looking for me.'

'He won't find you.' He pulled her into the middle of the floor just as the waltz began.

Magnus was light on his feet and he guided her towards the opposite side of where they'd last seen Gerald. Magnus's height gave him an advantage as he swung her round, for he could track in which direction Gerald moved. The music was romantic, and as he gradually pulled her closer while managing to avoid the rest of the dancers, she didn't resist.

'We dance well together,' he said, and she gazed up at him.

'I like the waltz. It's easy to remember.'

They were hemmed in by dancers now. He pulled her closer, so her head was resting against his heartbeat for a few moments, and she could have sworn that his mouth brushed the top of her head. The next moment the crowd opened out and he swung her out and around. She saw Gerald eyeing the dance floor and Magnus chuckled as he swung her in the opposite direction.

He looked into her eyes and she smiled, enjoying the game, but finding herself captured by their enigmatic darkness. Her smile faded and so did his, and they seemed to be the only people on the dance floor. What strange magic was this? It was as if she was alone with him in the middle of this crowd, and he was the only person she could see. They came to a standstill and he spoke her name in a whisper, 'Sarette.'

Gerald tapped him on the shoulder. 'You didn't think you were going to get away with it, did you? Hand her over, at once.' He was about to whisk her out of Magnus's arms and into his own when the music ended. 'Nice timing,' he grumbled.

Magnus gave a deep, satisfied chuckle that

made the roots of Sarette's hair tingle. 'It seems to me that I did get away with it.'

Clive Farrington claimed the next dance, much to Gerald's chagrin.

An hour later the ballroom was beginning to thin out. She bade farewell to Judge Huff, who'd turned out to be a jolly man. He pinched her cheek. Mrs Huff kissed her. 'It was lovely to meet a friend of John Kern, rascal though he was. I'd like to hear more about what he did in the Antipodes. You must ask Magnus to bring you over for a visit once New Year is over.'

'I should like that, Mrs Huff. Thank you so much.'

'Better still, I keep an open house on New Year's Day. Come the day before, I'm sure we can accommodate you,' Magnus said, as if they were what everybody thought – a couple!

Gerald finally got to dance a polka with her, and they galloped around the floor until she was dizzy and laughing. She collapsed in a chair while Gerald went off to fetch her some lemonade.

Now Sarette was resting she began to feel tired, and stifled a yawn behind her hand.

Magnus joined her. 'Tired?'

She nodded.

'Then I'll escort you up to your room and you can retire for the night.'

'But Gerald—'

'I'll say goodnight to him on your behalf.' He held out his hand to her and she took it.

'I've had a wonderful evening. Thank you,' she said when they reached the door to her room.

'It was entirely my pleasure.'

She placed her finger across his lips. 'Not entirely. Now, allow me to express my own pleasure without interruption. I enjoyed your company, and I'm glad you weren't so stiff and formal as you usually are, and that we didn't argue about anything of importance.'

He slanted his head to one side, appearing amused by her observation. Gently, he nipped the end of her finger. 'That's because you were a well-behaved child and I didn't have to evoke my strict rules of wardship.'

'Would you have preferred it had I been a child?'

His head slanted to one side and his observation of her was intense. 'No doubt you'd have made a damned nuisance of yourself by wanting to sit on my knee all the time. Besides which, you would have called me uncle, and I'd have had to pretend I liked you.'

Her stomach sank. 'You don't like me?'

'I adore you, and no, I wouldn't have preferred a child. That's the only compliment you're getting from me. You've had too much attention tonight as it is. Beware of Gerald, you can't trust him.'

'He said exactly the same about you.'

'I know. Perhaps you should listen to him. Sometimes I'm not so in control of myself as I appear.'

She opened her mouth to argue, then shut it again when he laughed. 'Oh, you.'

She was half expecting him to kiss her goodnight, but he didn't. He opened the door to her room, turned her round and gently pushed her inside. 'Goodnight, Sarry. Sweet dreams.'

Her head seemed filled with thoughts of Magnus, and she told Ada all about the ball as she was readied for bed.

'We're going to the Winter Gardens tomorrow to listen to the orchestra before we go home. They're to play Christmas carols.

'Then you must wear a warm coat. I'll leave it ready for you, Miss. George and I will be going straight back to Fierce Eagles after breakfast.'

No sooner had Sarette laid her head on the pillow than her eyes flew open and her heart began to pound. Gracious, she suspected she was beginning to like Magnus too much! What if he'd been telling the truth when he'd told her not to trust him? Perhaps Mr John *had* left her a fortune. Would Magnus really help himself to it? He might think he was entitled to it because John was his uncle. She wouldn't blame him if he did.

And what about Ignatious and Gerald? Surely they'd help Magnus obtain it, because they'd resent a complete stranger walking into Mr John's home and just taking it all. And it wasn't as if she'd wanted it in the first place. She realized that it would cause enormous problems if it were true.

But then, what were Magnus's plans for her? She couldn't live in his house indefinitely and allow him to support her. People were already gossiping about the nature of their relationship. Not that it bothered him, and he was too honourable to take advantage of her.

Her face grew warm as an insidious little voice in her head pointed out, *He wasn't very honourable with that Isabelle woman. He pretended he loved her then discarded her without a second thought.*

She said out loud, 'What if he does the same to me?'

Don't be stupid, he doesn't even find you attractive, and how do you know he pretended to love her?

She smiled at that. Go away, I'm tired and you're making me cross.

Resolutely, she closed her eyes, and was on the brink of sleep when the insidious voice said, *You're jealous of that contessa creature, aren't you? You've fallen in love with him.*

Her eyes flew open and she thought about it. Inevitably her mind went to Magnus Kern again. Her thoughts about him weren't at all ladylike or innocent, and her feelings, though designed to disrupt any notion of sleeping, were extremely and sinfully pleasant.

She cuddled her pillow against her, smiled and admitted to herself ... perhaps she had.

Sixteen

Christmas at the Grimbles was pleasant.

Most of the Grimble family and invited guests had gathered in the home of Ignatious, and it was a happy, laughing crowd of adults and children. Even Olivia was fairly polite to her – until the mood suddenly degenerated.

The problem for Sarette was Jessica Fenwick, who was all false sweetness in company, and who attached herself to Gerald's arm like a leech whenever she could.

If she caught Sarette alone she was rude and unpleasant, knocking her with her elbow as she moved past. 'Guttersnipe,' she hissed, on one occasion.

Anger rose in Sarette, and she felt like strangling Jessica. But she wasn't about to do anything to shame Magnus, who was deep in talk with Ignatious. Nobody seemed inclined to disturb them, least of all, her.

After dinner Olivia was persuaded to play the piano for carols and they all gathered around as she displayed her skills with several trills and flourishes. Jessica leaned on the piano in a pose that was designed to be noticed and admired, her face animated as she sang. She had a lovely voice, and made the most of the opportunity to show off her asset.

Sarette discovered Gerald by her side. His face was flushed and he was smiling too much, the result of a surfeit of Christmas spirit, she thought. She wanted to giggle when he winked at her. Gerald was priceless, and constantly made her laugh. As the other voices rose in song he took advantage to slide a hand under her elbow and steer her out of the room and into the hall.

'Gerald, what on earth are you doing? Release me.'

'I haven't had a chance to talk to you alone all day, Sarry, my love.'

'It's cold in the hall. Let's go back in and sing carols,' she suggested gently.

'It's Christmas, and I want to kiss you under the mistletoe.'

She laughed. 'Ah, so that's it. There is no mistletoe here.'

He brought his hand out from behind his back, flourished a small twig of mistletoe and said triumphantly, 'There, I brought one with me.' At the same time he pulled her close and kissed her. There was no escaping his embrace and she gave into it with good grace until he prolonged it and it became intrusive. Alarm filled her. She began to struggle and turned her head away and pushed against his chest. 'Stop it, Gerald.'

The next minute the door to the drawing room was thrown open and Jessica gave an outraged scream. 'You shameless hussy.'

Gerald staggered backwards, caught his heel on a rug and sprawled on his back.

The music suddenly stopped and people crowded in the doorway. Ignatious pushed his way through. 'Good gracious, Gerald. What's going on here?'

'That hussy was kissing him,' Jessica said shrilly, and pointed an accusing finger at Sarette.

Gerald laughed. 'Who's a hussy? Sarry? That's preposterous. She's as innocent as a newborn lamb. I was trying to kiss her and she was putting up a fight. How else d'you think I got down here?' Gerald began to laugh and Sarette nervously grinned.

'Explain please, Gerald,' Ignatious said, giving a hand to help his son to his feet.

'Certainly, father. I was attempting to kiss Miss Maitland under the mistletoe. She was reluctant. I was about to propose marriage to her. I must admit I was hoping for a bit more privacy than this, but there, I suppose this will have to do.' He fell to his knees, took her hand in his and kissed it. 'Will you marry me, Sarette, dear?'

Desperation filled her and she looked around for Magnus, her face flaming, before pleading, 'You're making a fool of yourself and you're embarrassing everyone, Gerald. I think you've celebrated Christmas too well. Please get up.'

'I can't. My head's spinning.'

Magnus stepped through the crowd and took hold of his collar. 'Stop making a horse's arse of yourself.' Unsympathetically, he hauled Gerald to his feet.

Gerald made choking noises until Magnus thought to loosen his grip. Two of Gerald's younger brothers took over the task of propping him up, grinning at each other.

Gerald gave Magnus a pathetic look. 'I feel a bit worse for wear, Mags.'

'I know you do. You never could hold your drink. Your brothers will take you upstairs to lie down for a bit, and I daresay you'll live to annoy us another day.'

Gerald wagged a finger at Magnus and grinned. 'I meant what I said. I'll marry Sarry if she'll have me. You will, won't you, Sarry? You can keep the damned legacy—'

Jessica advanced on Gerald and he cringed away. 'Get that harpy away from me.'

'You obnoxious cad!' Jessica said dramatically and, bursting into floods of tears, she flew into Olivia's arms. Olivia made soothing noises and glared at Sarette. 'See what happens when you invite a person of such low morals into the family home, father.'

'Enough, Olivia. Miss Maitland is entirely blameless.' Ignatious looked quite distressed when he turned to her. 'I'm so sorry this has happened, Sarette. Please accept my apologies.'

Sarette managed to smile at him, though she'd been embarrassed by Gerald's public declaration and felt like crying. 'It wasn't your fault, really. I'm not going to take the proposal seriously. He will have forgotten about it by morning, and we can all laugh about it. See how contrite he looks.'

But Gerald was far from contrite. He grinned at her from the stairs, and blew her a kiss. 'I'm not trite at all.'

Sarette couldn't help but giggle, albeit ner-

vously, and Magnus chuckled. 'It's about time we left, I think. I want to be home before it gets dark. Thank you for your hospitality, Ignatious.'

When they were under way Magnus said to her. 'You handled that well.'

'How can I be cross with Gerald when he makes me laugh? He's such fun to be with. I expect he'll have forgotten about it by tomorrow.'

'And if he hasn't ... what will your answer be?'

She shrugged. How could she accept Gerald as a husband when she loved his closest friend? 'I had formed an impression that Miss Fenwick had a claim to him. He was cruel to her.'

'Miss Fenwick has been given no reason to think that Gerald is interested in her. All the same, Ignatious will have him carpeted tomorrow, and he'll apologize to her, and to us. Despite his quirks, Gerald's heart is in the right place, and he'd make you a good husband.'

Sarette supposed it would be convenient for Magnus if she married Gerald and left Fierce Eagles. She wanted to ask him about the legacy, since it was the second time she'd heard it mentioned, but she didn't want to break the mood. In the meantime she chose not to respond to Magnus's question.

They were home just after dark, stopping to light the carriage lamps on the way. The dogs came bounding out from the kitchen to greet them and to be made a fuss of. Boots's voice had deepened, and he had a gruff woof in comparison to Patch's yap. He seemed to have grown six inches in a week.

The house was warm, a fire was glowing in the drawing room and the dogs followed them in and settled down in front of it. The flames sent out licks of light to reflect off the shiny surfaces and penetrate into the leaping shadows. Magnus didn't bother to turn up the gas lights.

There was a Christmas tree in front of the window. It smelled of pine resin and was decorated with tinsel stars, paper chains and wooden soldiers with drums, trumpets and pipes. On the top, an angel spread her wings as if she were about to fly away. Sarette felt contented, as though she'd always belonged here at Fierce Eagles.

'Can you remember your father and mother?' she asked Magnus.

He looked startled for a moment, then smiled. 'I can just remember my mother. I get little snatches of memory of her. I remember being sick once, and she put her arms around me and sang me to sleep. As for my father? I remember him better, but sometimes get him mixed up with my uncle. I was ten when he died, and lived in Swanage.

'Uncle John woke me in the middle of the night and told me what had happened. He was in practice with Ignatious Grimble then, and he vowed to give up the old ways, though I didn't know what he meant. He cried with me over the loss of his brother and my father, then wrapped me in a blanket and brought me here, to Fierce Eagles.'

'Were you lonely?'

'Sometimes. I spent two years with my cousin

for company, and Gerald often came over to stay. Then Uncle John's wife Annie died. When I was a little older I was sent off to boarding school with Gerald, then finished my studies at Cambridge University. I worked in London for a firm of lawyers and passed the bar exams, which qualified me as a barrister. My uncle went downhill after Margaret died, so I returned to Fierce Eagles to be company for him.'

'Sometimes Mr John was melancholy, but he was always good to me, and he talked about you a lot,' she said. 'I don't think he wanted to feel love any more.'

'He might not have wanted to, but he did. He said as much in his last journal.'

Her eyes came up to search for his in the twilight of the room. 'Will you tell me what he said?'

'He said he'd learned that he was dying, and that you were his heart and he didn't want to hurt you.'

'Mr John said that?' A lump came to her throat and threatened to choke her. 'How lovely ... and how very sad. I would have stayed and looked after him until the end.'

'Which was the very reason why he sent you away. He wouldn't have been able to bear seeing you suffer.'

Fiercely, she said, 'He would have lived longer if Flynn Collins hadn't shot him.'

Magnus sighed. 'If he'd survived that, the quality of his remaining life might not have been all we would wish for him. Did he seem to be in pain when you left him?'

'His stomach had pained him off and on for some time. When I left he seemed his usual self, though he looked a bit gaunt. Mr John was drunk when I first met him, and I don't think I ever saw him entirely sober. He drank too much, every day, starting just after breakfast. He needed it, he said. It stopped him from thinking too much. You're right. He wouldn't have wanted to be dependent on me. He was a very self-sufficient man.'

A knock came at the door.

'Come in, Branston.'

'You're sitting in the dark, sir.'

Branston's voice was a little slurred and Sarette smiled to herself.

'Yes, I suppose we are. It's pleasant, sitting here talking in the firelight.'

'Yes, sir. Is there anything you need?'

'Some cold cuts with bread and butter, a pot of tea and a slice each of that excellent fruitcake cook baked. The rest of the night is your own.'

'Yes, sir. Shall I turn up the light?'

'Not until you come back.'

The door gently closed behind Branston as he left.

'I'm not hungry,' she said.

'You might be later.'

She drew in a deep breath and called on some courage. He seemed to be in a mellow mood, and for her own peace of mind she needed to get to the bottom of this legacy question. 'There's something I wish to ask you, Magnus. When we were at the ball, someone mentioned that your uncle has left me a legacy. Today, Gerald mentioned the same thing.'

'Ah, I should have realized you'd notice his slip of the tongue. May I ask who told you at the ball?'

'The contessa.'

'Isabelle!' He cursed. 'How the devil did she know?'

'Perhaps you talk in your sleep,' she said drily, and could have bitten off her tongue when a frown coloured his voice, shattering the rapport between them.

'I haven't seen Isabelle for months. But why am I explaining something that is clearly none of your business?'

'Unfortunately, strangers seem to know more of my business than I do, and they're gossiping. Obviously they get their information from somewhere. Tell me about the legacy, Magnus.'

'My uncle has left you a house in Bournemouth, and some investments.'

'When were you going to tell me about this?'

'After the addendum to his will had been through probate, and the funds had been released and transferred to me, as your legal guardian.'

'What does addendum, and probate mean? They sound like medical terms.'

He laughed. 'The addendum is the addition he made to his current will, citing you as a beneficiary. It has to go through a formality to be proved legal and correct. It takes a little while.'

'Why didn't you tell me about this before?'

'I didn't see the need. The house was tenanted up until a few weeks ago. I was discussing it with Ignatious earlier today. I've suggested that

273

when a new tenant is found, that the rent be paid directly to you, to spend as you wish.'

'Perhaps I'll choose to live in the house.'

He rose and turned the lights up. The mood was lost and the room was filled with a brightness that made her blink. 'The house is fairly modest in size, but too big for one person to manage, and you wouldn't be able to afford the upkeep, or servants.'

'I don't mind getting my hands dirty. I could take in paying guests or turn it into a school.'

He gave an easy laugh and sat beside her, cajoling, 'Are you telling me you want to leave me, Sarry?'

'Yes ... no. Of course I don't. I love...' She only just stopped herself from telling him she loved him! 'I love it here at Fierce Eagles. I just wished you'd told me before someone else did. It was kind of Mr John to have made all these arrangements for me. I'm grateful that he sent me to Mrs Lawrence, clothed me and fed me. But I'm not a relative or anything, and I didn't deserve it, and all this time I've been feeling as though I was taking charity. Now I feel even worse.'

'You're miffed, aren't you?'

'Yes ... no. I don't know. I think my feelings are hurt, even though I've got no right to complain.'

'Has anyone ever told you that you have a pretty mouth?' He ran his finger gently over the curves then stopped in the middle of her lower lip. 'I like that little pout.'

She blushed. 'Stop trying to distract me. Magnus. Are you listening to anything I'm saying?'

'No, I have no inclination to be lectured. You're sitting under the mistletoe and I'm in the mood to kiss you.'

She groaned. 'Being kissed under the mistletoe has got me into enough trouble today.'

'Then the answer is no?'

'No...'

His mouth claimed hers in a tender caress. She gave a little sigh and her mouth parted under his. His palms cupped her face, his thumbs were a gentle caress behind her ears and his little fingers rested against her cheekbones.

When Branston gently coughed, they sprang apart.

'How long have you been standing there, Branston?'

The butler's eyes rounded in innocence. 'Who, me, sir?'

Sarette giggled when Magnus said, 'Yes, you, sir. I can't see anyone else called Branston in the room.'

Branston looked around him. 'Neither can I, sir. Where would you like your supper?'

'Place the tray on the usual table. Branston ... have you been drinking?'

'Yes, sir. It was the brandy you gave the staff for Christmas.'

'I gave you brandy for Christmas? I thought I gave you all a cash bonus.'

'You did, sir, and it was very generous of you. The staff are all pleased that you decided to carry on the brandy tradition that Mr John Kern began, as well. He was thoughtful, was the late

275

Mr Kern, and he brought you up well, if I may take the liberty of saying so. The staff of Fierce Eagles is pleased to be of service to you. Merry Christmas, sir, and to you, Miss Maitland.'

'Thank you, Mr Branston,' Sarette said.

Magnus opened his mouth, then thought better of what he was about to say and shut it again. 'Please close the door on the way out, Branston.'

'Yes, sir, and rest assured, I'll make sure the staff doesn't tell anyone about what I observed tonight.'

When the door closed behind Branston, they gazed at each other and began to laugh.

Less than two miles away Flynn Collins sat at the farmer's table and tackled a slice of fruit pudding swimming in custard. His stomach was already distended to capacity by the huge dinner he'd consumed.

He envied the farmer his plump, rosy-faced wife, and his comfortable farmhouse with the fire roaring up the chimney. It was a cosy rookery, and something he'd never have now. He was a criminal, sentenced to death for murder, and his only hope was to get away to America and start a new life. But first he had to make sure that the price on his head was no longer valid.

He'd barely finished his pudding when the woman of the house said in her round Dorset voice, 'Another slice of pudding, then, Mr Doyle?'

For a moment he wondered which bit of pudding she was referring to, for the farmer's wife had proved to have a need in her that her older husband seemed unable to satisfy.

'Thank you, Mrs Perkins, but it will take me a week to sleep off what I've already eaten.'

Cheerfully, she said, 'No sleeping on the job now, Mr Doyle. And you need your strength while there's still a furrow to be ploughed.' She plonked another dollop of pudding on to his plate.

Farmer Perkins sighed, scooped up the last spoonful from his dish and patted the expansion of his stomach as he moved to the rocking chair by the fire. 'Though I do say so myself, my Betty be the best cook around here. Not even the cook at Fierce Eagles can bake a pork pie like my Betty. It'll be open house there over New Year's Day. Annie and myself will be taking advantage of his smuggled brandy. The Kerns allus kept a good cellar. I've heard tell that Mr Kern has a woman staying with him, Betty. 'Tis said she's a pretty piece.'

'I heard she was the old man's fancy first. And Magnus Kern had his own fancy woman. I heard tell that she'd run off and married a foreign count. There's no accounting for taste. Mr Kern be keeping it in the family, I expect.'

Flynn remembered the girl who'd been with Kern in Dorchester. A pretty little thing. He wouldn't have minded a go at her himself, but she was quality, and girls like her didn't go for rough types.

Betty snorted. 'The gentry has different ways to ours, and it's not for us to comment on them if we knows what's good for us.'

'To be sure,' Flynn said, and sent Betty Perkins

a sly wink.

Betty placed a glass of port in the hands of the men and they sat in silence, sipping it and gazing into the fire. After a while Alfred's eyes closed and he began to snore loudly.

The empty glass was plucked from the farmer's fingers before he dropped it. It was placed on the table. Gazing at him, Betty smiled. Softly, she said, 'Well, Mr Doyle, do you have a little Christmas gift for Betty Perkins?'

Despite his full stomach, Flynn swelled against his trousers.

She placed her warm, plump hand against him and chuckled. 'That's a lusty little pigeon, and I've got just the place to hide him in.'

'What if Alfred wakes?' he whispered.

'He'll sleep for two hour, at least. If you delivered your gift right here on the table he wouldn't even stir.'

Flynn swallowed. He wasn't about to risk it.

'Come out to the stable in a little while.'

He shared his accommodation with the plough horse, an amiable creature with a broad back. The farmer worked them both hard, but kept them comfortable. He had fresh straw for his stall every night. The stable was built of solid stone and was warmed by a stove.

Betty joined him in the stable loft and spread herself on the blanket-covered mattress between the bales, which kept out any draughts. Her thighs were thick, strong columns and her breasts large enough to hide his head between and suffocate, if he'd a mind to.

The first time, she'd approached him she'd

278

said, 'I've been wed to Alfred for five years and I have a pressing need for an infant to suckle at my breast. Don't reckon I'll get one from my husband after all this time. You're a good-looking feller with a brain between your ears. I could carry one of yours if you've a mind to be generous. No one need know.'

Her words had touched Flynn. Betty would be a good mother, and any child she had would be received into a loving home. He liked the thought of knowing that when he went to America he'd be leaving a little cuckoo in the farmer's nest. It would make up for the low wage.'

'No luck yet then, Betty girl?' he said now.

She gave a secretive little grin. 'There be signs, but it's early days yet. Anyway, I like the way you do it to me, with all the touching and stuff. It makes me feel real good. Two minutes and it's all over with Alfred. I reckon he learned how to do it from the ram. Do you love me, Mr Doyle?'

'Of course I love you, Betty,' he lied. 'And there's something I want you to do for me the next time you go into Poole. Deliver a letter. It's a secret, mind.'

'Not if it's to a woman,' she said sharply. 'I'm not sharing you with anyone else.'

He could have pointed out her own behaviour to her, but let it pass. 'No, it's not.'

'That'll be the day after tomorrow then.' She reached out and cupped him in her hands. 'But tell me where afterwards, Mr Doyle, for I've got a real pressing need on me now.'

Magnus had been right. Gerald did apologize for his bad behaviour.

'I got a frightful dressing down in Pa's study. He was furious, and threatened to send me up North to work in the Liverpool branch with brother Oscar if my behaviour doesn't improve. I felt as though I was still ten years old. Still, something good came out of it. Jessica Fenwick hasn't spoken to me since, but her injured expression says it all. Olivia gives me the cold shoulder. She'll come round eventually, I expect. I don't know what she sees in Jessica. The woman is a spiteful pest.'

Magnus laughed. 'Rather you than me.'

'Now, I must talk to Sarry. I want her to know that my proposal was sincere, and I need to know what her answer is.'

'Save it for New Year, Gerald. Sarette is dashing about the house like a gadfly. She's busy trying to sort out the guest bedrooms, something Verna forgot to do. She's very efficient, and has the household staff organized. You would have thought she was brought up to it. She's rewritten the menu, and has made me a list. She has me organized too. I'm to take her into Dorchester tomorrow to gather it all together.'

'Has she indicated any interest in my proposal?'

'Actually, I think she's forgotten all about it, Gerald. I wouldn't count on Sarry accepting. In fact, I'd wager she'll turn you down.'

'How much?'

'I wager ten guineas.'

'You're not risking much.'

'Fifty guineas then.'

There was a short pause, then Gerald said, 'She hasn't accepted *you*, has she?'

'Good Lord. I haven't even asked her. I'm much more subtle than you with a woman, my friend. In fact, I've been thinking that we should abandon this first wager we have on her. She knows about the legacy now, thanks to you. How would she feel if she knew we'd laid bets on which of us will marry her for it. Besides, I'm pretty sure she's enamoured by me.'

There was a sudden draught down the chimney and a click behind him. The papers on his desk flurried. 'Excuse me a minute.' He placed the earpiece on the desk, strode across the room towards the door and yanked it open. The hall was empty. It must have been a draft that closed the door. He went back to the telephone. 'What were we talking about?'

'You know very well. You said Sarry is enamoured with you? Did she say so?'

'I can tell.'

'You couldn't differentiate between love and concussion from a clout on the head. And it's not just the legacy with me, Mags. Sarry's a fetching little thing and we have fun together. I'm quite taken with her.'

'You're only taken with Sarry because you feel threatened by Jessica Fenwick.'

'Damn you then. I'll take your fifty guineas, and I'll take the girl off you.'

'The wager is still on then.' Magnus hung up.

* * *

281

From her position on the landing, Sarette watched Magnus stride from the library and cross the hall to the drawing room. He opened the door and looked inside. 'Sarry?' From there he went to the morning room and did the same.

She composed herself and began to descend. As he turned, she smiled and said, 'Magnus, did you call me?'

His gaze searched her face, then he smiled. 'You look flushed. You should stop rushing around.'

'Yes, I should. What did you want me for?'

'Gerald was on the telephone. He wanted to apologize to you. Too late now. He's gone.'

'Is that all he said?'

'Yes. Were you expecting something else? You can always call him.'

'It can wait until New Year.'

'You're not thinking of accepting Gerald's proposal, are you?'

'Of course I'm thinking about it. You said he would make me a good husband, and told me to consider it. Have you changed your mind about that?'

He hesitated, then said, 'I have. What if I enforced my guardianship and refuse to consent to the marriage?'

She needed to punish him for what he'd done. She needed to punish both of them.

'First, you could refuse until your eyes turned blue, for all the difference it would make to my decision. Second, I haven't agreed yet. Third, you'd have to give me a good reason, otherwise I'd simply ignore your advice and dispense with

282

your claim to guardianship.' She gave him the chance to confess about the wager. 'Do you have a good reason?'

He shrugged. 'Not one that I'd care to voice at the moment.'

'That's what I thought. Excuse me now, Magnus. I need to go and make sure the tablecloths are free of stains.'

'Damn the tablecloths, I'm not interested in discussing domestic arrangements. Sarry, please, I'm asking you not to accept this proposal unless you're very sure you love Gerald.'

Like him, yes. Love him? Sarette was very sure that she didn't. She turned and gazed at him, waiting for him to explain, to lessen her hurt. *Tell me you love me ... lie to me. I'll believe anything you tell me*, she thought.

He did neither, and the shock in his dark eyes made her ache inside when she said, 'Have you considered that it might be possible that I am in love with Gerald?'

She walked away without another word.

Seventeen

The summons to Magnus's study came just after he returned home from Dorchester.

Sarette had been helping Verna dust the rooms and make up the beds for the overnight guests expected for New Year's Day.

She finished what she was doing, then presented herself to him, pink-faced from her exertions and straightening her apron. She blew a stray strand of hair from her face, and smiled at him. 'Branston said you wanted to see me.'

'You shouldn't be working in the house. We have extra servants.'

'Verna won't allow them in the bedrooms. She's worried they might steal something. I don't mind helping her. I'm enjoying it.'

'Are you managing the arrangements, all right? My former housekeeper always used to do it all before.'

'Verna is very efficient, and we're managing everything together. I'm learning from her. It might hold me in good stead one day, in case I need to be a housekeeper.'

'Which is doubtful. But it might stand you in good stead when you're married, and have a home to run.' He indicated the seat by the fire, and took the one opposite. 'Remember me telling you that I had someone searching for any relative you might have. I'm afraid nobody has been turned up. Do you want me to continue the search?'

'Thank you for trying, and for keeping me informed, but no, I don't see the point. My father never mentioned us having any living relatives.'

'We were careful not to reveal your circumstances during our enquiries. The world is full of fraudsters and trickery.'

Magnus and Gerald were living proof of that, she thought sadly. She said, 'It certainly is,' then she rose. 'I must go and help Verna, else your guests will end up having to make their own beds.'

He moved towards the door, barring her way. 'Are you still annoyed with me?'

Slanting her head to one side she gazed up at him. 'Would it worry you if I were?'

'Not particularly.'

She laughed, she couldn't help it. 'You know, you're the most arrogant man I've ever set eyes on. Move out of my way else I'll stamp on your foot.'

'I'm quite sure I deserve every snub, slight and physical offence you care to offer me.'

'Oh, please, Magnus ... humbleness just does not suit you.'

'I never know the right way to act around you.'

'Just be yourself ... you might be annoying, but I think I like you better that way.'

He grinned at that, and moved aside. 'By the way, Gerald will be here shortly. He intends to reprise his proposal.'

Her eyes flew open at the thought. 'He'll have to wait until I've finished what I'm doing.'

'Have you decided yet?'

'No.'

'If you're unsure, you shouldn't accept him.'

She didn't need his advice. What did he know about marriage, when his experience was limited to mistresses? How many women had he taken to his bed, promised them all they desired, then taken advantage of them, and taken their feelings lightly. Jealousy twisted its blade in her heart, then sliced into her tongue so every word she uttered was forked with insincerity. She hated herself for not being as honest as she wanted to be.

'Your advice is appreciated. Thank you for trying to find any kin I might have. I think you must be disappointed that I must still impose on your generosity.'

He drawled, 'Don't presume to know my mind, Sarry. You're wrong if you imagined I was trying to get rid of you.'

'I didn't imagine anything of the sort.' She shrugged, and altered her train of thought. 'Yes, I did think that. I'm sorry.'

'So you should be.' He stepped aside and allowed her to leave the room.

She was forced to find time for Gerald when he arrived.

'I apologize for embarrassing you.' Gerald shuffled the toe of his shoe in the carpet. 'My father said that I must honour the proposal. He is waiting in the study with Magnus.'

Sarette gave Gerald the opportunity to withdraw his declaration, sure that he would. 'You'd been drinking ... are you really sure that's what you want?'

'I wasn't too drunk to know what I was doing.' His eyes avoided hers and he gave a defeated sort of sigh. 'We get on well, and we have fun together, and my father likes you.'

'Which is immaterial because I wouldn't be marrying your father.'

He gave a bit of a grin. 'Just as well, I'd hate it if you became my step-mamma.'

Sarette laughed. 'Yes, I suppose it would be a bit silly to have a stepmother younger than yourself.'

'Then what's your answer?'

She wondered why saying yes to Gerald was so difficult when he was a perfectly presentable and clever young man. 'Do you love me?'

'Lor, yes ... I forgot about the affection bit. Would I have asked you if I didn't care for you?'

She couldn't bear to hear him avoid the one issue that should be at the core of a happy marriage, and she hardened her heart as she remembered the demeaning wager. 'I'm still thinking it over. Marriage to you was not something I'd ever aspired to, and your proposal was unexpected.'

His face flushed and he winced. 'The intention was always there, I was just a little premature in announcing it. What must you think of me?'

Sarette thought Gerald was not a very good liar, and she was not going to allow him to appeal to her heart. He was not a small boy who'd been naughty and obliged to beg forgiveness from his mother, while sure it would be forthcoming. He was a man, and a man experienced with women, no doubt.

Even so, the trapped expression in his blue eyes was hard to bear. 'I want to think about this. I'll give you my answer in March – on my birthday.'

The expression on his face became one of quiet resignation, and there was more than a hint of desperation in his eyes when he murmured, 'Of course.'

'You realize that there is already some unpalatable talk about me.'

'Which nobody who knows you believes, and for which, on behalf of my family I apologize profoundly. What about Magnus? He knows what I'm about and will expect to be informed.'

'When I've given you a definitive answer he will be.' Then he can collect his fifty pieces of silver, Judas, she thought. 'Besides, I'm not really interested in Magnus's thoughts on the matter.'

Gerald looked a bit worried. 'I thought he seemed quiet. Perhaps an affirmative news would cheer him up.'

'I daresay he'll be glad to get the problem I present to him off his hands. After all, if people are talking about me, then they must be talking about him, too, since I live in his home.'

'I'm sure he won't be pleased at being kept waiting for this issue to be settled between us. You're not being fair to him, Sarry. Magnus is a good, honest man.'

'Is he, indeed? Perfection must belong in the eye of the beholder I should imagine. You've been friends for such a long time that you've created your own mutual admiration society.'

He took her hands in his. 'Believe me, Sarette, Magnus holds your welfare dear to his heart, as we all do.'

She slid her hands from his and looked him straight in the eye. 'Does Magnus want us to wed?'

Gerald's glance skittered away, then came back to her. 'He wants what's best for you.'

'Then to do him justice, I shall take some time to decide what that best is.' She rose at the same time as he did, smiled, and said formally. 'Thank you for your proposal, Gerald. I'll let you know my answer in due course.'

He hesitated, clearly piqued. 'Is that what I'm to tell them, that you haven't made your mind up?'

'That's it.'

'How long are you going to keep me hanging on a thread?'

'I've already told you that you'll get my answer in March.' Colour touched her cheeks. She must remember that this was an intelligent man she was dealing with. 'Is that what you think I'm doing, keeping you on the thread?'

Amusement came into his eyes. 'All right, Sarry. I'll indulge you by playing your little game, but I don't know whether it will wash with Magnus.'

'Hah! to Magnus. It's nothing to do with him.'

A step brought him closer, his eyes were sharp

against hers. 'It's everything to do with him, since you're in his charge. We have always had the same taste in women and are rivals in love.'

'Is that what you both call your womanizing ... love?'

She bit down on her bottom lip when Gerald's gaze narrowed in on her. She'd nearly confessed that she knew about the bet. It had been too ambitious of her to take on these men and play them at their own game. What had she been thinking of?

However, she knew he'd misread her when he said, 'Mind you don't get your fingers burned trying to play each of us off against the other.'

'You're full of conceit,' she said angrily.

'I prefer to call it pride. You might have fooled John Kern with such tactics, since he was an old man. But you won't fool Magnus for long.'

'John Kern? *Fooled him?* I think you're fooling yourself, Gerald, if that's what you think. John Kern may have had a chequered past, but he was all heart. He rescued me when I was thirsty and hungry and ready to give up. In doing so he rescued himself, for he thought he had nothing left to live for. I would have given my life to save his.'

Gerald sounded slightly ashamed when he said, 'What else am I supposed I think? Most people think you were after John Kern, and when you heard he was dead you set your sights on Magnus.'

'And you said nobody who knew me would believe such a thing. Obviously you didn't include yourself in that.' Sadly, she asked him,

290

'Have you been listening to gossip, Gerald? Funny, but I really thought you were above that.'

'I am ... don't know why I said it. I'm jealous, and despite that, my proposal still stands. Once you're married nobody will dare criticize you.'

'Ah, so you want to save me from the gossips. I was thinking, Gerald, perhaps I should sue these people who are slandering me. Should I retain you for the task now I have the resources to pay for them?'

'I do have *some* dignity. I wouldn't take the case.'

'Would it be a conflict of interest, perhaps?' she asked gently, for she was certain that his sister Olivia, and the obnoxious Jessica were behind the gossip.

He didn't answer.

'Perhaps I should ask Magnus then.'

'He wouldn't take it either, and he'd crucify you for suggesting such a thing.'

'Are you certain about that?'

He stared hard at her, then said slowly, 'Magnus is too sure of himself where you're concerned. Has he ... made certain advances to you?'

She wondered, would a kiss or two be classified as certain advances?

'Touched you perhaps?'

Her blush became a furnace. This had become a no-holds-barred conversation, and she didn't like it. 'Gerald, stop this. It's upsetting.'

But he was relentless. 'Taken you to bed ... *Ouch!*' he said when her palm flattened against his cheek.

The door swung open and the dogs came in.

They picked up the tension in the room. Boots came between them and leaned against her skirt, his head pressed to the side of her knee and his hackles raised. Patch sniffed at Gerald's legs and gave a short, rattling growl that revealed a row of sharp teeth.

Gerald took a step backwards, his abused cheek burning bright, his eyes filled with his own shame. 'I think I deserved that.'

Magnus entered. He was wearing black trousers and a frock coat over a double-breasted ruby waistcoat. His cravat was fixed by a matching ruby tie pin. His imposing presence brought with it its own tension, and even though he looked quite relaxed he dominated the room.

Gazing from one to the other his mouth twisted in a wry smile when his glance settled on Gerald's flaming cheek. 'Oh dear, have we had a falling out?' he said, irony saturating the deep chuckle he gave.

The dogs deserted her for him, making ingratiating little noises and wagging tails. One strong hand came down to fondle their thrusting muzzles and Sarette felt a response in herself when he caressed Boots's floppy ears.

'I've come for Sarette,' he said and gave her a slow, beautiful smile that melted her insides as well as lifted her spirits.

She reminded herself that she was still as furious with him as she was with Gerald.

'Mrs Carradine and her daughters are about to arrive, I saw their carriage coming along the road and thought you might like to be introduced, then show them where they're to sleep

292

tonight. Gerald, if you've finished your business here, your father is waiting for you in my study. I'll join you there in a little while.'

Gerald gazed from one to the other, then gave a sardonic little bow and left.

Sarette was detained by Magnus's hand loosely circling her wrist. 'You look upset, Sarry, girl.'

'Do I?'

'You know damned well that you do. The tips of your ears turn red when you're angry.'

She touched one ear lobe with her fingers, managing a smile when she felt their heat. 'You notice too much.'

'Talk to me without throwing barbs. It will ease the tension in the atmosphere if you do.'

She gazed up into the dark turbulence of his eyes. 'Don't you want to know what passed between Gerald and myself?'

'I know what passed between you. He stepped over the mark and you slapped him. I daresay he deserved it.'

'Specifically?'

'That's between you and Gerald.'

She wished he cared enough to want to know what had happened. The edge had gone from her anger and she felt a little soiled. 'We argued.'

'And Gerald was relentless in his attack, and he wounded you.'

'How did you know?'

'I know Gerald's style of questioning.' He took her chin between finger and thumb, turned her face to the light and gazed reflectively at her. 'You're lovely, and I'm glad you turned him down.' His mouth came down on hers in a tender caress that turned her blood into bright, shining beads of quicksilver that pulsed through her veins.

She should push him away before it went any further, but he brought her hand up against his heart before pulling her closer, so she fitted snugly into his firm body. Love surged through her like warm honey and heated into sizzling lust. She felt herself grown-up with a vengeance. At this moment she knew exactly what she wanted. She wanted this man to love her. She wanted to be his woman. His everything. And for the rest of her life.

There came the sound of a carriage, and he pulled apart from her, then gazed ruefully at her. 'Are you not going to slap me too?'

When her heart was hopping like a kangaroo that had taken fright, and her mouth was feeling bereft by the loss of his, and her body...? But better to not think of the exquisite fusion of feelings inside her, of the hungry need to take it, shape it and feed it.

She touched against his face with her finger tip instead, and her voice was husky when she whispered, 'I'm still angry with you.'

'I don't want us to be at odds, anger is too destructive.' He kissed her again, his mouth taking all so she was weak and trembling and breathless – and had been made aware that she was his for the taking, any time he decided he would.

The doorbell suddenly clamoured. Branston coughed discreetly as he padded past the open drawing room door, letting them know that guests had arrived. The house staff were bound to gossip amongst themselves. What would they think of her behaviour?

There came the sound of female voices before Magnus released her. They gazed at each other for a moment, then he touched her nose and gave a small huff of laughter. He left her standing there, quivering like a newly hatched dragonfly stretching its wings to the sun. Mr John had forgotten to tell her about the devastating effects on the body of being in love.

'Mrs Carradine, Alice, Emily and Jane, how lovely to see you all again.'

As if she hadn't been folded in his embrace just a minute or so ago, she straightened her skirt, patted her hair in case it had suddenly lost its style.

'You haven't met Miss Maitland yet, have you. I'll see if I can find her.'

Sarette pulled a smile to her face and abandoned the drawing room for the hall, certain she was surrounded by a shining glow. She touched her mouth and felt it tingle, as if there was a star twinkling there.

There was a small company of chattering females in the hall; around them lingering the smoky winter chill of the day. 'I'm here, Magnus. How do you do, Mrs Carradine. I've heard so much about you all.' As if she was the lady of the house come to greet them. She saw Magnus grin and raise an eyebrow.

She took the Carradine family up to the room that used to belong to John Kern's wife. Mrs

Carradine would share it with her two youngest daughters, while Alice used the second bed in her own room.

'I hope you won't mind, Alice. Mr Kern has invited such a lot of people to stay that I was hard put to find room for everyone. It was his suggestion that you might like to share my room, since you'd all be rather uncomfortable crowded into the other room.'

'I'm sure I'll be comfortable, and it was kind of you to put yourself out. Mr Kern is well liked and respected by us all.'

Alice Carradine had fine eyes and skin, and had a soft, gentle way of speaking. Sarette liked her. She touched her mouth where Magnus had kissed her with her finger tip and a pulse throbbed. 'I've made some room in the wardrobe. We shall have to make do without a maid because the servant who usually helps me will be needed for other duties, but we have a bathroom we can all share.'

'We have only brought one dress apiece for best. That is all we have. My mother does her best but my father...' Alice drew in a heavy breath. 'My mother's income is limited.'

'If you wish, you may all borrow one of mine. Mr John Kern made sure I was fitted out. But Magnus Kern didn't like me in the gowns with bustles, and he insisted on having his own way. He said that the gowns Mrs Lawrence had chosen for me were much too fussy. There is one in blue and another in pink, which would suit your sisters if they would care to wear them. And there is a gown of apricot taffeta that is very pretty. Magnus said it doesn't suit my hair.'

'Your hair is a lovely colour. It has just a faint glow of chestnut in it. Miss Maitland ... Sarette?' Alice burst out, 'I hope you will excuse me when I say that I expected you to be much younger.'

'Ah yes ... Magnus thought I was going to be a child, you see, and he got quite a shock when it turned out that I wasn't ... now, I'm sure he can't wait to get rid of me ... forgot to tell you that I prattle when I'm nervous, and it was probably an awful insult to offer you a gown to wear, but I shall never wear them all, and nobody has seen me in them so the company wouldn't know. They are going to dreadful waste even though they are quite beautiful, and the moths will probably eat them before too long ... oh dear, you look quite taken aback. Have I said something wrong? I often do.'

Alice Carradine recovered quickly and kissed her on both cheeks. 'Not at all. It's generous of you to offer us a gown. Be sure we will be pleased to take advantage of you. My sisters have always felt disadvantaged in company, and will be delighted to have something fresh to wear. So will I.'

Having experienced that feeling quite often herself, Sarette was happy to throw open the doors to her extensive wardrobe and be generous with her good fortune. 'Wear anything you like.'

She began to pull clothes out on to the bed until Alice placed a hand on her arm. 'If you pull everything out we'll have to spend time hanging it all up again. Allow me to choose gowns for my sisters to wear. Perhaps the pink and blue ones you mentioned in the first instance. They'll be happy with my choice.'

Sarette pulled in a deep breath. She had never had a female friend, and liked Alice. 'I'm so pleased you're here. It will be such fun to have you to talk to. There are gloves and accessories in those drawers.'

She thought of Olivia and her friend, Jessica Fenwick, and her heart sank. She hoped they hadn't been invited. She had quite enough to cope with.

There came a knock at the door and Verna appeared. 'Cook's having a fit in the kitchen.'

That was the last thing she needed. 'Oh, dear. What about?'

'She said a pie has gone missing and she's blaming it on the temporary staff. She said she's not going to do anything else until the culprit owns up. Can you come, Miss?'

'Excuse me, Alice. Perhaps you could take charge of your family.'

She followed the housekeeper downstairs to the kitchen, where the atmosphere was frosty despite the heat coming from the the fat black stove, and the temporary servants were all lined up. Cook had her arms folded over her chest and a determined expression on her face.'

'What is it Mrs Mayberry? Can I help?'

'Somebody's eaten my pie.' Her gaze roved fiercely over the servants. 'This here's the mistress of the house. Own up, you lot.'

Mistress of the house? Was that how they regarded her? How odd.

Boots came from the basket in the corner, his tongue lashing over his snout. Patch followed and they went into their usual routine. Her hand came away sticky when she fondled them. She gazed down at Boots. 'I think these are the culprits, Mrs Mayberry.'

'Well I never ... those damned varmints, anyone would think they never got fed. I'll have to make another pie. What have you done with the plate, you bad dogs? I wouldn't put it past the pair of you to have eaten that as well.'

The dogs looked suitably chastened. Cook pressed her lips together and said sharply, 'What are you waiting for? You can get on with your work now that's cleared up.'

'I'm so sorry, cook. I'll take the dogs out from under your feet. Can I do anything to help? Peel vegetables perhaps.'

'Bless you no, Miss. That's what we pay the temporary staff for. You go off and enjoy yourself.'

Enjoy herself. Hah! She seemed to have been given the task of hostess, something she was ill-equipped to deal with.

The dogs followed her out and she took them to Magnus's study and knocked at the door.

'Come in.'

She stuck her head round the door while the dogs competed with each other to squeeze through the gap to get to Magnus first. 'Would you take the dogs please, Magnus? They're causing trouble in the kitchen, stealing food. The cook is about to cut their tails off.'

'I'll take them out for a walk. Coming Gerald?

Ignatious?'

'I'll stay by the fire,' Ignatious said. 'Sarette, have you time to talk to an old man for a moment or two?'

'Of course. Only you're not as old as you think. You danced my feet off at the ball.'

'Stop trying to flatter me, my dear. You know very well we sat it out.' He sounded so offhand that her heart sank. She supposed he was about to tell her off about the way she'd treated Gerald. Well, let him. It was really none of his business.

Gerald walked past her with a wary expression on his face. Magnus winked at her and she blushed.

When the door had closed behind them, she said, 'I suppose you're going to chastise me for my behaviour, Mr Grimble.'

'When a man proposes marriage he does her great honour. I would have thought Gerald deserved more than a slap on the face.'

'With respect, sir, you were not present. A slap on the face was exactly what Gerald deserved. And he would be the first to admit it if you'd asked him.'

His head slanted to one side. 'I did ask, and his answer concurred with yours. Would you care to elaborate?'

'I'm afraid not. Far from it that I should be the cause of trouble between friends or family. Gerald knows exactly why I slapped him.'

'I see. Will you be accepting his proposal in due course?'

'As I told Gerald, he will have his answer in

March.'

'Am I to take it that, at this moment, you consider Gerald not good enough to be a husband to you?'

'I assure you, Mr Grimble. It has nothing to do with Gerald's suitability, or otherwise.'

'Then?' he prompted.

She was tempted to talk to Ignatious about the wager because he had always – well, *almost* always – been scrupulously honest with her.

'I'm sorry Mr Grimble. This is a private matter between your son and myself. You should allow perhaps that Gerald is not a child.'

'But sometimes he can be childish.' Ignatious spread his hands. 'I want to see him settled and happy.'

'Then I will tell you that it will probably not be with me. I know Gerald is your son, and I'm grateful to him for saving my life. I like him a lot when he is not pursuing me. I have no intention of telling him yet, but I doubt if his feelings will be hurt. He doesn't love me, you know. And I do not love him in that sort of way.'

'Then I'll not push for a relationship between you. Is it Magnus?'

His perception startled her. *'Magnus...?'* She tasted his name on her tongue, it was as dark and passionate as red wine, as durable as leather and as soft as velvet. 'Magnus has made no declaration. Tell me, Mr Grimble, is the house I own still untenanted?'

'It is.'

'Will you sell it for me?'

Now it was his turn to look startled. 'Sell it?

When?'

'As soon as possible after the New Year.'

'Best to wait for summer, that's when people come to Bournemouth to spend their holidays. The sea air is beneficial for the health.'

'I want the house disposed of as soon as possible. I will also want the proceeds, and any money John Kern left me, donated to a suitable charity.'

'But that will leave you with nothing.'

'Exactly the way I started out. Then I will look for work and find suitable lodgings.'

'Does Magnus know of your intentions?'

'No.'

'You have a good home here, my dear.'

'No, I do not. People are talking about me. My reputation is in tatters, and you know the reason behind that. It was not what Mr John intended. There is something else.'

'Which is...? And be warned, Miss Maitland, I will do nothing that is detrimental to the welfare of my family or friends.'

'John Kern was your friend,' she reminded him bitterly. 'And you owe me something for what your family has brought about.'

'John is dead, and his will is open to my interpretation of it. I will not allow his assets to be disposed of on what is little more than a whim.'

'Then you and I are about to have a falling out, Mr Grimble, because if you refuse my request I'll have to find another lawyer. Think of what that will do to your reputation.'

'In the past, people have died for trying to bring down the Kern and Grimble families.'

Her blood chilled. 'Are you threatening to kill me, Mr Grimble?'

He snapped his fingers under her nose, making her jump, 'Miss Maitland, I could break you like that. But I won't. Magnus will be furious when he finds out about this request.'

'Not half as furious as I am just at this moment.' And because she didn't want him to think too badly of her, she told him the reason. 'I have no wish to hurt you or your family, Mr Grimble. But allow me to tell you something that you don't know. I overheard a phone call between Magnus and Gerald. They have wagered fifty guineas on Gerald's proposal being accepted or turned down. I also learned there was an earlier wager on which one of them would marry me and collect my legacy. Magnus has yet to follow through with his proposal.'

'And when he does?'

'He'll get the same answer that I gave Gerald.'

'Ah, now I see it all. You're going to punish them for the wager by keeping them in suspense.'

'I need to. I feel so insulted and ... so crushed. I don't want to come between them by choosing one over the other.'

'And the legacy? Surely you don't think getting rid of it will make any difference to the outcome of this silly wager.'

'I think they'll withdraw their favours once I've got rid of the cause. If they don't, then I'll know that it's me and not the legacy they're interested in. Mr John would bang their heads together if he knew what was going on.'

Ignatious's hand closed over hers. 'You should choose the man you truly love, my dear, and we both know who that is. As for the wager, put it from your mind. The only people who will benefit from it is the charity that they started together. It benefits impoverished victims of crime. Children who have a breadwinner in prison, and need shoes to go to school. A grandmother who needs a warm blanket.'

Was he telling her this to excuse how she'd been made to feel? If so, it wouldn't work. 'You don't understand, Mr Grimble. If I had a choice, I'd prefer the man who truly loved me. I'm afraid that the pair of them are so used to this rivalry that they're forgetting that the object of this wager is a woman who will suffer if it all goes wrong.'

'Try not to punish yourself, my dear. You're right, the wager is unseemly and irresponsible. There, it is settled, and we shall see what happens.'

It wasn't until after he'd left that she began to wonder exactly what had been settled.

Eighteen

Dear Mr John,

You might not have noticed, but I am now writing my journal on a fortnightly basis.

Something terrible as well as wonderful has happened. I have fallen in love with Magnus Kern. I am quite besotted with him, although he is a most complicated creature.

However, it's disagreeable to find myself the object of a wager, like a flitch of bacon hanging from a hook in the ceiling waiting to be claimed. As soon as Magnus does his proposing I shall tell them both that I've given my fortune away, and will release them from any obligation they consider themselves to be under. I have decided I shall make my own way in the world.

It was a pleasant New Year party. It was nice to see Mrs Lawrence again, though she is now Mrs Taggard. Olivia came with her husband and children and I was pleased to learn that her friend, Jessica Fenwick, had returned home. Olivia apologized profusely for her earlier behaviour. For the sake of Mr Grimble, I am trying hard to like her.

The Huffs were very jolly. Mrs Huff and I spoke about you. She says you were a rascal in your youth. Alice Carradine is my guest at Fierce Eagles. Gerald pays her much attention and I think they are falling in love. It's comforting to have a friend of my own in whom I can confide. She is very sweet and calm.

You are still a special memory in my heart, Mr John, but I miss you less, and see Magnus with a clearer eye as a result. I no longer compare him with you, and find fault as a result, but appreciate him for his own good qualities. He has a kind heart, but so likes to provoke.

We had some snow in early February, the first I've ever seen. It's nearly March now and soon I will be nineteen. I'm looking forward to spring.

Dear Mr John, they have not yet caught the murderer who shot you. I will not rest until he has been found and dealt with.

A month later Flynn Collins was becoming restless. He should have done the deed by now, for the longer he stayed in the district, the more likely he'd be recognized and caught.

He gazed around him at the field, now sown with wheat. There were carrots, potatoes and turnips to plant. He was deriving a certain satisfaction from his field labours. He was comfortable in his relationship with Betty, who demanded nothing except what he'd given her, a little pleasure and an infant growing under her snowy white pinny.

He envied the farmer who would bring up that child as his own, for he walked with a new spring in his step and a smile on his face. Flynn wished he could change places with him, for he'd be content to live a life with Betty Perkins. She'd fed him well, and he'd gained considerable weight around his middle.

Now he must get what he was here for over with. For the last few weeks he'd been watching the routine of Magnus Kern, and the coming and goings at Fierce Eagles. Magnus Kern stuck to a regular route and always came home at the same time. At the moment he had a young women guest. Flynn thought she might have been hired as a companion to the younger girl.

He didn't know who they were. He'd been told that Kern was unmarried, and he didn't have a sister. One of them must be his woman, then.

Flynn was uneasy. Notwithstanding that he'd shot the old man in the back when his dander was up, shooting a young man in cold blood didn't sit lightly on his shoulders. But if he didn't shoot him the price on his head would remain and he'd be fair game for anyone who recognized him, and for the rest of his days. He'd arranged for the dinghy to pick him up in the cove the following night, and hoped the weather improved.

Perhaps he should leave without killing the man. If he just left, the chances of him being recognized in America were slim.

The fact that Betty carried his child was pulling at him. He'd felt as though he'd achieved something worth having, but it would be snatched away from him. He'd never know what the infant would be, and the child would never know his true father.

He'd be better off not knowing. Flynn experienced a swift, remorseful pang in his stomach when he remembered the child he'd left to starve on the goldfields. She'd been a plucky little creature and he wondered – what had happened to her?

Buffeted by a capricious breeze Sarette was walking along the cliff top with Alice Carradine.

Now Mrs Carradine had suggested that it was time Alice return home to London, and her friend would be departing after the weekend. Sarette knew she would would miss Alice.

The expected proposal from Magnus had not eventuated, and now she found it hard to maintain the momentum of her anger. She had decided to release Gerald from the proposal – if not for herself, for the sake of Alice.

Alice's face took on a quiet glow when she was in Gerald's presence, and she hung on his every word. How could she keep up this farce when it was obvious that Gerald and Alice adored each other, Sarette thought. Gerald gazed at Alice like a lost puppy every time they were together. He couldn't do enough for her.

She placed a hand on her friend's arm, bringing her to a halt. 'I want you to be the first to know that I'm going to turn Gerald's proposal down when he arrives for the weekend.'

The joy that momentarily flared in Alice's eyes was replaced by doubt. 'Are you quite sure, Sarette? He would make you a worthy husband.'

'I don't want someone worthy, Alice dear. I want a man who will love me wholeheartedly, who will make me his mistress as well as his wife. I want to be adored, possessed, fought and played with, then chased around like a mad March hare until I surrender myself.'

Alice's blue eyes widened, but her voice was full of laughter when she admonished, 'Sarette, you shouldn't say such awful things!'

'Oh, there are only the two of us to hear. Don't pretend that spring hasn't got the better of you too. I see you with Gerald, and his eyes make love to you and you blush and stammer and your heart stops beating like that of a spinster and starts pounding like that of a woman in love. You and Gerald were made for each other. He knows it, and so do you. So does everybody who sees you together. I'm beginning to feel guilty for keeping you both apart with that silly proposal of his.'

'You would give Gerald up for me?'

'How can I give up something I never had in the first place? Gerald holds a special place in my affection, as I do in his, I think. But we don't love each other, you goose. It was a wager they had between them. Magnus tricked Gerald into proposing, so he could get me off his hands.'

'What if Gerald doesn't want me? I have no money, no position.'

Amusement filled Sarette and she gurgled with laughter. 'Then you're no worse off than you were before you came here.'

She gazed down at the farmhouse nestled in the valley. 'Let's go and visit Mrs Perkins before we go home. She makes wonderful scones, and I promised to drop in on her the next time I was over this way. She told me she thought she was expecting a baby, and I want to know for sure. Let's race.' And she was off, Alice chasing after her.

They flew down the hill, skirting a muddy field where a man was digging in the earth. He straightened, his hands easing his back, then turned to gaze at them.

His face was vaguely familiar, but Sarette wasn't close enough to see it clearly. She waved to him then picked up speed.

'Sarette, wait!' Alice shouted. 'I've got a stitch in my side.'

Laughing and breathless Sarette clambered on to the stile so her skirt was out of the small patch of muck beneath it. As she waited for Alice she noticed that the man was staring at her intently. Her smile faded.

Her memory triggered a vision of a snake. She recalled that there were adders in England and gazed into the undergrowth, trying to stifle the prickling chill of dread that ran up her spine into her neck.

The man turned, then walked rapidly away.

'Sarette, are you ill? I've never seen you look so pale.'

She managed a smile. 'I shouldn't have run so fast. I'll be all right in a minute.' And she was.

There was no response from Farmer Perkins or his wife to their knock. 'I'll check in the stable to see if the cart has gone.'

The only horse in the stable was the plough horse, who turned to stare amiably at them and blew out his breath in a manner that made his lips flap. She giggled. It was warm in the stable, and a ladder led up to the loft.

'Mrs Perkins,' she called out.

There was a slight shift in the dark shadows of the loft.

'Mrs Perkins, is that you? Is anybody there?'

Her ears tuned in to the quietness. It was uneasy, as if someone was standing in the shadows ... listening ... waiting. Sarette wondered where the man from the field had gone, and was unnerved when the door behind her banged in the wind. She jumped, wrenched it open and ran out into the blustery day.

Grabbing Alice's hand she said, 'Quick,' and the pair began running away from the farmhouse to the road, until they were both out of breath and were forced to stop and bend forward to catch their breath.

Alice said, when she'd recovered enough to be coherent, 'This was supposed to be a walk, not a race. What on earth made you take fright?'

'I don't know. I had the feeling that there was someone in the stable watching us. Then the door banged in the wind.' She giggled. 'Don't tell Magnus, he'll only tease me.'

A splatter of rain was borne to them on the wind. She gazed up at the tumultuous streamers of dark ragged clouds racing each other across the sky. 'We'll have to hurry if we don't want to get wet.'

'I don't think I've got any hurry left in me.'

But they'd barely started on the two-mile trek to the house when Magnus appeared from behind them in the gig. He drew the vehicle to a halt and jumped down, saying, 'I think we're in for a dousing. Sarry, you drive yourself and Alice home. I can walk.'

Soon they were on their way. Sarette enjoyed handling the horse and gig. She deposited Alice down on the doorstep of Fierce Eagles, then said, 'I'm going back for Magnus.'

'Mind you don't get soaked.'

'It's not very far.' Turning the light vehicle around she set out, back in the direction she'd come from. Nearly a mile of road had trotted under the horse when Sarette suddenly remembered exactly who the man in the field had been.

'Flynn Collins,' she said out loud and the blood began to pound in her ears. So it *had* been the Irishman she'd seen in Dorchester. And although he hadn't given any indication that he knew her, she remembered Alice shouting out her name just a moment or two before, and remembered the way it had caught Flynn's attention, and brought about his reaction.

What was Flynn Collins doing here? She was overcome by a thrill of fear when she realized that she was probably the only person who could identify him as the man who'd been convicted of the murder of John Kern.

It was not a coincidence that he was here in the district and working on the land adjoining the estate belonging to the Kern family. He had not come for her, though she was certainly in danger now Collins knew who she was. Lord! What about the price on the Irishman's head? Did Collins suspect that Magnus had posted the reward, and was about to kill him?

Had Magnus posted it?

She packed her curiosity away as the rain began to sweep across the landscape in miserable, slashing grey curtains. She was drenched and cold when she came across Magnus, who was also dripping with water as he trudged through the storm.

After she'd turned the gig round he climbed up beside her, gave her a wide smile, then kissed her on the cheek. 'You're a bedraggled looking angel.'

'There's something urgent I need to tell you, Magnus.'

'When we get home.' He was about to take the reins from her hands when a shot rang out. Simultaneously he slumped in his seat, his hat spun off into the undergrowth and blood began to run from under his hair.

Horrified, she stared at him, not quite comprehending. She gave a scream when there was another report and something whined past her ear. It chipped some bark from a tree. She flicked the reins, thinking, bless him for being so calm and well-trained a horse as he responded instantly. Magnus slipped sideways, his head lolling into her lap, where he bled profusely on her skirt.

'Oh, my God, tell me you're not dead, my poor love,' she whispered trying to keep the horse under control. As soon as she'd put some distance between them and the shooter she pulled the gig to a halt and placed her hand against Magnus's heart. It was still beating. Peeling off her stockings she tied them together, then pulled the makeshift binding under his waist and tied his body to the handrail. At least it would stop him from slipping off. The frill from her petticoat served as a bandage for his head – though didn't staunch the blood.

She drove carefully and steadily, trying not to panic and praying all the time that he'd survive. She was overjoyed to see Robert waiting to take the horse and gig. His face registered his horror at what he saw.

'Call George out to help you carry Mr Kern up to his room. He's been shot. Then stable the horse, and lock the stables and house. And we must load all the rifles and pistols in case the murdering Irishman who did this comes here to finish us off.'

When Robert gave a shout Branston opened the front door and came running.

Sarette threw at him. 'Telephone Mr Grimble and tell him that Magnus Kern has been shot by Flynn Collins, the escaped murderer who killed John Kern. Ask him to send a doctor to the house, and some armed constables to hunt the man down. And to tell them to be very careful, because Flynn is armed. Tell him I'm in danger too, because I can, and will, identify the man.'

Her orders were carried out without question. While Branston hurried off do her bidding Magnus was carried upstairs and George began to remove his master's wet clothing. The rest of the servants scurried around, locking windows and closing shutters.

Storm clouds had darkened the house prematurely, the wind had begun to howl. Rain lashed against the house like a cat-o'-nine-tails across a convict's back, and the tension in the atmosphere was almost palpable.

Alice blenched when she saw the blood on Sarette's dress. Sarette hoped she wouldn't faint. 'It's not me who's bleeding, it's Magnus.' And she quickly explained what had happened. 'Would you find me something else to wear while I go in the bathroom and sponge the blood off? Then you can help keep a look out for strangers, but stay out of sight behind the curtains. Branston will tell you which window to guard.'

A few minutes later and cleaned of blood under the running tap, she left her ruined clothes in the bath and stepped into the checked brown skirt, cream blouse and velvet bodice Alice had left on the bed for her. She couldn't spend much time on her appearance and quickly tied back her damp hair. Her body began to warm up now her clothes were dry, and her shivers gradually subsided.

Fetching some towels she went to check on the condition of Magnus. He was lying in his bed, looking pale and helpless, his shoulders naked. George had managed to slow down the flow of blood with a towel, but Magnus was still unconscious. She placed a fresh towel against the wound and bound it in place with some linen strips.

'I don't think it's as bad as it appears, Miss. The bullet creased his scalp, but I think Mr Kern is stunned and will soon recover his wits.'

'Let's hope he does, and before too long, then.

Can you handle a gun, George?'

'I think so, Miss Maitland.'

'Good, that makes four of us.'

'Are we to shoot the man down in cold blood, Miss?'

There was a slightly nervous tone in his voice that would have made her grin if the situation hadn't been so serious. Her glance went to the unconscious Magnus and anger began to build in her. Collins had already taken the life of one man she'd loved. He wouldn't get this one. Would she shoot the man in cold blood? Yes, she knew she would if he came within striking distance of Magnus.

'If he gets in the house we can't take chances, George. This man is a convicted murderer. He killed John Kern by shooting him in the back and has nearly killed Magnus today. He also shot at me and his bullet missed me by an inch. He doesn't deserve to be given a chance. If you're too squeamish to shoot him, call me. I'll do it myself.'

'But you're a ... lady.'

'Thank you, George. First and foremost I'm an orphaned brat from the Australian goldfields. Mr John Kern taught me how to fire both a pistol and a rifle. Don't worry. I don't expect Flynn Collins to come here, since he's proved himself to be a coward who shoots men in the back. The guns are a precaution in case he does, and will be used only in defence. Robert and Branston are loading them. We'll take one apiece and cover four sides of the house.'

'Have the authorities been informed, Miss?'

'Mr Grimble has been contacted by telephone. He will do the rest.'

'Then there will be reinforcements coming?'

'Yes ... of course there will.' She hoped so. There were many entrances to the house, and few of them to guard them.

Magnus mumbled something.

She lent him her ear. 'Tell me again.'

'Aches ... head.'

'I know it hurts, Magnus my love. The doctor is on his way. Rest now and your headache will soon get better.' Her mouth was just an inch away from his and she gently kissed him. She pulled the sheet up over his shoulders so he wouldn't get cold, before turning to George. 'We'll ask Verna to sit with him. I might need you, George.'

'Yes, Miss Maitland. And if I may say so, you keep a calm head on your shoulders when needed.'

'Thank you, but I was nearly hysterical when Mr Kern fell, and when the second shot missed me by an inch that startled me into action. I thought he'd fall off the rig, and if he had, I wouldn't have been able hold him.'

She heard the phone ring and took the stairs down two at a time, just in time to hear Branston say, 'Miss Maitland is fine, Mr Grimble.'

Sarette almost snatched the instrument from his hand. 'Mr Grimble?'

'Gerald ... I've just heard ... how's Magnus?'

'Unconscious, but we've almost stopped the bleeding. He was lucky. George said the bullet creased his scalp, and the second one missed me and hit a tree. Magnus did speak once,' she said and felt like crying. 'He said his head ached.'

Calmly, Gerald said, 'Probably a bit of a heroic understatement on his part. How are you holding up, Sarry?'

She inhaled a deep breath to steady herself. 'I'm fine. We're all armed to the teeth and keeping a watch out. If Collins comes within a mile of here and I see him, he's got a nil chance of survival.'

'And Alice. Is she all right?'

'Yes, she is. She's been allocated watch-keeping duties on the north side of the house and will ring a bell if she sees anyone approach.'

'I'll be there soon, and with reinforcements – a couple of soldiers, two constables and a doctor. The soldiers and constables are already on their way. I'm just waiting for the doctor to gather his things together then we'll set out.'

'Be careful Gerald. Collins got to Magnus on the road when he was on his way home from Dorchester, so he must have been watching his movements. If he has, he'll know your face as a visitor here. He's got nothing to lose.'

'I'll be careful.'

'And Gerald. I was going to tell you tomorrow, but I'll tell you now. You're released from any obligation you imagine you had towards me. I had no intention of marrying you.'

'Rather crushing, but I can't say it was unexpected, my love.'

'You don't have to sound so horribly relieved.'

He chuckled. 'Neither do you. You didn't have to punish me by making me wait for an answer,

318

you know.'

'It was revenge. You've got to admit that you gave me just cause.'

'Ah ... the bet with Magnus,' he said with great satisfaction, 'He said that the winner would be the loser, because he'd lose his freedom to win John Kern's legacy.'

'Aren't you operating under an assumption, Gerald? What have you actually won? Nothing, because you were free to begin with. What has Magnus actually lost? Also nothing. That's what he had to lose in the first place. So you see, it was all a waste of time. He hasn't proposed, and I haven't accepted.' And neither had she any intention of accepting under the circumstances.

'But he will and you will, since you've declined to take me.'

Her eyes narrowed. Gerald didn't admit to defeat easily. 'Good Lord, Gerald don't be so vain. There are other men in the world beside you two. As for Mr John's legacy—' she didn't want to play her ace by telling him she'd asked his father to dispose of it – 'it was left to me, not to Magnus.'

'But Magnus will have control of it, and he always liked the Bournemouth house. He's keeping you for himself, I tell you. He meant to win this wager ... or lose it, whichever way you care to look at it. He's tricky.'

'You may not have noticed, but I have a mind of my own. Now, we can't stand here talking while all this is going on. That man might be creeping up on the house, and I'm just in the mood to blow his murdering head off his shoulders.'

'You're an impressively bloodthirsty little cat when you're aroused to passion. I hope Magnus appreciates what he's getting.'

She refused to bite. 'I'll give Alice your love, shall I? She's unnerved by what's going on, you know. You're very good at rescuing damsels in distress. She'll be impressed when you arrive with your soldiers and constables ... as I was impressed when you risked your life by jumping into the stream to pluck me out.'

'For goodness' sake. The water only came up to my thighs.'

'But my head was under water, and you were soaked through.'

'You were dragged under and pinned to the bottom by a rolling branch. I had to duck under the water to free you. If you hadn't been so intent on saving Boots, you might have thought to undo your skirt and step out of it.'

'I'm still impressed.'

There was a short pause, then he chuckled. 'Not impressed enough, obviously. You know, I think you'd make a good lawyer, Sarry. Take care, and don't worry. We're leaving in about two minutes, so I'll see you in a little while.'

The telephone went dead.

Flynn Collins was in the farmhouse. The farmer and his wife were locked in the cellar, and it was peaceful now they'd stopped their bellowing. He'd been tempted to shoot the farmer and take the woman with him, but she'd prove to be a hindrance to him.

He didn't know whether he'd killed Magnus Kern or not, but it didn't matter now. The game was up. The girl had certainly recognized him earlier. By now she would have alerted someone in authority and they'd know he was abroad. He was under no illusion that they'd hunt him down, then shoot him on sight.

The only place he could think of to hide was in the cave in the cove, though he'd have to move the shingle that had built up against the opening – make it big enough to crawl through, anyway. He'd explored the cave before, as far as it went, and it should keep him high and dry. The farmer had told him that they'd been used for smuggling goods through the tunnels to the cellars of Fierce Eagles, but they'd been blocked by John Kern.

He wondered how far back the caves went, how thoroughly they'd been blocked and how far the tide took the water up the tunnels. The thought of hiding under the house of the people who were hunting him down was appealing. It would be the last place they'd look. He had a fishing boat coming for him the day after tomorrow, one that his cousin in Poole had arranged. Once he reached the quay he could slip aboard the ship that had his stoker acquaintance on. He hoped the storm would blow itself out before then. He wasn't a good sailor.

He filled his pockets with any cash he could find then thrust some food and a bottle of water into a bag. He took the farmer's bottle of whisky from the sideboard as he left, and stuffed a blanket from the farmer's bed under his coat.

With the rain pelting down and the sky glowering dark grey, he headed across the field, keeping to the shelter of the hedgerow. He stopped when he saw movement down by the farmhouse. Sinking to the muddy soil of the field, which stank of the muck he'd spread the week before, he gazed down at the farmyard.

He'd got out just in time. There were soldiers, two of them. When they went into the farmhouse Flynn turned and ran, bending double to the ground. He wasn't going to have the head start he'd thought he'd have. He made it undetected to the copse that sheltered the field from the wind coming off the sea, stood in the shadows and took his bearings. The soldiers had come out. So had the farmer and his wife. The woman was waving her arms around, and she pointed towards the stable. The soldiers headed for it, guns foremost.

She was like everyone else, he thought. She'd got what she wanted from him. Now she was eager to hand him over to the authorities.

Flynn didn't like being used and his eyes narrowed. If he had a rifle he could have picked them off from here one by one, he thought. But then, the soldiers and the farmer had rifles too. They could pick him off just as easily if they clapped eyes on him. Besides he didn't want to hurt the woman who was carrying his kid. Flynn liked the thought of his byblow inheriting this farm. It would give the kid a good start in life, which was more than he'd been given.

Sarry Maitland came into his mind and regret pinched at his guts. He should have stayed in the goldfields and looked after her, not given in to greed. She'd grown into a pretty little thing, and he was glad the bullet had missed her.

He was relieved when he reached the copse, and was able to disappear into the shadows. He headed along the path that lead downwards to the cove on the other side. He just hoped the tide was out.

Nineteen

Magnus opened his eyes. He was in bed ... his own bed. Something wasn't quite right. It took him a while to figure out what it was. He remembered Sarette meeting him with the gig. He couldn't remember coming home in it.

He sat, and was rewarded by a steady throb in his head. He felt bandaging and groaned as he remembered her slapping Gerald. Had he gone too far with her and she'd brained him?

The light was turned up and she was standing there, a rifle in her arms, her face pinched with worry.

Alarmed, he whispered, 'Do you intend to shoot me, Sarry?'

'Don't be ridiculous.' One lonely tear trickled down her cheek like a bright diamond. 'Thank goodness you're all right, Magnus.'

'Why are you crying then?' He swung his legs out of bed and stood up.

'*Oh!*' Her eyes widened and she turned her back on him. '*Magnus Kern! Get back into bed at once!*'

Her scandalized expression made him grin. It was as if she was his governess instead of his... 'Lor...' he groaned as he realized he was naked. His backside hit the edge of the bed and he swung his legs back under the blanket. Spots appeared to dance dizzily before his eyes and he felt slightly sick. 'My pardon ... I didn't realize I was... What happened ... did a tree branch fall on me? Who took my clothes?'

She sniffed prissily and turned back towards him. 'Certainly not me. George did. No, a tree didn't fall on you. You were shot.'

There was little light in the room, but enough to see that this snippet of femininity was blushing furiously, and biting down on her lip as though she was trying not to laugh at him for hopping back into bed on her order.

He chuckled. 'I'm in danger of being shot again if you don't put that gun down.'

'No you're not. The safety catch is engaged and I can shoot the eye from a snake. Mr John taught me how to shoot.' She placed the gun on a table between him and the door and, then came to his side to check his bandage. 'Lie still, Magnus. You'll make the wound on your head bleed again. The doctor is on his way, and so is Gerald.'

His heart jumped, then he denied what she'd said. Being shot didn't happen. Sarry was getting her own back for all the times he'd teased her. 'That's not funny. Tell me what really happened.'

'Flynn Collins really happened. He's been working at the Perkins farm, biding his time and lying in wait for you.'

Now he knew she was teasing. 'For what reason?'

Her scowl would have frightened a fox and she growled. 'I'm beginning to think the bullet punched a hole in your skull and took off with your brain in tow. Flynn Collins doesn't need a reason except you have the same name as Mr John. He's a murdering scoundrel, that's what he is. His second shot missed me by an inch. He knew I'd recognized him when I saw him in the field, then Alice called out my name.'

'He recognized you. Oh God,' he groaned. 'You're in danger. He might come here after you. I must get up and get dressed.'

When he was about to rise again she placed her hands against his shoulders and pushed him down on to the pillow. 'Kindly stay put. You've lost a considerable amount of blood, and ruined my favourite gown in the process. Everything is under control, Magnus. The windows and doors are all locked. We're keeping a look out and everyone who can shoot is armed to the teeth. Gerald is on the way here with soldiers, constables and a doctor.'

'And you're here guarding me.' He felt very tender towards her. Placing an arm about her waist he pulled her down and against him. 'Where's George?'

She resisted. 'Keeping watch. Behave yourself, Magnus.'

He kissed her on the nose. 'You haven't given him a gun, have you?'

She could feel his body against hers, his heat and his hardness. 'Yes. He said he knew how to handle one.'

'Knowing how to handle one and actually doing it safely when it's loaded is two different things. He'll probably put it in his pocket and shoot off his ... *his foot*.'

She tried without success not to giggle at his near slip, and said. 'George is just keeping a look out.' This time she kissed him. 'Allow me to rise, Magnus. You shouldn't excite yourself.'

'It's too late for that,' he said with a wry laugh, but he released her.

'Verna will be here to sit with you in a few moments.' She moved away, picked up the rifle and went back to the window, the weapon slung over her forearm to point at the floor in the safety position.

Fatigue stole through him as what had happened became real to him. What she'd done had taken a great deal of courage. Most women would have fallen into a seething heap of hysteria. He thought to ask her, 'How did you get me back here by yourself?'

'I tied you to the rail with my stockings, and held your head in my lap so you wouldn't fall to the ground.'

He grinned. He'd never been tied up with a woman's stockings before, and to think he'd missed that little treat.

She came back to him then, tears in her eyes. 'This is not funny. You might have died ... we both might have died ... I was terrified.' She placed the gun across the end of the bed and held out her hands. 'Look, I'm still trembling.'

He took her hands in his, pulled her gently, so she had no choice but to seat herself on the bed next to him. Her luminous green eyes were set in the longest of lashes, and the lashes were clumped together with tears.

'You're the bravest woman I've ever met, and I owe you my life,' he said, wondering if the way his body was reacting to her at that moment was quite decent. How would she respond if he pulled her into his bed and ravished her? She'd respond wonderfully, he suspected, but just at the moment she needed reassurance and tenderness. The pounding in his loins began to equal the pounding in his head when he pulled her into his arms. She smelled like crushed violets and rain, and felt as though she belonged there.

There was a whisper of breath against his bare shoulder as she sighed, 'Oh, Magnus.'

The moment of sheer bliss was lost when she seemed to remember what she was about, and sprang to her feet, all flustered and womanly and aware of the feelings building in her. The look she gave him was dark and accusatory, as if it was his fault. 'Is there anything you need?'

There was a pressing need in him, but that could wait. For now he was content to be in her presence. The darkening day pressed against the window, the wind blew its worst, the rain splashed and roared as it travelled the gutters and spouted out of the gargoyles on the corners of the roof. The fire cracked and spat tongues of fire in the grate. The dogs came in and settled on the rug in front of the fire.

Where better to be at this moment than within the walls of Fierce Eagles with the woman he loved? When love had first made itself felt he didn't know, and he didn't much care. It existed inside of him, dark and warm, a euphoric emotion that was everything a man in love should feel for a woman. Sarette Maitland was a gift from his uncle. She was his if she would have him, and he was hers for ever. Gerald and the stupid wager could go to hell!

His eyelids began to droop as tiredness pressed in. He fought it. He didn't want to sleep – sleep kept him apart from her. He wanted to be awake so his eyes could consume her image. But the world insisted on getting greyer and greyer.

He forced his eyes open, to see her gazing down at him.

Her smile was that of an angel, though a slightly wicked one. 'Rest, Magnus Kern. I insist.'

'You're delicious when you insist.'

His words brought a gurgle of laughter from her. 'You're delirious. Go to sleep at once.' There was a whisper of her breath against his forehead. His eyelids. His mouth.

She'd kissed him, and he wanted a thousand more of her kisses, he thought. He smiled inside, and did what he was told.

The doctor had stitched the wound on Magnus's head, then left during a break in the storm.

Magnus waited until the carriage had gone through the gates, then with the help of George, had dressed and come downstairs for dinner.

The constables and soldiers were invited to dinner, then when the storm had intensified were invited to stay the night. They would take it in turn with Gerald to keep watch during the night.

The soldiers stated their intention of going back to the farm in case Collins returned there seeking shelter.

The four of them intended to meet and resume their search in the morning.

'Collins would have gone to ground, I imagine, but where?' Gerald wondered out loud.

One of the constables asked Sarette, 'Are you sure that the man was the convicted murderer, Flynn Collins? The farmer said he called himself Doyle.'

'Of course Miss Maitland is sure,' Magnus said. 'He was her father's partner. He was calling himself Jack Maitland when we saw him in Dorchester, and must have stolen her father's papers after he died. There's a picture of him in some newspaper cuttings in the desk drawer in the library. Fetch them for us, would you please, Branston.'

'Yes, sir.'

'Why didn't you let the police know you'd seen Collins, Miss Maitland?'

'At the time I wasn't sure it was him because his face was so dirty, and the last time I'd set eyes on him he'd had a full beard. Mr Kern thought I might have been imagining it.'

Magnus sent her an apologetic smile.

'You look pale, Magnus. Do you feel all right? You lost an awful lot of blood.'

He nodded. 'The doctor said a head wound always bleeds profusely, and usually looks worse than it is. And what about you, angel? You've had an eventful day.'

There was a faint grin from Gerald at the endearment.

Branston came back with the newspaper cuttings and handed them to Magnus. It was obvious the men wanted to talk amongst themselves, so she exchanged a glance with Alice and rose. 'I must admit that I'm tired. Would anyone mind if I retired?'

Taking that as a cue, Alice rose. 'Me too.'

'Mr Branston, please thank the staff for being so heroic today,' Sarette said.

The butler smiled broadly. 'You're welcome, Miss, and I'll tell them. If I may say so, your own example was inspiring.'

Gerald rose too, tall and graceful. 'I'll make sure you reach your room safely, ladies.'

Magnus's eyes came alert. 'Surely you don't think that Collins has gained entrance to the house. The dogs would kick up a racket if they saw a stranger wandering around. The cur would not be so foolhardy as to take us all on.'

'No I don't, Mags. I'm just being cautious. My guess is that Collins is on the run, and he might be desperate enough to try anything if the opportunity presents itself. If he can make the quay at Poole he can find himself a ship.'

The policemen smiled at each other. 'Customs are keeping a look out for them.'

'Has the cellar door been locked and bolted, Branston?'

'Yes, sir.'

'Good, but we'll search the cellars in the morning as a precaution.'

There came a banging at the door. Gerald turned the light down and gazed out through a chink in the curtain. 'It's all right, Branston. It's one of the soldiers. You can allow him entrance.'

The soldier had stopped to inform them, 'The farmer's woman said that the Irishman had a cousin in Poole. She delivered a note there not long ago, arranging for a fishing boat to pick him up in the cove. She gave me the address. I'm off there now to see if the cousin can throw any light on the man's whereabouts.'

'We'll do that,' the two constables said together. 'Can you manage with one soldier, gentlemen? We need the other at the farmhouse in case Collins goes back there.'

Gerald nodded.

When they reached their room, Gerald kissed her fingers and smiled. 'Thank you for everything, Sarry.' He turned to Alice and his smile grew warmer and much more intimate. 'I have something I wish to say to you in private, Alice.'

'Anything you wish to say can be said in the presence of Sarette.'

'Who has declined my offer of marriage, because she so rightly realized that my affections had become engaged by another.'

Alice looked from one to the other. 'Is this true, Sarry? You have turned down Gerald's proposal of marriage?'

'Would Gerald lie?'

Gerald knew he had on occasion. His eyes

331

opened wide in a vain attempt to look innocent, then he gave a shamefaced grin and shrugged. 'I never promised to be perfect, but I promise I'll try and improve.'

'Did anyone say they wanted you to try and improve? Honestly, Gerald. Haven't you heard that leopards never change their spots?'

Gerald looked pleased with the comparison.

'That was not a compliment, Gerald, dear. What was it you wished to say to Alice?'

'Oh ... that. Allow me to accompany you to your home in London next week. I would very much like to speak to your mother.'

'I've never seen you so lost for words, Gerald.'

'Lor, Sarry, can't a man have a bit of privacy. Go away and keep your nose out.'

He pushed her inside the room, pulled the door shut, then in the darkness of the hall drew Alice into his arms. He kissed her, then said, 'I adore every inch of you, Alice, my love. Will you marry me?'

'How absolutely romantic. Of course she will,' he heard Sarry say from behind the door panel.

Flynn Collins was spending an uncomfortable time huddled against a rotting wooden barrier made of planks.

The tunnels were draughty and smelled of decomposing seaweed and fish. The shingle had been built up by the high tides, and if he dug down an arm's length the pebbles were damp, as if the tide was seeping under them like a giant mouth to suck them out from under him. The roof pressed suffocatingly down in the darkness, so he couldn't stand up straight. The worst thing was that he couldn't see the high tide mark in the darkness. He was trapped until the tide subsided, unless it filled the tunnel and drowned him.

With the blanket pulled tightly around him, he ate the bread and cheese he'd taken from the farmhouse and washed it down with the water. As the chill sank into his bones he realized that his backside was damp and cold. He was filled with fear. Was he to die here, trapped like a rat in a flooded hole while the water crept relentlessly up from under him, to fill his mouth, his nose and his lungs? Was his body to be left to the mercy of the tide, stinking while the crabs feasted on his rotting flesh?

He thought he could hear the water seeping through the stones, reaching for him, then creeping back and gathering strength for a longer reach.

'Mary, mother of God, save this poor sinner,' he prayed. 'Get me to America and I'll repent my sins and never do a bad thing again.'

Frantically scooping the pebbles with his hands he tried to pile them up as a barrier in front of him. But it wasn't going to keep the water from filling the tunnel. Lying on his back he thumped a heel against the planks of the barrier and felt it give a fraction. Another few frantic thumps and the top plank fell from its rusting nails. The second plank was easier now he had more grip. Wriggling through the gap he'd made he dropped down the other side, to find himself up to his knees in water.

It was pitch black, but he could stand up. He reached out and his fingers encountered the sides. He kept his hand against the left side and cautiously made his way forward, the water getting shallower and shallower until he found himself on a dry floor. The tunnel seem to slope upward, and under his feet were metal tracks to take the grooved wheels of a wagon.

The sea water didn't reach this far up, but water dripped from the roof and roots stretched down to clutch at his face. The air was warm and clammy, and he imagined the weight of the cliff just above him and began to sweat. Then he remembered the props his hand had encountered, and knew that the tunnels had been properly constructed and maintained over the years. Flynn stopped to take a swig from the whisky bottle. The liquor warmed his stomach and relaxed his mind, and he began to feel better.

'Thank you, Lord,' he said humbly. 'All you need to do now is calm the storm and send the boat, and I'll be on my way in the morning with no further need to trouble you.'

And it seemed that his prayers were to be answered, for by dawn the storm had blown itself out, and although Flynn didn't know it when he woke, a small ship was standing off the cove and a dinghy waited on shore for his use.

Magnus was up before dawn the next day. Apart from a sore head he'd suffered no ill effects from the events of the day before. He stroked his prickly chin. He needed a shave. But then, so did Gerald. His friend was curled up on the couch, his head on a cushion.

He'd slept long enough. Magnus nudged him with his foot and Gerald came blearily awake. 'Oh, it's you.'

'Who were you expecting at this time of morning, Miss Alice Carradine?' He handed Gerald a cup of coffee. 'Collins' cousin wanted no part of the escape arrangements, so it's been arranged by the authorities. The constables arrived back at the crack of dawn, bringing reinforcements, and there's a customs' cutter hidden behind the promontory. Once they sight him he won't get far.'

Taking a gulp of the coffee Gerald let out a heartfelt sigh, then grinned. 'The revenue men, eh? Your ancestors will turn in their graves like a bull on a spit.'

Magnus laughed. 'So will yours. We must be a great disappointment to them. I've been told we're to stay home and keep our noses out.'

'The devil we are!'

Gerald looked so disappointed that Magnus laughed. 'Better we don't attract the attention of the revenue men. The constables deserve to be in for the kill, and the soldiers, too. I bet you ten guineas that the soldiers get him rather than the constables or the customs.'

'My money's on the constables. Don't forget I still owe for the last wager.'

'Our usual charity, Gerald?'

'Where else.'

'Just remember that I haven't proposed to Sarry yet. She might refuse me. In fact she'll probably box my ears for me now she knows about the wager. I might have to lock her in the cellar until she accepts that I know what's best for her.'

Gerald grinned. 'We were going to search the cellars this morning.'

'And we shall, but only as a precaution. I can't see that anyone can get in via the cave since my uncle had that boarded up at the beach end and filled with shingle. We'll go down there now.' He set his cup down on its saucer and stood, yawning as he stretched to his full capacity. 'Afterwards, George can tidy us up before the women wake up. Alice will change her mind if she sees you looking like that. You know, Gerald, you've got a sweet-natured and sensible woman there. She's more than you deserve.'

'Nonsense.' Gerald punched him lightly on the arm. 'Sarry doesn't know what she missed by refusing me.'

'You knew she would. But *your* loss is going to be my gain.'

'As you always meant it to be. Will you show her the cellar room?'

'It's part of the history of Fierce Eagles, and so will she be when she accepts me.'

Sarette rustled down the stairs in pastel green taffeta. She'd left Alice soaking in a bath of scented water. After a hearty breakfast she went to find Branston, who informed her of the latest gossip.

'Where's Mr Kern and Mr Grimble?'

'They've gone to check the cellars.'

'Oh, I see.'

She was about to return upstairs when her glance fell on the cellar door standing open, and she remembered the secret room Mr John had told her about. She stood and looked down a steep flight of stairs. The gas lighting extended into the cellar, and the place was brightly lit, revealing racks of bottles.

She went down and looked around. She'd never seen so many wine and spirit bottles gathered in one place. No wonder Mr John had drunk so much, she thought inconsequentially.

One of the racks had been swung open like a door. Beyond was darkness, except for a faint light flickering in the distance. There was a small scuffing noise and she shuddered. Rats?

'Magnus,' she called out.

The gaslight suddenly went out and she was plunged into darkness. The next moment an arm came round her neck, nearly choking her.

'Make one fecking sound and you're as dead as a doornail,' a voice growled.

She froze.

'You're going out before me and I'll have a gun in your back. Understand?'

'Oh yes, Flynn Collins,' she sneered, as loudly as possible. 'You're good at shooting people in the back.'

'You think you've gone up one in the world, don't you? Miss Maitland is it? People don't bother about whores like you. First it was the old man, now the nephew. I'm glad your father didn't live long enough to see this.'

'My father was worth a dozen of you, and so was John Kern, you thieving, murdering snake

337

in the grass.'

'One more word from you and you'll get my fist in your teeth.' He shoved his kerchief as far into her mouth as he could get it, so she wanted to gag, then tied her hands behind her back with a piece of cord. Something cold and hard was shoved against her spine. 'Walk.'

Sarette managed to stagger up the steep stairs. As luck had it, the hall was deserted and the dogs were still in the kitchen begging for scraps. Collins closed the door to the cellar until it clicked gently, then turned the key in the lock. 'Help me get down to the cove and I'll spare your life.'

She doubted it. And she knew that nobody was going to spare *his* life if he killed her. And even if she escaped, Magnus would follow him to the ends of the earth to take his revenge if she was so much as harmed. He had fallen in love with her – she just knew it.

She took Collins out through the French windows in the morning room, which was at the side of the house and directly under her bedroom. They kept behind the shrubbery and skirted the grounds as they sloped gently down towards the cove.

The landscape was battered by the storm and there were mud patches everywhere. She walked through them, leaving many footprints for the soldiers to follow, her bright gown collecting dirt and rips as they went. Her hair was snatched at by twigs, her style unravelled and the length of it falling about her body, where it became tangled more with every step.

The day was bright. Too bright to die. But the day didn't show any mercy to its victims. It had been a bright day when the snake had killed her father.

There was no sign of anybody on the cliff. What had happened to the soldiers and the constables?

A movement caught Alice's eye and she stared at the shaded patch on the other side of the shrubbery. She caught a glimpse of two faces as people passed a gap between plants. Sarette? Her friend's arms were held at an awkward angle behind her back, and she was with a man.

Alice knew without asking who the man was. Pulling on the rest of her clothing she hurried downstairs, bursting into the dining room. 'Where's Mr Kern? The Irishman has got Miss Maitland.'

Branston paled. 'I thought she was with you, Miss Carradine. Mr Kern and Mr Grimble are in the cellars.'

There came a sudden banging and shouting from the hall and they hurried to release the lock.

'Miss Maitland has been taken by the Irishman, and I think he must have locked you in,' Alice told them.

Magnus swore. 'This is my fault. I should have checked last night.' He gazed around at everyone. 'We've just discovered that the shingle my uncle put in the tunnels has been gradually sucked out by the tide, and the barrier had been kicked in where the wood had gone rotten. We

339

found an empty whisky bottle, obviously the one stolen from the farmer's house. I'll never forgive myself if anything bad has happened to Sarry.'

With Gerald on his heels, Magnus hurried through to the gun cabinet and began to load the weapons. One rifle and one pistol apiece.

'They went along the side of the garden, using the shrubbery for cover. Be careful,' Alice said, her alarm clearly written on her face.

'We will.' Gerald touched her face. 'Ring my father and tell him what's happened. Then go to the kitchen and wait there with the servants until I get back. I don't want to have to worry about you.'

'Promise you'll bring her back safely, Magnus.'

'Even if I have to swim to Ireland to get her,' Magnus growled. 'The authorities have got the cove covered and we'll go down through the tunnel. The tide is out, and if Collins can get in through the tunnel, then we can get out the same way.'

The beach was piled high with seaweed washed ashore by the storm.

Collins smiled when he saw the dinghy loosely tethered to a rock, and pushed Sarette down the precarious path in his haste to get to it. Sarette half slid and half ran in the scree that formed the path. When she reached the bottom she tripped and sprawled face down in the shingle. His fist closed around her hair and he hauled her upright.

'Let the woman go, Collins,' someone shouted.

On the cliff top were some half-a-dozen men with rifles. A quick glance showed her that they were surrounded. Collins brought a gun up against her ear. She didn't even flinch when he clicked the safety off. Coward, she thought.

She caught a glimpse of Magnus in a small gap between two rocks. He was gazing down the barrel of a rifle, his eyes dark, and downright deadly. When he caught her glance he became uncertain.

Sarette smiled to reassure him that he had her trust, then closed her eyes.

It seemed a long time coming. It was a time in which she heard the safety catch of Flynn Collins's pistol being released. It was a time in which she smelled his fear and experienced her own moment of resignation, followed by calmness. This gun had killed John Kern, who was stronger and braver than she was. It was fitting that she died the same way. This might be her last second alive.

A shot rang out.

Sarette's knees buckled and she sank like a stone.

Two seconds later Magnus gathered her up in his arms and turned his back on the scene. He began to carry her away from it, up the cliff path, seagulls wheeling and shrieking in the sky above her. He didn't say anything, and that made her nervous.

She clung to him, beginning to shake. 'There's something you should know first. I've told Mr Grimble to sell the house in Bournemouth.'

'I know. It was his duty to inform me. I've

341

rescinded the request.'

'I didn't want you to think I was a gold-digger, you see. Well, I was one, but the mining gold out the ground sort of gold-digger – not that I mined much, mind you. I'm really not the sort of gold-digger that befriends rich old men ... or rich *young* men come to that ... just to shove my diggle into their pockets.'

His mouth twitched. 'You mean, dig your shovel into their pockets, don't you?'

'I thought that's what I said. And I'm going to give Mr John's legacy away, too, because before you propose to me I want you to be aware that I won't allow anyone to marry me for my money.'

'I've rescinded that request too.'

'I knew you would. I wanted you to marry me for love ... rather than my legacy. You do see.'

He gazed down at her. 'Yes ... I see everything perfectly. It just happens that I'm in love with you, so everything will work out fine.'

'And remind me to talk to you about those wagers when I feel more able,' she said. 'I'm a bit nervous at the moment. Will you take me home now, please?'

'Happy birthday.'

She gazed into his eyes and smiled. 'It is indeed, since I'm still alive. Did I hear you say you loved me?'

He nodded, then said, 'And despite Uncle John's legacy.' He kissed her so very tenderly that she forgot everyone was watching until a cheer went up. Then she broke down and began to cry.

Twenty

Alice fussed over her. Alice who was so shining with happiness over the fact that they had all survived the ordeal that her quiet glow warmed Sarette's heart. She was grateful for Alice's friendship and hoped it would endure for the rest of their lives.

The bath water was relaxing against her skin and when she emerged Ada was waiting for her with a warmed towel.

'Oh, your poor face,' she wailed. 'It's scratched to pieces, and so are your arms. And look at your hair, all tangled. I'll never get all those knots out.'

'The scratches are superficial and will soon heal when some salve is applied,' Alice said calmly. 'As for her hair, it will take a little while but I'll brush it free of tangles.'

An hour later they went downstairs arm in arm.

Ignatious Grimble had arrived, and he clucked over her injuries.

'They're nothing, really. Just superficial scratches.'

She crossed to where Magnus stood, smiling at her. 'Is he dead?'

'Yes.' He took her hand in his and caressed her

knuckles. The others hesitated to shoot in case they hit you.'

She said quietly, so the others couldn't overhear, 'You were unsure.'

'Hell yes ... what if I'd misjudged...? I knew you'd told me to go ahead as soon as you closed your eyes. My main fear was that Collins would move you into the line of fire. As soon as he pulled back the hammer on his pistol I knew I had to take the risk.'

'Do you still love me ... really love me, I mean?'

'Do I love you, Sarry girl? I absolutely adore you.' He tipped her chin up and gently kissed her on the mouth for everyone to see.

She grinned when Ignatious Grimble cleared his throat and said, 'I wonder if you'll get the reward offered for Collins's head.'

Magnus lifted an eyebrow as he gazed at Gerald. 'It was a rumour someone started to flush Collins out, I imagine. I won't expect payment for an act that I didn't relish, and which was made purely in defence of someone else. In fact, the money would best serve charitable services.'

'So it would.' Ignatious smiled. 'It would make a nice addition to the victim's fund the pair of you administer between you.'

Magnus shrugged. 'So it would. By the way, the constables require a statement from you, Sarry. Ignatious will accompany you and advise you.'

It didn't take long. When they came back she found a small heap of gifts for her birthday. An embroidered handkerchief case from Alice. Silk gloves with pearl buttons from Mr Grimble, an enamelled box from Gerald and an emerald and diamond ring from Magnus.

He slipped it on her finger, saying, 'My uncle requested that I give you his gift when I thought you were settled in enough to appreciate it. He said he found it just before the pair of you left Coolgardie, and he had no need for it himself.' He indicated an object on the table covered in a velvet cloth.

When Sarette pulled the cloth aside a large gold nugget shaped like a heart was revealed. She stared at it for a full minute, then whispered, 'Oh, Mr John. You did it.'

'Smuggling unregistered gold into the country is not legal, of course...' Magnus shook his head.

'How could I have smuggled it when I didn't know what was in the trunk? No wonder it was so heavy.'

Ignatious smiled. 'I'm quite sure I can get round the legal question if need be. I know one or two people in the gold trade who would melt it down and—'

'*Mr Grimble!* I'm shocked that you'd suggest something so dishonest when I've looked up to you as a good example for all this time,' Sarry exclaimed.

She grinned when Ignatious blinked and appeared taken aback, pleased she'd managed to nonplus him at long last.

Gerald and Magnus exchanged a smile when he said lamely, 'Did you, dear?'

'The gold must stay as it is.' Sarry smoothed

her hands over the lumpy metal, knowing Mr John's hands must have done the same. She closed her eyes and imagined his palms under hers, and she could almost feel the steady tick tick inside the metal.

'It's a heart ... Mr John's heart,' she said. 'He doesn't want it to be melted down. He sent it back to the place he loved and it must stay here for ever.'

Magnus's eyes were filled with laughter. 'I can't remember my uncle as being that sentimental. Still, if that's what you want, I know the very place for it. We will go there together, after the weekend, you and I.'

Sarry was reluctant to descend into the cellar again. But they carried lanterns. Branston lingered in the hall to make sure nobody inadvertently locked them in.

Magnus slid a rack of shelves to one side to reveal a door behind it.

'I expected it to be in the tunnel,' Sarette whispered.

'It is, but not in that tunnel to the cove. The connecting tunnels to this one were blocked by Alexander Kern. My uncle filled in the one to the cove, but it needs attention. The sea has eroded it and it won't be long before the cliff above it falls. I'll just encourage that process with some explosives.'

The door opened into a wider tunnel. She could see the glow of light in the distance and thought that perhaps a beam of sunshine had found its way through the hill.

They skirted the solid foundations of the house and headed for the light, which they followed for a short way down hill. A left turn and the tunnel opened up into a cavern.

Sarette blinked. The place was lit by hundreds of candles, their light twinkling and winking on the stalagmites and stalactites, and reflecting on a pool of still water.

'It's beautiful.'

'Branston and I came down to light the candles earlier.'

There was a pool where the stream had gone underground and as her eyes adjusted to the light, she gasped. 'Look, there's a ship!'

'It's the pirate ship, *Fierce Eagles*.' And indeed, Sarette could see two eagles on the figurehead. 'It's the ship used by Alexander Kern and Esmerelda Rey. They lived to a ripe old age, but when Esmerelda died Alexander had the ship dismantled and brought up the tunnels from the cove, where it was rebuilt. It's his shrine to her. Alexander's journals are in the library if you'd like to read them.'

'I would like to. Can we go on the ship?'

'No, she's unsafe now, full of rot and resting on the bottom. If you stepped aboard her you'd probably fall through the deck.' Magnus took her hand in his and led her around the pool to where water steadily dripped from the roof of the cave to form a basin. The golden heart had been placed under the water, and each drip made the water pulse ripples to the edge of the basin.

'That's a lovely spot, Magnus. It looks as though the heart is beating.'

He took her hand in his and placed it against his chest. 'As mine is beating for you. I've waited until we were alone before I formally propose, and thought this a fitting place. The Kern men always marry for love, and I'm totally in love with you. Will you become my wife, Sarry?'

She slid her arms around him and hugged him tight. 'Mr John said I'd love you as much as he did. It was a lie. I love you more.'

She accepted his proposal, his kiss, and later ... because he was a very persuasive man and she was a curious woman ... his complete and passionate attention. Funny, but she hadn't imagined that being loved could feel so good, or had known that she could blush all over.

But she wasn't going to put that in her journal for future members of the Kern family to read.

Mr John, today Magnus and I will be wed in the village church. I'm to be given away by Ignatious Grimble, who said he would act in loco parentis, whatever that means. My gown is elegant, fashioned from cream satin and Brussels lace. I'm wearing a tulle veil kept in place with pink silk roses. You would not recognize me.

The church bells are ringing. You know what a stickler Magnus is for being on time. He said he'll throw me over his knee if I keep him waiting at the church. By now he'll be looking at his watch and swearing under his breath.

You once told me that life is a journey made up of many chapters. I know you'll understand when I tell you it's time to put our chapter aside.

It is over now and a new one is about to begin. I know you will wish me much happiness in my journey with Magnus.

Your heart of gold is pulsing beneath our home even as I write. I will not forget you, Mr John, for we will call our first son after you.

Sarette Maitland

A knock came at the door. 'Are you ready, Sarette?'

'Yes, Mr Grimble.'

She gently closed the journal on her words. A flutter of excitement filled her. Picking up the photograph of her friend and mentor, she ran a finger over his dear face, then sighed and placed it in the drawer. 'Goodbye, Mr John,' she whispered.

The author invites comment from readers
via her website:
http://members.iinet.net.au/~woods

or by post:

PO Box 2099
Kardinya 6163
Western Australia